Peril at the Pleasant

Peril at the Pleasant

Judith Alguire

Doug Whiteway, Editor

EDITIONS

Cover design by Doowah Design.
Photo of Judith Alguire by Taylor Studios, Kingston.

This book was printed on Ancient Forest Friendly paper.
Printed and bound in Canada by Hignell Printing Inc.

We acknowledge the support of the Canada Council for the Arts and the Manitoba Arts Council for our publishing program.

Library and Archives Canada Cataloguing in Publication

Alguire, Judith, author
        Peril at the Pleasant / Judith Alguire.

(A Rudley mystery)
Issued in print and electronic formats.
ISBN 978-1-927426-26-5 (pbk.).—ISBN 978-1-927426-27-2 (epub)

        I. Title. II. Series: Alguire, Judith. Rudley mystery.

PS8551.L477P47 2013   C813'.54   C2013-905424-3
                                               C2013-905425-1

Signature Editions
P.O. Box 206, RPO Corydon, Winnipeg, Manitoba, R3M 3S7
www.signature-editions.com

To my great-niece Molly

and in memory of
Wendy Piper (Trew)
KGH School of Nursing '71

Chapter One

Six weeks before Christmas, Donnie Albright, administrative assistant and general gofer, lost his job when the small company he worked for in Fredericton succumbed to the recession and managerial ineptitude.

January — The Pleasant Inn

Margaret and Trevor Rudley, co-proprietors of the Pleasant Inn had a conversation that, to the latter, seemed inconsequential at the time.

Margaret came to the front desk with a bundle of mail. She proceeded to open the letters. She paused over one and smiled. "Rudley, look."

Trevor Rudley, who had been rummaging under the desk for his pen, stood up and smacked his head against the edge. "Damn."

"This card is from Mr. Morgan," Margaret said. "He writes a lovely note saying he has never enjoyed himself as much as he did during his stay. He especially mentioned Music Hall. He says he was delighted at the opportunity to play the piano in public. It's been a dream of his since he began lessons with Mrs. Scott in the first grade."

"Somehow, a card, however lovely, seems inadequate compensation for the torture he put us through."

She waved him off. "The quality of the performance doesn't matter. The idea of Music Hall is for people to enjoy themselves."

"Margaret, the man played for twenty minutes."

"We often have extended performances at Music Hall."

"But not by someone who knows just one song. Now, Margaret, I revere 'God Save the Queen' as much as any man, but twenty minutes is a bit much."

She tilted her head. "I found it rather stirring."

"If you say so."

"Mr. Morgan also comments on the beauty of the floral arrangements. I agree. Mrs. Blount did a wonderful job with the holiday flowers."

He crossed his eyes. "Yes, Margaret. After I laid down the law. 'Christmas, Mrs. Blount, red, white, and green with only the occasional subdued bit of gold, brass, or silver. No fuchsia, no teal, no chartreuse or anything else that looks as if it came out of a Hawaiian cathouse!'"

Margaret pretended not to hear him. "Frances is a wonderful businesswoman."

"Margaret, the old bat couldn't make a living in a brothel if she were the last woman on earth."

"Frances is creative. She believes in pushing the envelope—for those whose tastes have not fossilized."

"The only thing that's fossilized is that woman's grey matter. Teal and fuchsia," he fumed. "It's as if she went on an LSD trip in the sixties and never recovered. I suspect she's still on something. Probably narcotics prescribed by her doctor for no other reason than to get her out of his office."

"And here's a postcard from the Sawchucks," Margaret went on, ignoring what he had said. "They're having a splendid time in Florida." She passed the card to Rudley.

"Lovely."

"And a note from Miss Miller. She's planning a wilderness adventure."

"Better her than me."

"Yes, dear." She gave him a peck on the cheek and took off into the dining room.

As the weeks wore on, Donnie Albright realized something had to give. His unemployment insurance would soon expire. He had exhausted his savings. He had no prospects. His job search had yielded only two interviews and no return calls. Time was running out. He knew he would soon have to consider taking a McJob, but the idea of flipping burgers paralyzed him. Worse was the reality he would have to give up his pricey apartment.

He opened a new file on his computer and began to type in the address of yet another company that wouldn't want him. He stopped. *His apartment…* The letters he'd typed disappeared into the screen saver.

He had grown up as the only kid of a single mother. They were always moving from one lousy place to another. He spent time in foster care. The foster houses were nice, but he didn't belong in them. He turned his chair to look out the window. His apartment was on the second floor above a boutique pharmacy on a pleasant street that ran parallel to the main commercial avenue. The apartment consumed an exorbitant portion of his salary, but it was the only place he had ever lived that felt like home. His mother would say he was trying to live above his station.

He swallowed hard. He liked to think he had risen above his station. There'd been times he could have fallen in with the wrong crowd. Those summers at the fresh air camps helped. He looked forward to them every year like an addict to his next fix. Then he got older and they wouldn't let him come back. He spent a couple of summers at a wilderness camp for teens, then the wrestling coach at the high school took him under his wing. He wasn't big enough for football or tall enough for basketball, but he was quick and strong and turned out to be a good wrestler. He worked hard to get into a business program at the community college, convinced the diploma would lead to what he craved—a decent life and security. And now, looking out the window, he knew that was threatened.

He watched as a young couple emerged from Pritchard's Jewellery. The woman held out her ring finger. The man laughed and put an arm around her.

During these weeks of typing job applications—punctuated by lengthening periods of staring out the window—Donnie had ample opportunity to view the passing show. He observed many things. Mr. Pritchard opened his store at nine a.m., five days a week, and closed at five every afternoon. He did not do business on Sundays. On Wednesdays he closed at noon and did not reopen until nine the next morning. Donnie didn't understand why Mr. Pritchard kept the Wednesday routine. He was too young to remember the convention of the medical half-holiday. Doctors traditionally had taken the half-day to go golfing. Mr. Pritchard had, for many years, golfed with Sam and Bert, a pair of GPs, and Mike, an orthopedic surgeon. Those days were long past. Doctors no longer took the half-holiday on Wednesdays. Bert and Mike had passed on. Sam had moved to Victoria to be near his children. On those half-days, Mr. Pritchard would hand the shop over to his apprentice, Tommy Wells, and after Tommy moved to Toronto, to his wife, Effie. After Effie died and everyone else either died or moved away, Mr. Pritchard no longer went golfing, but he continued his habit of closing early on Wednesdays. He would put up his closed sign at noon and pull down the shade. Fifteen minutes later, he would reappear, walking through the breezeway that separated his shop from Around The World With Tea. He would turn left and not be seen until nine the next morning.

Donnie thought—idly at first—how simple it would be to rob Mr. Pritchard. The shop, like several others on the block, had entrances off the rear parking lot in addition to those facing the street. How simple it would be to walk in and wait in the shadows by the back room until the last customer had left and Mr. Pritchard closed up. A gentle tap on the head, grab whatever he could get, and exit through the rear door.

He wasn't sure how much money Mr. Pritchard would have on hand, but it would be more than he had now, which was almost nothing. He took a deep breath. It had been a long time since he hadn't been a few dollars ahead. He remembered his mother opening a can of creamed corn and telling him that was supper for both of them. When he saw the can of creamed corn on the counter, he knew that meant the wolf was at the door—as his mother would say. That meant there wouldn't be enough money to buy food until the end of the month, sometimes several days away. He was part of the breakfast program at school and that meant having other kids looking at him as if they felt sorry for him, which wasn't nice, but better than the ones who made fun of him. It meant being dragged down to free dinners at whatever church was offering. By the time he was ten he thought he had seen the inside of every church in three towns. He dug his knuckles into his eyes to hold back tears. He had worked too hard to go back to that life.

March — The Pleasant Inn

Margaret Rudley bustled up to the desk with a letter in her hand. "Rudley, I've got a note from Miss Miller. She's researched the wilderness canoe excursion and thinks it would be a splendid adventure for the Pleasant."

"Wonderful, Margaret. Can you imagine lugging the Sawchucks through the woods? They have enough trouble getting around the grounds."

"The Sawchucks wouldn't need to go on the trip, Rudley."

"What are we going to do with them? Leave them here to run the inn?"

Margaret smiled. "Here's what we're going to do. We're going to offer a week-long adventure as part of the regular package. We'll hire a professional guide. Those guests who choose not to accompany us will be looked after by the remaining staff."

"What if the staff wants to come?"

"They don't."

"Why do I get the feeling that this venture has already been discussed behind closed doors and is a virtual *fait accompli?*"

Margaret reached into her pocket and took out a handful of brochures. "It's going to be wonderful, Rudley." She opened one of them and pointed to a map of Northern Ontario. "Miss Miller selected this as the most feasible route."

"And who do you propose to accompany you?"

"Miss Miller and Mr. Simpson, of course. Norman and Geraldine Phipps-Walker. And a few others, I expect. We've added the brochure as a supplement to our usual announcements for the summer season."

"How did I miss all of this, Margaret?"

She patted his arm. "We didn't want to worry you with the details, Rudley. We wanted to have a firm proposal to put before you."

"What if I were to squelch the whole thing?"

"You wouldn't. Not with everyone so keen."

He considered this, then brightened. "I agree, Margaret, it's a splendid idea. I think you should go ahead and enjoy yourselves."

"Rudley."

"Let's be sensible, Margaret. There's no reason I need to come. I'd just be in the way, a wet blanket."

"I know you would, Rudley, but do it for me."

"I'd do many things for you, Margaret. I can't say this is one of them."

"Rudley, you'll love it. I want you to at least think about it." She pushed the brochure in front of him. "If anyone's looking for me, I'll be at the High Birches."

Rudley planted his elbows on the desk, letting his hands form a ledge for his chin. The High Birches, Margaret's sanctum sanctorum. She was clearly annoyed with him. She hadn't deserted him for the High Birches—the cabin so named because it perched on the rise near the woods—for over a year. She'd stayed away two days that time and all he'd done was telephone Mrs. Blount and question her aesthetic sense. He thought he'd been remarkably restrained when he'd viewed the floral arrangements for that year's Valentine's Day Ball. She was lucky he hadn't gone down to the flower shop, leapt across the counter, seized Mrs. Blount by the throat, and roared out what he thought sounded so much more restrained on the telephone: "Who in their right mind could imagine that dusty rose and cream would be an appropriate combination for Valentine's Day? Red, Mrs. Blount. White,

Mrs. Blount. Those colours only, Mrs. Blount. The red is symbolic of the human heart. If your heart were dusty rose, Mrs. Blount, you'd be completely dead instead of just from the neck up." He put his hands over his ears and let his forehead sink down onto the desk. Margaret had been furious for his outburst. So angry he hadn't dared yell at Mrs. Blount since. He knew such restraint wasn't good for his blood pressure. He paused, brought his head up, and stared at the wall.

He was standing there when Tiffany Armstrong, the housekeeper, came out of the drawing room. She stopped in front of the desk. "Mr. Rudley?"

He looked at her, morose. "Do you need to do something here? Dust the desk, for example?"

Tiffany shook her head. "I'll do that later. I just wanted to let you know I'd be at the High Birches."

He regarded her with hound-dog eyes. "You too?"

Her eyes widened with bewilderment.

"What did I do to offend you?" Rudley continued.

"Nothing in particular. I promised Mrs. Rudley I'd help her take some measurements."

Rudley's forehead crimped in perplexity.

"Mrs. Rudley is making new curtains for the High Birches."

Rudley sighed with relief. "I thought it had to do with this wilderness thing."

Tiffany clapped her hands. "Oh, won't that be exciting? I'm sure you'll love it."

"So, you plan to go?"

"No."

"If you're so sure I'll love it, why aren't you going?"

"I know you'll love it, Mr. Rudley. I wouldn't care for that sort of thing at all."

He looked after her, dumbfounded, as she headed down the back stairs, then slumped over the desk.

Tim passed the dining room door with a stack of napkins. Gregoire followed, gesticulating wildly. Rudley clapped his hands over his ears.

Tim McAuley, the young Paul Newman, and Gregoire Rochon, the incomparable chef, had been working together for several years. They were a bit of a Laurel and Hardy act. Rudley doubted if a day passed without the two of them having an argument. Tim was always cool; Gregoire was always frazzled. Tim worked hard and had a talent for pleasing the most difficult guests. He was handsome and fit. Rudley was sure Tim could have had a significant career on stage. He had done a terrific Macbeth at the inn's summer theatre, Margaret having successfully made the leap to Shakespeare.

Rudley paused in thought. He hoped she would take a leap out of it soon. As much as he appreciated the Bard, he had had quite enough of him in high school. "Give me Broadway any day," he said aloud. He loved the choreography. "How much dance do you see in a Shakespearean play?" he asked Albert, who had rolled over on the rug in the middle of the lobby and was regarding him fondly.

The commotion in the dining room faded as Tim and Gregoire retreated to the kitchen. He cocked an ear but caught only the occasional word, none of them particularly illuminating. "Albert," he said, "I think it's time for a cup of coffee."

As he approached the kitchen door, the conversation came to a halt. He opened the door. Tim was sitting on a stool, picking at crumbs from a cookie sheet. Gregoire was leaning over the stove, peering into a saucepan.

"What was all that commotion about?"

Gregoire stepped back from the stove, mopping his forehead with the tail of his apron. "He has been taking my most luscious strawberries, the ones I had chosen myself for the fondue."

Rudley looked at Tim.

"I did not take his luscious strawberries," said Tim. He returned his attention to the crumb tray.

Rudley thought for a minute. "Were those the ones in the yellow bowl by the sink?"

Gregoire turned and looked at him suspiciously. "Yes?"

Rudley coughed. "You're right. They were luscious."

Tim laughed. Gregoire rolled his eyes and returned to his saucepan.

"I suppose you've heard about this canoe trip," Rudley added hastily.

Gregoire froze, spoon in hand. "We are not going."

Tim sniffed. "I was keen on going until I found out I'd have to carry a canoe and wear khaki. But," he hastened to add, "you'll love it."

"And you?"

Gregoire huffed. "I do not mind cooking over an open fire once a week for the fish fry. I would not care to do it three times a day for seven days or so—although I would, if absolutely necessary. But it will not be necessary because I am sure you will enjoy preparing your own meals as part of the camping experience over an open pit with kindling you have ignited with mirrors."

Rudley paused. "I'm sure Lloyd will be coming."

Tim shook his head. "Lloyd doesn't like travelling."

"Besides," said Gregoire, "we need him here to fix whatever is broken."

"I see." Rudley poured himself a cup of coffee and returned to the desk.

Fix whatever is broken? Surely they didn't expect the inn to fall apart in a week. He sighed. He knew he would have to go on this damn trip—better to suffer a week with mosquitoes and camp toilets than suffer an eternity of guilt for disappointing Margaret and ruining her enjoyment of the adventure. And it was probably just as well that the staff remained at the inn. He was sure they would cope very well in the wilderness, but they would drive him insane.

He slumped over the desk, defeated. He had no desire to spend a week in the wilderness. He was perfectly happy where he was— at the front desk with his coffee and his illicit package of cigarettes, presiding over his kingdom with a firm but benign hand.

He sighed. The year had got off to such a promising start. A New Year's Eve with an outstanding Music Hall. Melba Millotte had wowed the audience with her mastery of the flute, although, to his mind, she'd always been rather good at puckering her lips. Tim and

Gregoire had done a superb dance routine to a medley of songs from *Guys and Dolls*. Tiffany had performed several études from Bach. He wrinkled his nose—toe-tappers they were not, but he had to give her credit for being an excellent pianist. Then Lloyd with his creepy rendition of "Maxwell's Silver Hammer." Aunt Pearl had warbled through a heartwarming version of "White Cliffs of Dover." The old judge had done "It's a Long Way to Tipperary" on the spoons, a performance he had favoured them with for at least the past fifteen years. Then—he smiled—he and Margaret had put the frosting on the cake, waltzing to a selection of Broadway show tunes. He did a few steps behind the desk. Ah, if there were anything that would keep him from that desk, it would be dance. He glided out into the lobby, did a pirouette, and almost tripped over Albert, who had chosen that moment to roll over.

"Never took a dance lesson in my life," he told Albert. "I learned from watching the best. Fred Astaire, Bill Robinson. I might have been a dancer too, he thought, if it hadn't been for my father. He'd wanted to take tap dance lessons as a boy. His father suggested instead that he play hockey, football, baseball, basketball, tiddlywinks. "Anything, Trevor," he had said, "anything but dance. People might think you were peculiar." He was thirty years old before he realized what his father meant. Hell of a thing to think someone was peculiar because they danced. Dance is in our souls; it's an expression of joyous abandon. He wouldn't have met Margaret if it hadn't have been for dance.

Rudley smiled in recollection. There he was at that gathering in London, putting up with the pretentions of a band of arty twits, standing in a corner with a bottle of Irish whisky, when she approached and asked him to dance. A bit cheeky of her, he thought. She told him later—once their romance was well-established—that she couldn't bear seeing everyone in the room having such a good time while this Canadian grump stood in a corner, swilling whisky, and looking ready to kill. He hadn't been swilling whisky—he'd had only three shots—and the grumpiness was the result of his feeling out of place. But he didn't tell her that when she approached him he had been reduced to a blithering idiot. That he'd been watching her all evening while pretending he was not. It wasn't because she was the most beautiful woman in the room—although after he had known her a few minutes he was sure she was—it was because she seemed so vibrant and devoid of airs. And—as he quickly discovered—she was also kind and thoughtful.

People were always telling him how lucky he was to have married a fine woman like Margaret. More like a miracle, his father once said. He knew he had snared the blue ribbon when Margaret said yes. His smile broadened. Not bad for a boy from Galt.

Aunt Pearl came out of the drawing room at that moment and paused. "So nice to see you looking happy, Rudley. And so rare."

Rudley picked up a stack of mail and began to sort through it. "Just because I'm not grinning like the Cheshire cat all the time doesn't mean I'm not happy, Pearl."

"You're a grouch, Rudley. You've been a grouch as long as I've known you. You probably were a grouchy baby."

"Perhaps I was," he said. "And in a world overflowing with calamity, I think a little gravity is called for." He cleared his throat. "Will you be coming on the wilderness adventure?"

Pearl fixed him with a myopic stare for a moment, then broke into laughter. "Of course not, Rudley. The Pleasant is sufficiently rustic for me. Why, when I lived in London, I thought Hyde Park was the frontier. I was never one for mucking about in straw hats and Wellingtons."

"I suppose we'll be wearing Tilleys and hiking boots, but I appreciate your sentiment."

"Besides," Pearl continued, "Tim and Gregoire aren't going. I like to be close to my boys."

Because you can twist them around your little finger, he thought. "I see you're aware of the details of our trip, Pearl. I was apprised only a few minutes ago that the whole damn thing had been arranged."

"That's all right, dear. Sometimes it's better to go with the flow. Besides, you have more important things to worry about than a journey into God-knows-where."

He gave her a dubious look.

"Better to have it arranged and presented for your approval."

"Pearl, you're laying it on a bit thick."

"All right, then. Everyone knows you're a killjoy, Rudley. Better to go ahead and make plans and let you carry on about it afterwards than have you throwing cold water on the project from start to finish." She brightened. "Oh, there's Mr. Patry. I promised him a game of cribbage."

"How much do you plan to take him for today?"

She smirked. "He's not much of a gambling man but he has lovely eyes."

Rudley watched as Pearl intercepted Mr. Patry and steered him toward the drawing room. The woman's like a spider spinning her web, he thought. If I were an older gentleman, I'd worry about becoming the latest fly. Of course, he'd never had any complaints from these older gentlemen. He smiled. Wonderful woman, Aunt Pearl. Everyone adored her in spite of the fact she was a souse and an unreformed kleptomaniac. He supposed that had something to do with having had a bomb dropped on her during the war. She didn't travel much these days, apart from that trip to Pago Pago, where, according to Ralph, Margaret's brother, she turned the island on its ear. Won one of the villagers in a card game, Ralph reported, although she gave him back before she left.

Rudley had never understood the itch to travel. Why anyone would want to be anywhere other than the Pleasant stumped him. Where else could you find so much beauty? A pristine lake, a forest brimming with flora and fauna, beautiful grounds, wonderful food, and—he smiled a self-congratulatory smile—a firm but gracious innkeeper. He'd heard that travel built community and erased ignorance and misunderstanding. Nonsense, he thought. If we hadn't travelled in the first place, we'd never have discovered how much we loathed one other.

The Pleasant was idyllic, soothing. True, there had been the odd murder on the premises. But none of them were his fault and he saw no reason to apologize for them. He did think, however, that there had been quite enough of them and he was determined there would be no more. The last thing he wanted was another go-around with Detectives Brisbois and Creighton sticking their noses into his Eden.

Lloyd, the handyman, came by the desk

"What do you want?" Rudley asked.

"On my way to the kitchen. Gregoire says he has lemon pie for me and some jam-jams."

"Oh." Rudley sagged against the desk, deflated. He was in the mood for confrontation and Lloyd's reasonable response had taken the wind out of his sails. "By the way," he said peevishly, "how did you get out of this canoe trip?"

"Told Mrs. Rudley I didn't want to go. I like being at home."

"And what did she say?"

"She said, 'I understand, dear.'"

Rudley sighed. "You may go now." He shooed Lloyd away, reached under the desk, and took out a crumpled pack of Benson & Hedges. "I told Mrs. Rudley I didn't want to go, that I liked being at home," he muttered. "That didn't work for me." It would have been handy to have Lloyd on the trip. He could fix anything, improvise all sorts of contraptions. And if they ran into a bear? Lloyd had a way with animals.

Lloyd would have come if Margaret had coaxed him. He was responsive to Margaret. More than to me, Rudley thought with chagrin. Of course, Margaret pampered Lloyd, let him have whatever he wanted—because he was an orphan. Margaret had read too much Dickens.

Lloyd's probably an orphan because he murdered his parents, Rudley considered. The man looked enough like a psychopath to make that notion plausible. He pondered the idea for a minute, then reluctantly dismissed it. Even if Margaret had insisted on taking Lloyd on the trip, even if she could have persuaded the rest to come along, she still would have wanted her husband to accompany them. "We can't leave you alone here at the inn, Rudley," she would say. He paused, a blissful look crossing his face. All alone at the Pleasant. He could stand at the desk all day, reading his paper, sipping his coffee, smoking as much as he wanted, and enjoying the odd glass of whisky. No one to bother him.

He was about to light a cigarette when Margaret returned from the High Birches, coming up the back stairs, measuring tape in hand. He threw the pack of cigarettes under the desk. "Perhaps this canoe trip isn't such a bad idea. It'll give me a break from the staff."

"And vice versa." Margaret smiled and went on into the drawing room.

Chapter Two

Donnie finally had to move from his cherished apartment into a basement bachelor in a seedy part of Fredericton. He kept a stiff upper lip as the truck from the used furniture store carted away his belongings for a fraction of the price he had paid for them. The truck dropped him and the few things he had retained off at his new place. It wasn't until he was inside that he broke down. He allowed a few tears, then wiped them away stubbornly. He'd learned a long time ago that showing emotion had a high cost; when things were most dire, that was the time you could least afford to give up and fall apart. He washed his face and promised himself he would not grieve for his home again.

For the first few days he existed in a state of quiet paralysis. He sat on his cot, watching the legs of people passing and dogs sometimes doing their business on the weedy patch in front of his window. Sometimes he would close his eyes and pretend he was on his old street with its pleasant trees and flowerpots, breathing in the fragrance of cedar and geranium, taking in the quiet opulence of the jewellery store window.

Holding onto that image helped him block out the reality of the dog poop. Some people did pick up after their dogs, and if they didn't, he did—at first. Then one day he didn't until later. The day after that he didn't bother at all.

May—The Pleasant Inn

Margaret stood at the desk opening the mail, placing the envelopes to one side. She unfolded each letter, smoothed it, scanned it, and set it aside for Rudley. "Well, here's the last piece. Mr. Turnbull has confirmed with his cheque."

"Another one for the expedition?" Rudley asked.

"Yes. So we're all set. We'll have Miss Miller and Mr. Simpson, Geraldine and Norman, Eric Turnbull and Vern Peters, and, of course, you and me. That's eight, not including our tour guide."

"Whom did you sign up with?"

"That friend of your father's."

"Mr. Jackson?"

"Yes. Archie put us onto him."

"So my brother's involved in this?"

"He agrees you should get away."

"Old Clifton Jackson. Well, I do like a man with experience."

"I doubt if it will be Clifton himself."

"He's foisting us off on a stranger?"

Margaret shook her head. "Rudley, Mr. Jackson is in his eighties. He's titular head of the enterprise, but he no longer leads expeditions."

"I don't see why not, Margaret. I plan to be leading this enterprise when I'm in my eighties."

"No one is apt to perish if a linen order gets mixed up." She patted his arm. "Rudley, Mr. Jackson's company has a good reputation. Our guide will, at the very least, be competent."

"If you say so."

"That's it, Rudley. Mrs. Millotte will do a wonderful job while we're away. We have nothing left to do but attend to the details of getting our kit together."

"Our kit bags and matches."

"Now you're getting into the spirit, Rudley."

He sang a few bars. "Pack up your troubles in your old kit bag and smile, smile, smile." He hummed a few more bars, then stopped. What in hell were they smiling about? They were in filthy, rat-infested trenches, trying to warm themselves with matches. His grandfather had signed up for World War I, but had been thrown off his horse and broken his leg before his division left England. Then, by the time he had recuperated, the war was over. His father had volunteered in World War II, but had been rejected because of his flat feet. If it hadn't been for Aunt Edie, we'd have no history of war service at all, he thought. Aunt Edie was a nurse in a field hospital. The old bat was still alive, driving everyone nuts, checking them for trench foot. He emitted a short laugh.

"What's so funny, Rudley?" Margaret looked up.

"I was thinking about Aunt Edie up there in Preston, driving Archie and Betty to distraction with her weekly foot fungus check." He paused and gazed toward the far wall, troubled. "You know, Margaret, when we're Edie's age, we won't have anyone to drive to distraction."

"Nonsense, Rudley. You'll have the same people you have now."

"I don't know, Margaret. Tim and Gregoire will probably elect to spend their retirement in a warmer climate. Tiffany will probably marry. If she ever finds anyone she deems suitable."

"Perhaps her standards will soften a bit."

"Perhaps."

Margaret ran a finger down the registry entries. "We'll always have Lloyd."

"Perish the thought."

"And Ralph has been making noises lately about retiring near here."

Rudley paused. Ralph. Margaret's brother. King of imported plastic junk. "How near?"

"Quite near, Rudley. And" —Margaret hastened to add —"we have Officer Semple. He plans to retire here."

"That idiot."

"He seems to enjoy our company."

"I don't enjoy his."

"And then, of course, we have Elizabeth and Edward. They're practically family."

"Fine young couple."

"There you have it. Our golden years will be filled with people. All the young people we see regularly. Officer Semple, Officer Owens, Officer Vance, Officer Petrie. They're like old friends too."

"We only see them when someone is murdered."

"Nonsense. They often drop by when they're in the neighbourhood."

"Just in case," he murmured.

He let Margaret go on about the trip, pretending to share in her enthusiasm with the odd "hmm" and "ah."

It was true, he thought, that there had been murders at or near the Pleasant, in addition to the more prosaic risks of cottage life, the drownings, the boating misadventures, the accidental poisonings, and the occasional exotic mishap. He could still see that man dangling from the ski lift by his scarf.

Why did they happen to him? Why not to Ott at the Bridal Path or to the MacPhersons at the West Wind or to one of the proprietors of the many B and Bs? Why should the anal retentive, the ordinary, and the insufferably stupid avoid these mishaps? Possibly because no one who patronized these places had a whiff of imagination or the heart and spirit for risk taking. Even his dullest guests—and the Sawchucks were high on his list of dullest guests—showed more stomach than the brightest of his competitors' clientele. And Norman Phipps-Walker, in spite of his failings, was always up to a challenge. He didn't have to aim his sled between the boulders and the bramble bush. He didn't have to be in the sled at all. Norman seemed as invulnerable as a teenager. And then there was Miss Miller, who was not only always up to a challenge but often precipitated the excitement. Ott would close down if someone broke a leg. Rudley smiled a jaunty smile. Why, around the Pleasant, a broken leg was a badge of honour.

Not that he had any desire to have bodies piling up around his establishment. It wasn't that it discouraged business. It didn't. But he didn't like the police crawling around, taking over his office, and interrogating his staff and guests. Murder disrupted the smooth functioning of the Pleasant and having the order of the Pleasant disrupted was why he hated the notion of this damn trip.

He sighed. How simple the world would be if everyone were more like him. People would, therefore, mind their own business and stay where they belonged.

Chapter Three

Donnie thought a lot about Mr. Pritchard's jewellery store while he sat in his basement apartment staring at the walls. The memory of the subdued sheen of the display window gave him pleasure, if not hope. He had pretty much given up hope. His unemployment insurance cheques were about to run out. The only jobs available were in fast-food establishments and every time he imagined wearing one of those uniforms and working with a bunch of teenagers—worse, waiting on people who were used to seeing him in a suit and tie—he cringed. A counsellor had suggested he might go back to school to brush up on his skills. He didn't have the energy for that. Then something happened one night that drove him out of his funk.

He'd sat in his apartment terrified while the couple upstairs fought. They were new to the building, a whip-thin woman and a stringy punk with a perpetual scowl. They had a baby and a girl about five. The fight—about nothing more than glass of milk the kid spilled—started in the usual way, with raised voices, but it soon escalated, growing louder and more incoherent, with the baby wailing and the little girl screaming. Then someone got slapped hard. Furniture was knocked over. A door slammed and the man pounded down the stairs. The baby continued to wail but the little girl no longer screamed. He listened for the sound of her feet skipping across the floor and was relieved later when he heard them. The fight jolted him out of his torpor, reminded him of who he was, and told him he had to get out of there. At that moment, the only way out seemed to be through Mr. Pritchard's jewellery store.

He told himself it would be easy.

What Donnie didn't count on was Mr. Pritchard standing in front of a mirror when he crept up on him and he didn't count on Mr. Pritchard turning on him and clawing the bandana from his face. He responded by punching the man in the face, hard enough to send him reeling back against the wall, breaking the mirror, and collapsing to the floor, unconscious. Donnie strangled him with the bandana. He grabbed the bag Mr. Pritchard had been about to empty into the safe, stuffed it into his shopping bag, and walked out the back door. He discarded the gloves he'd worn and the bandana in a garbage bin and went home.

Back in his apartment, he put the bag into the closet, put on the kettle for a cup of instant coffee, and sat down on the cot. He held his hands out in front of him and stared at them. He didn't regret killing Mr. Pritchard. He had no choice. The old man could have identified him. He had no intention of going to jail. He'd struggled too hard to make a life for himself. He didn't deserve to be punished for events he had no control over.

He made his coffee, took a few sips, then got the bag from the closet. He found a roll of bills and a smaller canvas bag he assumed contained jewellery or stones. He counted out the cash. Three hundred and fifty-two dollars. He chuckled ruefully. He'd killed the old man for grocery money. He checked the smaller bag, hoping for unset gemstones, and started. The small bag contained a gun and a box of bullets. He checked the gun carefully. It was loaded. He emptied the magazine and returned the bullets to the box. He put a few dollars on the coffee table and returned the gun to the canvas bag with the rest of the money. He emptied the vacuum cleaner bag and stuffed the money and gun into it. Finishing his coffee, he lay down on the bed, and had a nap.

He woke two hours later feeling hungry. Although he was disappointed with his take, he felt cheered by the prospect of a decent meal out.

He chose a Korean restaurant several blocks away, eschewing the places he usually frequented when he seldom had more than enough for a plate of fries and a cup of coffee. He also thought he would be less likely to be remembered. He had heard that Asian people had a hard time identifying Caucasians and vice versa. Something to do with the facial features each group focused on. He had a nice but not extravagant meal, was polite but remote, and left an appropriate tip. He had brought a newspaper with him and pretended to be absorbed with it as he ate. No one seemed to pay any particular attention to him.

It was only after he got home and removed the money from the vacuum bag to recount it that he noticed every bill was marked with a red squiggle in the lower right-hand corner. Every single one. He guessed Mr. Pritchard probably marked the bills so he didn't double-count.

He sat still, staring at the bills, holding his breath. The bank would know the squiggles. And if the bank knew, the police would soon know. They'd sweep the neighbourhood, asking if anyone remembered seeing the marked bills. He squeezed them hard. He wasn't going to be able to spend any more of the money for a long time. He took a deep breath and tried to relax. He reprised his visit to the restaurant and decided he had acted appropriately.

Then he remembered the woman at the cash desk. She had examined the bills, turning each to face her, smoothing them, then dealing them into the cash drawer like a veteran card shark. He assumed it was her way of screening for counterfeits, but someone as precise and practised as she would have noticed Mr. Pritchard's little red squiggles. No matter what nationality she was, if she could take in details of paper money that quickly, she could have taken him in too.

He checked his wallet, hoping he had used only his own money. He still had forty dollars. That meant he had used three fives and a ten with the red squiggles.

He wanted to get up and leave, pack a bag, and walk away. But any abrupt move on his part might raise red flags. He decided to wait for his last unemployment cheque, then let the landlord know he would be moving on at the end of the month. He'd go to the landlord and hold out the cheque helplessly. "This is my last cheque. I guess I'll have to move in with my mother for a while." The landlord would ask about his mail. He'd tell him he'd arranged to have the post office forward it.

He stared at the money. He should get rid of those bills with the red squiggles, take them out to a vacant lot and burn them. Instead, he bundled them together with the gun and returned them to the vacuum cleaner bag.

Lloyd appeared at the desk, pulling a load of suitcases on a dolly.

"I see that the Sawchucks have arrived," said Margaret.

"You'd think those grandchildren of theirs could have carried the luggage," Rudley sniffed.

Lloyd grinned. "They ain't very big."

Margaret lowered her voice. "Are they little people?"

"Guess so," said Lloyd and added, "I guess 'cause they're just little kids."

"How little?" Rudley demanded. "The Sawchucks implied they were teenagers."

"Little," Lloyd persisted. "Maybe eight."

"Damn."

Margaret gave Rudley a nudge as the door opened and Doreen and Walter Sawchuck hobbled in. "Rudley, mind your manners." She came out from behind the desk to greet the new arrivals. "Mr. and Mrs. Sawchuck. It's good to see you."

"It's good to see you too, Mrs. Rudley." Walter peered at the desk. "Rudley?"

"Did you have a good trip?"

"Exhausting," said Doreen as Margaret trotted across the lobby to get her a chair. "Our son-in-law drove all the way from Rochester. We wanted to fly but they wanted to take the car to Montreal to catch their plane to Europe."

"He never wants to stop as often as we need to," said Walter.

"Which must be every ten minutes," Rudley murmured, cognizant of Walter's prostate problems.

"He's all right," Doreen said. "But…"

"Our daughter likes him, I guess," said Walter.

"That's a nice arrangement then," said Margaret. "Why don't we just have Rudley sign you in. You can rest a bit, then we'll help you to your room." She patted Mrs. Sawchuck on the arm. "I'm going to run out to the kitchen and get you a nice, cold drink. What would you like?"

"Just sparkling water," Doreen said. She paused, waving her hand. "No, lemonade. But no ice."

"It hurts our teeth," said Walter.

"My teeth are starting to hurt too," Rudley muttered. "From clenching them." He put on a smile. "You usually enjoy your trip from Rochester."

"Yes," they said in unison. Walter started to say something, then stopped as Doreen tugged at his jacket.

The door opened and a tall man with a beard and a short woman with frizzy hair entered. The man turned and said impatiently, "Come on."

The woman turned and said, "You know what we discussed."

Two children entered, their hands clasped behind their backs. The man stepped forward. "I'm Jim Danby. My wife, Delia, and our children, Ned and Nora."

"Trevor Rudley."

"Say hello to Mr. Rudley," the woman cued the children.

"Hello, Mr. Rudley," they chorused.

The man sighed.

"We were expecting teenagers," said Rudley.

"Oh," said the man, "not teens, twins. I guess you didn't catch that."

"No, I didn't."

"Well, no matter," said Danby. He turned to the children. "Now, I want you to pay attention to Grandma and Grandpa Sawchuck."

"Yes, sir," the children murmured.

"Good." He reached into his pocket and slipped the kids each a bill. They looked at them, shrugged, and stuffed them into their pockets.

Mr. Danby turned toward the door. His wife was already halfway out.

"Will you be staying for lunch?"

"No, Mr. Rudley. We have to be on our way. We have a plane to catch."

"I hear you're going to Switzerland," said Margaret, who had returned with the drinks and was fussing over Mrs. Sawchuck, who was fanning herself vigorously with a newspaper.

"Yes," Danby said and disappeared out the door after his wife.

"That plane must be taxiing as we speak," said Rudley.

"He's always hell bent for leather," Walter said crossly.

"He's anxious about being on time," said Doreen. "It isn't easy in the airports these days."

"Which is why I try to avoid them," said Rudley.

"Will the children be having lunch?" Margaret gave them an encouraging smile.

They smiled back.

"If they want to," said Walter. "Although I don't know how much more they can stuff in."

"We stopped at McDonald's," said Doreen.

"Perhaps some dessert," said Margaret. "I know Gregoire has a lovely chocolate pie chilling in the refrigerator. If you'll come into the dining room, I'll get you some pie and something to drink."

The children followed her into the dining room.

Doreen stopped them as they passed her. "Remember," she said. "Six o'clock."

Nora rolled her eyes. "Yes, Grandma."

"Say 'thank you, Mrs. Rudley,'" said Doreen.

After a pregnant pause, both children turned and said, "Thank you, Mrs. Rudley."

Lloyd escorted the Sawchucks to their room and returned for the luggage.

"Twins," Rudley muttered.

"Both of them," said Lloyd.

Margaret came out of the dining room. "They seem like nice children, Rudley."

"I'm sure Doreen told me they were teenagers when she made the reservations."

"Perhaps in her mind they are, Rudley."

"That could be true," said Rudley. "After all, in her mind a spider is a matter of national security."

"And children grow up so much faster these days. Eight-year-olds today probably seem like the thirteen-year-olds of yesteryear."

"I'm not sure how I feel, Margaret, about the Pleasant being responsible for such young children in their parents' absence."

"The Sawchucks are responsible for them."

"That would be a novelty. I haven't known them to be responsible for anything since I met them."

"Now, Rudley, the children are quiet and polite. I'm sure they won't be a bit of trouble for anyone." She gave him a peck on the cheek. "I'm going up to make sure the Sawchucks are settled in."

He listened to her quick steps up the stairs and grinned. Most nimble feet west of the Bolshoi, he thought. Then the children came to mind and the smile vanished. It was a shame to see children at eight being thought of as teenagers. When he was eight, he couldn't even imagine being a teenager. His days were full of bicycles and sleds and baseballs and tramping around in the woods with his pal, Squiggy Ross. He shook his head with nostalgia. Dear old Squiggy, that winsome lad with the blond curls and gap-toothed grin, now bald and toothless, squatting on a corner in downtown Galt. But at eight, he and Squiggy didn't have a care in the world. He found it repulsive that children as young as seven were tarted up and expected to take an interest in the opposite sex. He barely knew he was supposed to be interested in girls until he turned thirteen and his father gave him the talk. Not easy for his father, who, although an affectionate father, was not accustomed to intimate conversations with his sons. Of course, it helped that he was a medical doctor with charts and diagrams. He delivered the talk as if he were lecturing a class of medical students. When the lecture ended, Rudley was horrified but not much better informed. And to think that five-year-olds were subjected to such information!

"Rudley"—Margaret appeared in front of the desk—"you look as if you've swallowed something disagreeable."

"Children grow up too fast these days, Margaret."

"That's what my mother used to say."

"Makes me long for that age of innocence."

"Yes, children were working in the coal mines then." Margaret turned toward the dining room. "I'll nip in and see how they're getting along."

Rudley shook his head. He didn't agree with child labour, not that he discounted the discipline such work encouraged. The Victorians had one thing right: Children should be seen and not heard. He paused and smiled a cheery smile. Preferably not seen and not heard. Preferably several miles away. Preferably on their own continent. People should be incubated in cocoons, he decided, and emerge as complete adults. He thought for a moment, then nodded. Yes, a much more sensible arrangement.

Chapter Four

Five days after Mr. Pritchard's death, the Fredericton newspapers reported that a woman had witnessed a man crossing the parking lot behind the jewellery store at about the time the murder was believed to have occurred. She couldn't offer a good description as he was wearing a floppy hat that obscured his face. Besides, she was mainly focused on the shopping bag. It was brown with a big purple iris on it. She remembered that because it came from a gourmet food shop where she sometimes bought gifts but couldn't afford to frequent on a regular basis.

The newspaper item left Donnie cold. He never imagined anyone would notice the bag. He'd taken it because it was the sturdiest shopping bag he had. He'd been in the store just once, to buy a Christmas gift for his boss, who had a thing about smoked salmon. His gaze darted over the coffee table, the newspaper he was holding now collapsed in his lap. He shook his head, incredulous. What if he went to jail because of a five-dollar bill with a red squiggle and some foodie with an eye for bags with logos?

He had to get rid of the bag and hope that no one else had paid any attention to it. He knew his thinking wasn't logical but, in his mind's eye, he saw thousands of people watching the news item and discussing it at water coolers, people at the Gourmet Shoppe straining to remember likely suspects, people in the neighbourhood trying to remember who they'd seen carrying that bag. He was glad he had worn the hat but now he'd have to get rid of that too.

He waited until dark, tore the incriminating logo off the bag, and flushed it. He rolled up the brown bag and put it into a plastic one along with the floppy hat. He ducked out of his apartment and deposited the bag in a garbage bin. Then he went into Harvey's and ordered a burger. He noticed one woman staring in his direction but then he realized she was near-sighted and was trying to read the menu. He went home, ate his burger, and considered his situation. In the end, he decided it was best to proceed with his previous plan: collect his last cheque, which was scheduled to arrive in the next couple of days, wait out the few days until the end of the month when the rent was due, then hand in the key to his landlord, reasoning it would look suspicious if he left precipitously.

But something would happen two days later that would change his mind.

The auxiliary police officers in their bright yellow vests were merely calling at a house where a citizen had reported an abandoned bicycle. Donnie didn't linger at the window long enough to see them take the bicycle and wheel it to their truck. When he saw the officers he closed the blinds and went into the bathroom, anticipating their knock, waiting for them to go away.

Maybe they were searching the neighbourhood for clues. Maybe someone saw him walking home with the bag and its faded purple iris. Maybe they had found his hat in the garbage bin. He couldn't imagine they would check every garbage can, but maybe in a murder case they did, especially since—if the newspapers were correct—George Pritchard was a much-loved man and the community, in the words of the police chief, was incensed at the killing of an eighty-five-year-old. And for what? the proprietor of Around the World with Tea was quoted as saying. The few dollars his old friend George would have had in the till after the half-day Wednesday?

He thought about the crumpled bills with the red squiggles. He took the money because he needed it. He hadn't planned to kill the old man. He froze as he heard a knock at the door, then relaxed when the door across the hall opened to a girl's voice and laughter.

He took a deep breath and ventured out into his sitting room. He thought for a moment, then started to pack a bag, hesitating before he took the gun from the vacuum cleaner and shoved it into his shaving kit. He spent the night roaming his apartment in the dark with the curtains drawn, praying that his cheque would arrive on time.

The cheque was in his mailbox the next morning. He cashed it, picked up his suitcase, and left.

Rudley was at the desk when the children came down.

"Grandma said you have a games room," said Nora.

Rudley looked up from his paper. "I suppose she meant the drawing room." He pointed in that direction.

"What kind of games?"

"The usual, I suppose."

"Do you have Angry Birds?"

"No, I would say ours are usually quite benign."

Nora and Ned gave each other a look and went off to the drawing room.

Twenty minutes later, the kids returned. They stopped in front of the desk, arms folded. "There's nothing in there but a bunch of board games," Nora said.

Rudley looked at them over his paper. "I beg your pardon?"

Nora stamped her foot. "You heard us."

"And there's an old lady in there who wanted us to play cards for money," said Ned.

"And she cheats," added Nora.

"I see you've met Aunt Pearl," said Rudley.

"Our father said there'd be computer games and an arcade."

"I'm afraid your father was misinformed."

"We want something to do."

"You could read a book."

"We didn't bring our Kindles. Dad said we wouldn't need them. He said you'd have all that stuff."

"You could watch television."

"Where?"

"There's one in the drawing room."

"That little thing? You've got to have a bigger one somewhere," Nora complained.

"With cable," said Ned. "That one has three channels."

"I'm afraid that's all we have," said Rudley. "We don't watch much television."

Nora heaved an exaggerated sigh. "Come on"—she poked Ned in the ribs—"let's go."

Margaret came out of the kitchen and said hello to the children as they passed. They ignored her.

"I think their manners are slipping," said Rudley. "And rather quickly."

"Oh, I think they're just out of sorts from their trip or not feeling comfortable in an unfamiliar place. Children of that age aren't very good at hiding their emotions."

"You're a forgiving woman, Margaret."

"Just well practised."

While Rudley was trying to decipher the meaning of that comment, the front door opened to a smattering of chuckles and chatter revealing Norman and Geraldine Phipps-Walker, each laden down with a backpack and two suitcases. Norman paused to inhale the aroma from the dining room before arriving at the desk.

Rudley turned the register to face him. "Mr. and Mrs. P.-W., are you planning to take all of that into the wilderness?"

Norman offered a bucktoothed smile. "Of course not, Rudley. Most of this is for the rest of our stay. I can assure you, Geraldine and I will be stripped down to the essentials. We've taken excursions where our entire kit fit into my hip pocket."

"I take it you're talking about your American Express Card."

Geraldine waved him off. "Oh, Rudley, you're so wry."

"Looking forward to the trip, Rudley?" Norman asked.

"Not particularly. I think these jaunts are disruptive and ghastly. Why would anyone want to go anywhere when they can stay here?"

"I have heard, Rudley, that it is necessary to seek out new experiences to keep life from falling into a predictable pattern. Falling into predictable patterns makes our lives mundane. Novelty keeps our lives from flowing away on us."

"If you say so, Norman."

"They say travel is broadening, Rudley."

Rudley folded his arms across his chest. "I travelled once, Norman. I went to England. I met Margaret. I saw things that were less grand than I had imagined them to be. I decided travelling was not all it was cracked up to be."

"I suppose that's possible, Rudley," Norman responded, "if you expect real life to resemble picture postcards."

Geraldine patted him on the arm. "Oh, you'll love it, Rudley." She cast a fond look into the dining room. "I'm glad we decided to check in a day early. It gives us a few hours to enjoy Gregoire's cooking before we're reduced to living off the land."

"He's preparing quite the feast tonight with that in mind."

"We'll just stow our gear and be down for lunch in a flash," said Norman.

"I'm guessing salmon quiche," said Geraldine, inhaling deeply. "And do I detect a hint of chocolate cake?"

"I'm sure you do."

Geraldine and Norman went on up the stairs, laughing and chatting.

"That woman could ferret out a lemon tart at a hundred paces," Rudley told Albert.

Geraldine Phipps-Walker was a big woman, not obese, but tall, big-boned, and substantial. She ate like a lumberjack, and with gusto. She did everything in a large way. He cocked an ear. He could hear the Phipps-Walkers twittering away all along the second-floor corridor.

"Geraldine and Norman just checked in," Rudley told Margaret, who had come out of the dining room. "They seem to be in especially high spirits." He paused as Geraldine's shout of "Oh, Norman" floated down the stairs. "Exceptionally high spirits."

"It is their anniversary this week, Rudley."

"It's amazing how you remember these things, Margaret," Rudley responded, thinking he could barely remember his own.

"It's wonderful to see a couple who have been married so long and who so clearly enjoy each other's company."

"I hope she doesn't expect him to carry her over the threshold. For old time's sake."

"I'm sure she doesn't, but I know he'd be game for it."

"I'm glad you didn't expect me to perform that silly ritual, Margaret."

"I had other plans for you, Rudley. A wrenched back wouldn't have fit with them." She gave him a peck on the cheek. "I'm going to see how Tiffany's doing."

He smiled a lopsided smile. "I think I would have managed somehow."

Donnie Albright bought a ticket from Fredericton to Montreal, planning to transfer to a bus to Toronto. But when he arrived in Montreal, he found he would have to change stations and the bus was a milk run. He decided to proceed instead to Ottawa and from there catch an express to Toronto, which would be quicker. If questioned, he would say he was planning to look up one of his foster brothers. He knew one of them still lived close to a house they had shared. Their foster mother sent him a card every year. He never responded. He supposed she did it out of some sense of duty. He guessed she thought he was fond of her. Maybe because of his smile. He learned early that the way to get more of what he wanted from her was to smile.

He almost fell asleep on the bus. He must have dozed off for at least few minutes because when he came to, his head was on the shoulder of the lady in the next seat. He took a deep breath and sat up straight, forcing himself to keep his eyes open.

Tim came out of the kitchen, rolling a trolley laden with food.

Rudley looked up from his newspaper. "It looks as if everyone ordered in."

"It's for the Benson sisters," Tim said. "And their guests."

Rudley looked at him blankly.

"They've invited the children to join them."

"Senility has finally won out, I would say."

Tim rolled his eyes. "The children discovered the sisters have their very own fifty-inch television with an unlimited supply of DVDs. Right now, they're engaged in a *Rocky* marathon. They've ordered Philly cheese steaks, cherry cheesecake, made, of course, with Philadelphia cream cheese, litres of Pepsi, heavenly hash ice cream, and a special platter of Gregoire's dream fudge."

"We'll find them all dead in the morning from a sugar coma or a coronary."

"Nothing is too much for such sweet children," Tim said. "I'm quoting the sisters, of course. You wouldn't believe it, but those little monsters are absolutely mealy-mouthed around them."

"Our problem is solved."

"For a few hours anyway." Tim shook his head. "The kids thought you were lying about the television situation. So they went from cabin to cabin peeking in windows until they came to the Elm Pavilion."

"And there they found three ladies frozen in front of that hideous screen."

"More or less. Louise saw them at the window and waved them in."

"She probably couldn't see who they were."

"Oh, she saw who was there. She saw the most adorable moppets clinging to the window sill, their eyes wide."

"And she let them in."

"Of course. After all, they were merely seeking a kind adult to give them some attention—what with their parents away, with everyone so busy, with everyone misunderstanding them. And such an adorable little girl and sweet little boy."

"Maybe they're fattening them up for the oven," Rudley remarked.

"That's what I was hoping," said Tim. "But the sisters seem genuinely besotted with them."

"We'll have to keep an eye on that. Make sure they aren't after the old dolls' cache of laudanum."

"I'm on it, Boss."

Tim went on his way. Margaret came down the stairs with a list in her hand. "Rudley, the Sawchucks have presented me with a preliminary list of their concerns."

"Preliminary?"

"In case they think of something they need to add later."

Rudley checked the list, his eyebrows dipping into a 'V'. "'Who,'" he read aloud, "'will be responsible for arranging our boating outings while you are away?'"

"Well, how in hell do I know? Ask whoever happens to be hanging around the desk." Rudley looked again at the list. "'Who will be responsible for emergencies involving vermin?'"

He crossed his eyes. "The cat. We'll chain Blanche outside the door, Mrs. Sawchuck."

"I doubt if that would put her in a good mood," Margaret observed.

"That cat's a persnickety old thing. Couldn't you tell that when you adopted her, Margaret? She was the only kitten left. Didn't you wonder about that?"

"They explained, Rudley, that people kept passing her by because she didn't seem particularly cuddly. I don't think it's fair to shun someone simply because they're reticent."

"True, we can't all be charming."

She let that pass. "I'm afraid Blanche won't be available in any event, Rudley. The sisters want her as their guest while we're away."

"The sisters are losing their marbles." Rudley turned back to the Sawchucks' list. "'Who will make sure we have an adequate supply of prunes and prune juice on hand?'" Rudley threw his pen down, exasperated. "I'm sure Mrs. Millotte is capable of following a basic stock inventory."

Margaret patted him on the shoulder. "Patience, Rudley."

"They're acting as if they expect us to come back to find them upside down in the swamp, or eaten by rats, or bound up to the gills."

"Humour them, Rudley."

Rudley crumpled the list and tossed it toward the recycle bin. "I have another concern at the moment."

"What would that be?"

"The Benson sisters have befriended the brats. They're having them in for low tea, high tea, supper, whatever, allowing them to watch movies on that monstrosity they call a television. I'm sure those rotten kids are perfectly capable of taking advantage of three helpless ladies."

She gave him a reassuring pat on the arm. "I'm sure there's nothing more untoward going on than two bored children who want to watch television."

"I hate to leave the staff to deal with this sort of thing."

"I'm sure things will sort themselves out once we're out of the picture. Everything is topsy-turvy at the moment with everyone coming and going."

A few minutes later Tim returned with the trolley.

Rudley eyed him expectantly. "So?"

Tim pushed the trolley aside and came to the desk. "The Benson sisters are having the time of their lives. The children are behaving like angels. Yes, Miss Louise. Yes, Miss Kate. Yes, Miss Emma. Butter wouldn't melt in their foul little mouths."

"Perhaps we misjudged them."

"I don't think so. When the sisters weren't looking, they stuck their tongues out at me."

"Nervy."

"And thumbed their noses."

"Disgraceful."

Tim straightened. "Don't worry, Boss. We're on top of things."

"Perhaps I should stay here."

Don't worry," Tim said quickly. "If they step out of line, we'll fix their wagons."

When the bus pulled into the station in Ottawa, Donnie's plans changed. He was sitting as other passengers got off, staring out the window, when he spotted a man talking to a bus driver who had started toward the station for a bathroom break. The man looked familiar because he looked like everyone's idea of the law enforcement officer who rushes to the bus, train, or plane, hot on the heels of a fugitive. The man was wearing a business suit but he wasn't carrying a briefcase. The suit screamed police—not too expensive, not well tailored, too small in the shoulders, and with a tie that was neither the right width or colour nor too conservative or too flamboyant. The fact that the man kept glancing toward the bus added to Donnie's unease.

Donnie was wrong. The man he believed to be a policeman was actually a used car salesman who had come to pick up his daughter coming in from Toronto on a bus scheduled to arrive a few minutes later. He knew the bus driver, having once coached him in Little League, on the team he sponsored: Jerry Bumbry's Auto Sales and Service Bearcats. It was just a hello, how are you, remember the old days kind of conversation. But Donnie didn't know that and the way the man kept glancing toward the loading platform made him nervous. He got up, grabbed his suitcase, and tried to blend in with the other passengers leaving the bus.

He flushed and felt faint with the realization that Mr. Pritchard might have had some kind of surveillance camera in his store.

He left the bus station, forcing himself to act purposefully. He ignored the taxis and proceeded toward the parking lot. He heard the sudden eruption of a siren and saw lights flashing as a police car sped by on the street adjacent the bus station. But it passed without turning in and he exhaled sharply. His grip tightened on the handle of his suitcase. He needed a safe haven. Furthermore he was hungry.

He walked away from the station, past a line of commercial businesses, a five-pin bowling alley and poolroom, and a laundromat, then turned into a side street, feeling uncomfortable with the light and activity.

He walked several blocks past rows of three- and four-storey walkups and turned off again.

He found himself in a bastion of small bungalows with huge backyards, old trees, and mature hedges, a few of them trimmed, but many overgrown. Several of the houses had for sale signs out front. The cars in the driveways were mainly economy compacts, with a few old dinosaurs.

An elderly woman came out of a house across the street and retrieved a penny saver from the newspaper holder under the mailbox. He waited until she went in and closed the door, then crossed the street, walked up the driveway to the rear of the house, and let himself into the backyard through a gate. He eased up the back steps, glancing about to make sure he wasn't being observed. A six-foot board fence enclosed the yard. At dusk, the adjacent backyards were murky and silent.

A curtain busy with sunflowers obscured his view into the house. He strained to see through the narrow slit between the curtains but saw no sign of the old woman. He took a package of vinyl gloves from his pocket, pulled on a pair, and tried the door. It was locked. He slipped out a credit card and jimmied the lock. He opened the door a crack.

An old man sat at the kitchen table, his back to the door. Donnie slipped in and closed the door behind him. The man didn't move. Donnie crept to the table and clapped a hand over his mouth. The old man's slippers scuffled on the door, his fingers moved toward his watch. No, not a watch. A medical alert bracelet. Donnie tore it off and stuck it into his pocket.

He released his grip on the old man's mouth. He gasped for breath. Donnie crept to the door and looked around the corner. The old lady was sitting on a bench near the door, leafing through the penny saver.

"Mary."

The name was said in barely a whisper. Donnie turned and stared at the man. Then he heard footsteps. The old lady had a sixth sense.

"I'm coming, Will." She came through the door, stopped and gasped. "What…?"

Donnie was standing behind the old man, his hands on his shoulders. "I'm hungry," he said.

Chapter Five

The old woman cried out, "Who are you?"

"You don't need to know."

"You've got to leave."

Donnie dug his fingers into the old man's shoulders. The old man shrieked. "Mary!"

She reached a hand toward her husband. "You're hurting him. Please…"

"I need something to eat."

"I don't have anything thawed out."

"A sandwich is fine." He smiled, which emboldened the old woman.

"I'll fix you a sandwich," she said. "Then you'd better go. I'll put it in a bag for you to take with you. Paula will be here soon."

"Is that your daughter?"

"She's our home care worker. She puts Will to bed. She'll be here soon."

"What time?"

"Eleven, but she gets here earlier."

Donnie looked at the clock.

Mary got a package of ham wrapped in grease-stained butcher's paper from the refrigerator, then reached for a bottle of dills. "Do you want pickles?"

He hesitated. "Sure."

"Brown bread okay?"

He stared at her, incredulous. "Fine."

She finished making the sandwich and left it on the counter.

He stopped in front of her as she started toward the door. "Where are you going?"

"To get the rest of the paper. I read it to Will."

"I'll be watching." He stood in the doorway while she retrieved the paper. She returned to the kitchen, pulled her chair close to Will's, and read to him in a high-pitched quaver. Donnie shoved his chair back against the counter. From this position he could watch both doors as he ate.

The telephone rang, startling him. Mary scrambled up, but he grabbed the receiver before she could.

"I have to answer it," she said.

"Answer it, then. Tell whoever it is you'll call back."

Her hand brushed his as she took the receiver. The touch of her dry, thin skin made him shiver. He pressed close to hear the conversation.

"I'm sorry," she said into the receiver, "I can't talk now. I'll…"

He pulled the phone from her hand. "It's a robocall. Telemarketer," he added, as she looked dumbfounded.

She stole a quick breath. "They're terrible. They always call at supper. My granddaughter got put on a list. Maybe I should…" Something in his expression made her break off and scurry back to Will, who gave no sign he had noticed her absence. He was reaching across the table trying to snare Donnie's sandwich. Donnie pulled it away.

"I'll make you something, Will."

Will continued to stare at the sandwich. Donnie broke off a big piece and devoured it, his eyes never leaving Will.

"Maybe you'd like the rest of the soup Jena made for you." Mary said.

Donnie took another bite of the sandwich and gulped it down. "No, don't give him anything." He wiped his mouth on his sleeve. "We've got things to do." He pushed his plate away and rose. "We're going to call a cab." He grabbed the phone and thrust it at Mary. "Call your home care worker. Tell her not to come."

"She just comes."

He grabbed a card stuck on the wall near the phone. "Is this the place she works?"

"Yes."

"Call them and have them tell her not to come. Say you've got family visiting."

He dialed the number and held the receiver to her ear.

"Dot," she said as someone answered. "It's Mary Dack. Can you tell Paula not to come tonight? I've got company."

"Are you all right, Mary?" Donnie heard a pleasant voice ask. He scowled as Mary hesitated.

"Yes, I'm fine," she managed.

"You sound a little breathless."

"Oh, all the fuss."

"Oh, I know what you mean," Dot said. "You're glad to have them come and glad to have them leave. If you change your mind about Paula, give me a call."

"Okay."

Donnie grabbed the phone away from her before she could add anything else. "Now, I want you to call a cab."

Mary's head wobbled. "Why?"

"I have to catch a bus."

Donnie dialed the taxi number from another card near the phone and listened as Mary gave the information. "Okay," he said. "We'll wait for the cab in the front room. When it gets here, you're going to go to the door and ask the driver to come in and help you with your luggage."

She balked. "I can't go anywhere. I can't leave Will."

He smiled. "You and Will are going to stay here. I'm going to take the cab."

She looked confused. "You'll leave me here?"

"Yes."

The cab seemed to take forever. The old lady watched the window, turning anxiously at every sound from the kitchen. Finally the cab slid into view. The driver sat for a moment, then tapped his horn.

Donnie pushed Mary toward the door, whispering in her ear. "Ask him to come in and help you with your suitcase." As she hesitated, he whispered, "You don't want anything to happen to Will."

She stuck her head around the door. Donnie held his breath as her mouth worked soundlessly. The driver, a slight middle-aged man, came toward her, frowning.

"What's the matter?" he asked.

"Luggage," she croaked. "Help."

The driver came up the steps and into the living room. "Where's your…?" His breath left him as Donnie smacked him across the head with the fireplace iron. The driver wobbled, then crashed to the floor. Donnie closed the door, grabbed a pillow from the couch, and pressed it firmly over the man's face.

Mary grabbed a vase. Catching the movement from the corner of his eye, Donnie jumped up, caught her by the arm and flung her against the wall. She reeled back, her head slamming into a radiator. She collapsed and lay still.

Donnie felt for the cabbie's pulse. It was faint and erratic. He pressed the pillow over the man's face for a full two minutes, then rechecked the pulse. It was gone. He dragged the driver away from the door, locked it, and went to check the old woman. She was breathing irregularly. He held the pillow over her face for a few minutes, then went into the kitchen, pillow in hand.

"Mary," the old man whispered.

Donnie didn't answer. He tipped the old man's chair back onto the floor and pressed the pillow over his face.

The old man surprised him, putting up a vigorous fight, flailing about with his arms and legs, and sending a glass of orange juice on the table crashing to the floor. But Donnie clamped the pillow down hard, continuing to push even as he heard Will's nose crunch.

Leaving the old man on the floor, still in the chair, Donnie returned to the living room to make sure Mary and the cabbie were dead.

Once outside, he eased the cab onto the street. He felt anxious, as though other eyes were upon him. But no one was on the street and only the flicker of television light was visible from a few of the windows. Donnie drove toward the train station, following side streets, keeping an eye out for police cruisers. He spotted one two blocks away going in the opposite direction. No lights, no siren. Once at the station, he drove to the deepest, darkest corner of the parking lot. Before leaving the car, he paused to check his face in the mirror. Satisfied he looked neither harried nor otherwise suspicious, he checked his pockets. Reassured to feel the package of vinyl gloves, he left the cab, straightening his jacket down over his hips.

The cabbie's wallet had yielded two hundred and fifteen dollars. That, with the fifty he had found in the old woman's purse, would keep him going for a bit. He took a deep breath. He had killed four people for a little over five hundred dollars. It didn't matter how many more people he killed at this point. If they caught him, he'd never see the light of day from anywhere but a prison again.

He shifted his suitcase to his right hand and walked along the rear of the parking lot. Slipping through a line of trees, he walked along a grassy verge, trying to orient himself and not look conspicuous. Beyond the verge, a ramp led to the Trans-Canada Highway and below that that he saw the lights of a service station. As he contemplated where to go next, he heard a train whistle. Turning, he saw the train shuffle away.

Chapter Six

The service station Donnie had spotted consisted of a self-serve bay backed by a cafeteria. He hesitated before going in. He was carrying a suitcase, which made him uncomfortable. People didn't often go into rest stops carrying luggage. But he was still hungry and he was thirsty. When he got inside the cafeteria though, he felt reassured. The place was packed. He bought a coffee and a jelly doughnut. The clerk at the end of the line took his money without looking at him.

He sat near the back, facing a window, where, he reasoned, he could spot the police quickly and make an inconspicuous exit. He saw one cruiser but it was Ontario Provincial Police and it didn't slow down. It took the ramp and went onto the freeway. Donnie slouched in his chair, trying to look bored and weary while he considered his options.

He couldn't stay in the area long. The cab company would be looking for its driver soon. At first, dispatch would be annoyed, figuring he'd turned his radio off. Then they'd be worried. Within the next two hours, Donnie calculated, the bus and train stations would be flooded with police. He finished his snack and exited through the side door.

An RV pulled into the service station. Ricky Betts and his wife Monica were travelling from Nova Scotia to visit her family in Red Deer. Monica had developed a migraine and had been asleep in the rear of the van since they left Montreal. Though reluctant to wake her,

Ricky thought he'd better check on her. After filling the tank at the self-serve, he moved his vehicle to the side of the station and went to the back of the van.

Monica was stirring.

"Oh," Ricky said with relief, "you're awake."

She looked at him groggily.

"I'm going to get some coffee. Want anything?"

"Yeah." She strained to see the clock dial. "You go ahead. I'll be along in a minute."

"What do you want? I'll bring it back."

"No." She yawned widely. "I want to see what they have."

"Okay."

After Ricky left, Monica struggled to the side of the bed. A beam of light from the service station sign burned her eyes and she dropped back onto the bed, where she promptly returned to sleep.

Donnie slipped out the side door of the cafeteria just as Ricky Betts walked in the front entrance. He hesitated, trying to decide which way to turn.

Without warning, a police cruiser pulled into the service station. An officer jumped out and stepped inside the cafeteria. Donnie froze, his heart doing a stutter step against his breastbone. He knew he had to get away.

He stumbled along the row of cars, cringing as his suitcase banged against a fender, desperate to find one unlocked with the keys in the ignition. No luck. He came to the RV. The door was unlocked. No keys. He couldn't steal the van, but he figured he could, at least, hide out until the cop left.

He eased into the RV, crouching low to avoid being seen. The RV was substantial, with living quarters separated from the cab by a curtain. He slipped behind the curtain and sidled down the passageway past a kitchen nook until he came to a louvered window. He lifted a slat in the Venetian blind to check the cafeteria.

"Ricky?"

Rudley backed out of the Sawchucks' room, cardboard box in hand. "Yes, Mrs. Sawchuck, I'll dispose of him at once." *Oh, I don't know,* he added to himself, *perhaps I'll use one of Gregoire's meat cleavers.* He eased the door shut and pounded down the stairs to the main desk.

Margaret looked up.

"What was the problem, Rudley?"

"Mrs. Sawchuck saw a bat in her bathroom." He opened the box and turned it toward her.

Margaret looked away. "Rudley, don't let it out in the lobby. The poor creature will be frightened to death."

"There is no bat, Margaret. It was just the way the light struck the curtains. The woman can't see a thing without her glasses but has enough conceit to imagine she can."

"Sooner or later, Rudley, she'll catch you in one of your subterfuges."

"No, she won't. The woman is as dull as a bag of hammers. Walter isn't any better but at least he doesn't imagine things. Because he has no imagination."

"Now, Rudley, you like the Sawchucks."

He considered this. "I suppose I do, Margaret, but I prefer them when they haven't taken complete leave of their senses."

"Mrs. Sawchuck is simply obsessing. Once you're away and she realizes the staff is prepared to address her concerns, she'll settle down." Margaret sighed. "It'll be good to get away for a week." She trotted off into the drawing room.

"Once we're away she'll realize the staff is prepared to address her concerns," he repeated to Albert, who lay on his back, nose twitching. Rudley collapsed on the desk, propping himself up on his elbows, his hands muffling his ears. Tim could handle the bats and mice. For an unmitigated fop, he was surprisingly cool about such things. Gregoire, on the other hand, would throw a fit and start quoting public health regulations. Tiffany could deal with the mice but she had a problem with centipedes. Lloyd could handle any species.

Rudley raised his head and smiled blissfully—Mrs. Millotte had been handling the old asses for years. She could handle the

Sawchucks. But why do I have to put up with all this nonsense in the meantime?

He straightened, picked up a pen, and began noodling through the order forms. Because you're an innkeeper, Rudley. The guests have come to depend on your very high standards of service. Rudley sniffed. And what a pain in the ass that was at times. I could have been a dancer, he thought. I was good enough.

He picked up the grocery order. Fancy red and green peppercorns? Couldn't Gregoire make do with ordinary black pepper? He doubted if anyone around the place had a palate refined enough to detect the difference. Gregoire was like all chefs—a royal pain in the butt. Rudley shook his head. A cook was one of those things beyond the control of an innkeeper. Good chefs were always in demand. The possibility of being stuck with a terrible one with no recourse was an innkeeper's worst nightmare. He shuddered as a vision of Mr. Cadeau crossed his mind. He'd had to keep a running tally of every squirrel, raccoon, and frog around the place when Mr. Cadeau was in the kitchen. What a difficult bunch they were, these chefs.

I could have been a doctor, he thought. His father had wanted him to follow in his footsteps. Rudley shook his head again, reached under the counter, and pulled out a pack of Benson & Hedges. He lit up. Thank God, he hadn't gone into medicine. Imagine the hell of being stuck by yourself in a cluttered office trying to save people who were hell bent on self-ruination. He took a long drag. A fate worse than death.

When Monica's fingertips brushed against the back of Donnie's leg she assumed Ricky had returned with the coffee. She was still groggy and when the pillow was pressed against her face she was only able to flail helplessly. The knee rammed into her stomach just below the breastbone took any remaining fight out of her.

Donnie heard the RV door open and someone step aboard. He stuffed the pillow under the woman's head and turned her to her side, facing her away from the door, then flattened himself against the wall adjacent the divider. He could hear the man moving around, paper rustling, and smelled French fries. The footsteps approached. He held his breath. The man stopped in the doorway, so close Donnie could smell his aftershave, feel his body heat.

"Monica?"

The man stood for a few moments staring at the dim light, then turned and went back toward the cab. Donnie stayed still, pressed against the wall, listening. He heard a cupboard door open and close. He smelled coffee.

The engine started. He waited, expecting the RV to turn onto the ramp and onto the Trans-Canada. Instead, it turned in the opposite direction. Donnie sank to his haunches, all the time keeping his ears pricked. He took a deep breath. As long as the RV was moving, he didn't have to worry about being ambushed by Ricky.

Ricky. It was handy to know a man's name if he had to act quickly. People always hesitated if someone unexpectedly said their name.

He felt disoriented as the RV dipped and turned. Were they headed in the direction Ricky had come from? But then, the RV turned again and picked up speed. Donnie rose slowly and peeked out the window. They were headed out of town, toward farm country.

When the cabbie failed to respond to repeated prompts, the company notified the police. The officers went first to the origin of last call and discovered the bodies of Mary and Will Dack and the cabbie. Next, they went to the destination Mary had named on the phone, the bus station. When they asked the ticket agents if they'd seen anything strange, they rolled their eyes. They saw strange things every day. The officers changed their approach. Had the agents seen anyone who seemed nervous, hypervigilant? They thought about that but, in the end, had to say they hadn't seen anyone who stood out.

While the police were questioning people in the bus station, they got a call from an officer who had gone to the train station to check out a report on an empty cab. They decided the murderer had tricked them and boarded a train instead.

Donnie strained to see the numbers on the luminous dial of the clock beside the bed. The RV had been travelling for over an hour. He eased back against the wall and tried to unwind while images flitted through his mind of the dead woman in the bed sitting up and pointing a finger at him, shrieking "It was him!" He tried to focus on his purpose—to avoid getting caught. He would have to get rid of the man, of course. He didn't think that would be too difficult. Ricky was tall but slender. And not particularly observant.

He had been prepared to attack the man when he came to the door, expecting him to lean over the bed to check on his wife. Instead, the man had stood looking at her for a few seconds before turning away. Maybe she'd been ill and he didn't want to disturb her. Or maybe they'd had a fight. Maybe he was just glad to have some peace and quiet. Maybe she'd been nagging him about his driving—he wasn't exactly smooth, the way he handled the RV. People often argued when they travelled. He'd earlier glimpsed the RV's licence plate. Ricky and Monica had been stuck with each other twenty-four hours a day all the way from Nova Scotia.

His mother and various stepfathers always argued on trips. Donnie remembered travelling to Wawa with his mother and a guy called Jim. Jim had amused himself by driving erratically, threatening to plow the car straight into a rock cut while his mother screamed all the way. Donnie had clung to the back of the seat and cried. When Jim finally pulled into a rest stop, he kicked Donnie's ass all the way into the diner, his mother hanging onto Jim's shirt and begging him to stop. When he did stop, Jim slapped Donnie's mother and his mother slapped Jim back. After the police were called in, that was the end of Jim and the end of his mother for a while.

Donnie guessed Ricky would be tired soon and that would make things easier.

He allowed himself to relax as the RV rolled along. The window vent was open, bringing in the fragrance of cut hay and wild flowers. He thought everything would be all right. All he had to do now was keep a few steps ahead of the police. Once he got out of this pickle, he could make his way home. That would be Sarnia, the last he had heard. His mother was there and she would be glad to see him. He would stay around for a while and indulge her in her fantasy that they had reconciled and would finally have the life together they had been denied while he was growing up. Then something would happen—probably another useless man—and he would move on. That's the way they had always done it.

An hour after leaving town, Ricky pulled the van to the side of the road. Donnie eased to the window and peeked out. They were in the middle of nowhere. He heard a rustle of paper, a muffled exclamation of disgust, then paper being crumpled. Then silence. Donnie stood, cringing as his knees cracked, and peeked through the curtains. He could see Ricky sitting in the driver's seat, his head back against the headrest.

Donnie waited.

Five minutes passed, then ten, and Ricky started to snore. Donnie inched forward, put the man in a headlock and pulled sharply to one side, recoiling as he heard the neck snap. He took a deep breath, mopped his forehead with the sleeve of his jacket, then dragged Ricky's body to the bed and arranged it alongside his wife's.

Ricky's wallet lay on the dashboard. Disappointed to find less than two hundred dollars inside, Donnie searched for the wife's purse, finally finding it beside the bedside shelf. She had a hundred and twenty. He pocketed the money and climbed down from the RV to study his surroundings. He was standing in farm country close to a wooded area.

He returned to the RV and moved it cautiously into a crossroad that led into the woods. He eased along, looking for a place to pull into, finally finding what looked like an old service road. He steered onto it and tucked the RV behind a thicket.

He hunched his shoulders, then let them sag with relief. He went into the refrigerator, took out a few cans of soda, some vegetable juice, some packets of trail mix, and a couple of apples. He found a gym bag and stuffed the food into it, along with some toiletries he found in the RV's bathroom. Searching for other things to take, he spotted a pair of binoculars, a digital camera, and a Tilley hat, which fit well enough. Ricky's slacks didn't fit—they were too long—but his shorts did and so did his shirts. Donnie found a backpack and folded the clothes into it. He tried on Rick's hiking boots. They were a size too big but they would have to do for now. Donnie decided he could pass as a hiker until he got his bearings. He pondered what to do with his suitcase, and finally decided to empty its contents into the backpack and the gym bag. He wiped the suitcase down and slid it under the bed.

He paused. He hadn't slept a lot lately. Running on nerves as it were. He considered spending the night in the RV but thought better of it. The OPP would come across it eventually, especially if they were looking for it. Noting a survival kit behind the driver's seat, he removed a foil blanket and added it to his backpack. He decided to put a couple of miles between himself and the RV, blend back into the woods, and find a cozy spot to take a nap.

He made his way back to the main road and walked another half mile until he spotted a wood lot. Ducking in, he found a dry spot, wrapped himself in the foil blanket, and soon fell asleep.

Chapter Seven

Donnie woke to birds singing. He used a disposable razor to shave and brushed his teeth and washed up using bottled water and travel wipes.

The RV gambit had given him breathing space but anxiety was building again. He suspected that once the police got through the preliminary investigation of the cabbie and the old couple, they'd spread their net wide. He couldn't hitchhike. He would be too obvious. He'd have to pass as a hiker travelling through the countryside until he reached a town big enough to have a bus station.

He was trudging along a faded paved road in what seemed like no man's land when a car appeared on the horizon. He glanced up as it passed but the driver seemed intent on his surroundings. Then Donnie heard the car turning around.

He kept on walking, hoping the car would pass him again, but when tires crunched gravel behind him apprehension surged through his body. He expected an off-duty police officer to approach, his hand hovering near a shoulder holster.

"Hey, buddy."

Donnie turned and looked into a smiling face.

"Need a lift?" Smiley asked.

Donnie nodded and got in.

"You're lucky," the man said, "at this hour of the morning, you could be walking a long way. I got turned around coming off the bridge." He pulled onto the road. "I don't usually pick up hitchhikers," he added, his smile conspiratorial. "But seeing as how you're part of the nation."

"Pardon?"

The man tapped the logo on Donnie's gym bag.

Donnie recovered quickly and grinned. "Oh, yeah. Go, Red Sox."

Rudley was at the front desk, lingering over his morning paper, when Lloyd appeared down the hallway.

"Had to come in the side door," Lloyd explained before Rudley could speak. "The back door was bolted."

"At this hour?"

"The kids did it. They was running ahead of me. They went in and put the bar on the door so I couldn't get in."

Rudley crossed his eyes. The children. Suddenly the idea of getting away had more appeal.

The children. Hell One and Hell Two. Or, as their grandparents called them, Ned and Nora. They'd seemed so innocuous when their parents dropped them off. A pair of neatly dressed, well-groomed eight-year-olds who smiled shyly at him while their mother explained they would be away one month and that the children's grandparents, Doreen and Walter Sawchuck, would be responsible for them during their absence.

The children had behaved beautifully for the first few hours, carefully calculated, he guessed, to take into account the time it would take their parents to drive to Ottawa, catch their plane, and be halfway across the Atlantic before anyone noticed how hellacious they really were. And so far the Sawchucks hadn't taken a lick of responsibility for them.

Doreen and Walter were hobbling into the lobby as he contemplated how to handle the latest transgression.

Rudley cleared his throat. "Walter, Doreen?"

Doreen shook her head as if puzzling over some distant sound.

He raised his voice. "Walter, Doreen?"

Margaret came out of the dining room. "Mr. and Mrs. Sawchuck, how did you enjoy the paddle boat?"

"Wonderful," said Walter. "Great exercise for the knees."

"We think we'll try it again," said Doreen.

"We were just on our way to breakfast," Walter added.

"Could I have a word with you first?" Rudley practically shouted this time.

"I think Rudley's calling you." Margaret gestured toward her husband.

The Sawchucks turned, feigning surprise at finding him looming over the desk.

"It's about the children," Rudley began.

The Sawchucks' mouths formed O's.

"They locked Lloyd out of the basement."

"Doesn't he have a key?" Walter asked.

"He does. They threw the bolt."

Doreen smiled. "They're a lively pair."

"That's all very well and good, Doreen. Children are entitled to a certain amount of mischief making. But if they continue to amuse themselves in this manner, we'll all have to become proficient at climbing in windows."

"We'll have a word with them," Walter huffed. He took Doreen's arm and urged her into the dining room.

"You shouldn't bother the Sawchucks about an innocent prank. They were clearly upset."

"Balderdash, Margaret. They were upset because I delayed their arrival at the trough. I don't think they're at all worried about the trouble the children are causing everyone else."

Margaret looked doubtful. "The parents must have considered the Sawchucks capable of managing the children. Otherwise, they wouldn't have left them in their care."

"I think the parents were so desperate to get away from the little miscreants, they would have left them with Attila the Hun."

Margaret opened the register, then closed it. "Rudley, they're just children. What have they done that was so terrible?"

"They ran a pair of Tiffany's bloomers up the flagpole."

"She was a good sport about that."

"They put a frog in Lloyd's bed."

"Lloyd didn't mind."

"The frog might have."

"The children are at loose ends."

"How can they be at loose ends?"

"Children these days are accustomed to constant entertainment, Rudley."

"They're getting a daily dose of crap at the Elm Pavilion."

"Apparently, their father promised there'd be a full complement of electronic devices and an arcade. He inadvertently left their games at home."

"The man's a sadist, Margaret. Leaving us to cope with those brats in electronic game withdrawal." He paused. "I hate to leave the staff to deal with them."

"They'll be fine, Rudley. There's Tim and Gregoire and Tiffany and Lloyd. And Mrs. Millotte, who's had more experience with children that anyone. She'll have them in hand in no time."

"Margaret"—Tim appeared in the doorway—"Gregoire has some scrumptious French toast for you."

"Lovely. Shall I bring you some, Rudley?"

"Perhaps just a muffin and some coffee when you're finished, Margaret."

Rudley turned the page of his newspaper and smoothed it along the top of the desk. "Mrs. Millotte will have them in hand," he murmured, then added: "Mrs. Millotte will have them well in hand."

He raised his brows. "Mrs. Millotte will have them on their knees, begging for mercy if they make one misstep. Mrs. Millotte will lock in a closet and feed them liquid pap through a straw inserted through the keyhole. Mrs. Millotte will set them adrift on the lake with bread and water and no paddles."

He did a little pirouette. "Mrs. Millotte will hang them from the rafters by their toes."

He whistled a few bars of "Oh, What a Beautiful Morning," tapping out the rhythm on the desk.

"Glad you've perked up, Rudley." James Bole strode across the lobby toward the desk. "You've been down in the mouth lately."

Rudley resumed his position behind the desk. "As you know, Mr. Bole, it's always stressful contemplating changes in routine, but I've just had the most wonderful mental images."

"Ah, yes, the great boreal forest. Rushing water, pristine air."

"Yes, that sort of thing."

"Makes me nostalgic for spring in Kashmir, the rivers and streams engorged with water rushing from the snowmelt in the Himalayas."

"Spectacular, I imagine."

"Indeed." Mr. Bole paused. "Rudley, if you need some reassurance, I feel confident everything will run smoothly while you're away. The young people are reliable, Mrs. Millotte is stalwart, and I will be available to lend the wisdom of my experience as necessary."

"That's reassuring, Mr. Bole."

Mr. Bole tipped his hat and went on into the dining room.

Rudley considered Mr. Bole's words. He wasn't surprised. Mr. Bole had been coming to the Pleasant so long he probably considered himself innkeeper emeritus.

He frowned.

Really, they were all acting as if the place could run perfectly well without him—except for Mrs. Sawchuck. He retrieved her latest note from the trash. It read:

Mr. Rudley, please make sure the screens on my windows are in perfect condition before you leave on your vacation so the bats can't get in.

Rudley smiled. *The bats don't come through your windows, Mrs. Sawchuck. They come from under the eaves and enter your room through the heat registers.*

Mr. Rudley, would you remind the staff to keep the doors locked?

He considered this for a moment. *As you know, Mrs. Sawchuck, I have installed a Breathalyzer at the front door. Anyone too drunk to remember to lock the door behind them will not be able to get in. No, Mrs. Sawchuck, I have left explicit instructions that the doors are to remain wide open during my absence with arrows pointing toward your room.*

Mr. Rudley, I trust that Lloyd will not be too busy during your absence to help us into our boats.

Rudley ticked off the item with a flourish. *He'll help you in, Mrs. Sawchuck. If you tip him well enough, he might help you out.*

Did you remember to order my prunes, Mr. Rudley?

Rudley tore the note in two and dropped it into the recycle bin. *Mrs. Sawchuck, I've ordered enough prunes and prune juice to give every guest and member of the staff fulminating diarrhea until well into the next century.* Enough to keep the septic tank pump truck on permanent loan.

Well, he considered, at least I won't have to preside over the mess. I'll be up some godforsaken creek without a paddle. Mrs. Millotte will be in charge of this lunatic asylum. The thought made him laugh out loud.

"What's so funny, Rudley?" Norman Phipps-Walker asked as he came down the stairs.

"Mrs. Millotte will be in charge." Rudley couldn't help himself and broke into gales of laughter.

Norman looked at him, frowning. "It must be reassuring, Rudley, to know you can hand the inn over to someone like Melba and walk away."

"Oh, yes." Rudley wiped away a tear. "Tremendously reassuring."

Norman regarded him solicitously. "I'm glad you're able to get away, Rudley."

As Norman continued into the dining room, Rudley did a little soft-shoe behind the desk. Leaving Melba in charge was the only bright spot about going away. For some reason, Melba was under the impression it was possible to control this crowd of stinkers as long as you didn't give in to them. The name of the game, he told himself, was to let them think you were giving in to them, all the time keeping in mind where you've drawn the line in the sand. Mrs. Millotte was a fine woman, competent, respectful without being gracious, a woman of integrity, unflappable. He smiled. It was all very well to have a drill sergeant in charge for a week, just to keep people on their toes, but over the long haul the vocation of an innkeeper required finesse.

"Mr. Rudley"—Mrs. Sawchuck hobbled out of the dining room—"I want to add something to my note."

"Yes?" Rudley grabbed a notepad and picked up a pen.

"I wanted to make sure Mrs. Millotte knows to check for snakes."

He leaned across the desk toward her. "I assure you, Mrs. Sawchuck, Mrs. Millotte will do a complete inventory of all reptiles on the premises."

Doreen did not look reassured. "You know they can come in on the firewood."

"If the forecast is correct, Mrs. Millotte will not need to bring in any firewood."

"I've heard they come in on produce too."

"I think you're thinking of black widow spiders."

She gasped, then put a hand to her mouth. "I hadn't thought of those."

He crossed his eyes. "Mrs. Sawchuck, Gregoire has a special device to scan the groceries for such creatures. He would be hurt to think you could imagine him letting a black widow spider nestle into your salad."

She sighed. "I didn't know."

"Now you do." He smiled. "Is there anything else I can help you with, Mrs. Sawchuck?"

She stared into space, her mouth open as if to reply, her upper dentures slipping over her lower lip. Finally, she recovered. "You've been very reassuring, Mr. Rudley."

"Reassuring is my middle name."

When she had hobbled back to the dining room he took a celebratory cigarette from a battered pack under the desk and lit it.

"Rudley?"

He turned, smoke trailing through his nostrils, to see Margaret facing him across the lobby.

"You promised not to smoke unless absolutely necessary," she said, plopping his muffin and coffee down on the desk.

"I assure you, Margaret," he responded, tapping ash into his saucer, "it is absolutely necessary."

She raised an eyebrow.

"Mrs. Sawchuck is doing her best to see that I end up in an insane asylum," Rudley explained. "Now she's worried about snakes coming in on the firewood and black widow spiders on the produce."

"I suppose spiders could do that."

"Bite your tongue, Margaret. I've assured her Gregoire scans every item with a magic wand."

"I'm sure she didn't believe that."

"Margaret, the woman is so dense she'd believe we had a cupboard full of elves climbing through the lettuce with ray guns."

Margaret gave him a reproachful look. "Rudley, the Sawchucks aren't worried about snakes and spiders. They're anxious about you going away. They're getting older. They depend on you. They trust you to keep them safe."

He looked at the cigarette burning away in the saucer. "Nonsense, Margaret. They're anxious because they haven't figured out how to manipulate Mrs. Millotte." He took her hand. "Now, Margaret, I want you to go into the kitchen and apprise Gregoire of that magic wand situation."

She shook her head in reproval and left.

"And so I can enjoy the remainder of my Benson & Hedges in peace." He took a deep drag. Sublime.

He had just finished his cigarette when Margaret reappeared, waving her way through the haze. "If you're going to smoke, Rudley, you need to blow away the fumes." She got a fan from the hall closet and plunked it down on the desk.

"Yes, Margaret."

The door opened. A stolid looking man entered carrying two suitcases and stopped at the desk.

Margaret smiled. "Good morning."

"Bill Bostock," the man said.

Margaret hesitated. "Oh, yes, Mr. Bostock." She turned the register toward him. "If you would care to sign in. We have you at the Pines."

He grabbed the pen and scribbled his name.

"And how was your trip?"

He stared at her. "Fine."

"Have you got a car?"

"Should I?"

She glanced at Rudley, who turned and began to busy himself in the cupboard. "No, no, it's just that if you have a car we take down the details, show you to your spot, and so forth."

"I took a cab out."

"Well, then." She handed him the key. "I'll call Lloyd to help you with the luggage."

"I can carry my own luggage." He continued to stare. "Where's the cottage?"

"Oh, out the front door, turn to your left, follow the path. You'll see the sign."

He weighed the key in his hand a moment, then stuffed it into his pocket. He picked up his suitcases and left.

"Pleasant chap," said Rudley.

Margaret frowned. "What a strange man."

"Oh, I don't know, Margaret. Most of our guests are insane, eccentric, or at least interminably irritating. He should fit in."

"But our guests are usually more social." She sighed. "He's probably just one of those types who takes a bit to warm up." She shook her head. "Frankly, Rudley, he was rude."

"Not everyone is as blessed with social graces as I am."

She ignored this. "I suppose it doesn't matter. Our guests have a right to be as rude and nasty as they wish."

"Some of them have even been murderers, Margaret."

"Yes, but they were always congenial."

"He's just booked in for two weeks, Margaret. He shouldn't bother anyone too much. The Benson sisters won't know he's here. Mr. Bole will find him intriguing. The Sawchucks exist in their own realm. If he irritates the children, that's a bonus."

"He could be a tragic figure, Rudley. Perhaps he's suffered some trauma, lost his entire family or such, and has taken on an uncivil veneer to protect his tortured soul."

"Or perhaps he's just an ignoramus."

Pearl came out of the drawing room at that moment, bumping into the doorjamb. She teetered as Rudley rushed to her aid.

"Are you all right, Pearl?"

She gave him an aggrieved look. "I wish people would stop moving things."

"You ran into the doorjamb, Pearl." He coaxed her toward the desk. "Now, where were you headed?"

"The dining room."

He took her arm, escorted her into the dining room, and sat down opposite her at a table near the kitchen. "I think it's time for cataract surgery."

She waved him off. "I left my glasses at Whittingdon's for new frames. I'm wearing an old pair that aren't quite up to snuff."

"Didn't you break your most recent pair walking into the newel post?"

She gave him a withering look. "I took them off to clean them and Tim stepped on them."

"I see your memory's going too," he said. "And did you know your lipstick was askew?"

She whipped out her compact to see mirrored a blurry image of Unbridled Passion. "It looks perfectly fine to me."

He rolled his eyes. "Will you be safe if I leave you here?"

"Of course, Rudley."

He returned to the desk. "Margaret, if that woman doesn't have cataract surgery soon, she'll break her nose."

"She's never had surgery, Rudley."

"No time like the present."

"She's apprehensive."

He shook his head. "What could possibly happen to her during cataract surgery?"

"It isn't the surgery," she said patiently. "It's what happens before. The doctors order scads of X-rays. The X-rays show an abnormality that leads to surgery for a condition you could have lived perfectly well with. Or they find your blood is low. The iron pills make you sick so the doctor orders iron injections. The nurse hits your sciatic nerve. You are in agony the rest of your life and still iron deficient. You then get influenza because, after the injury to your sciatic nerve, you won't let anyone come near you with a needle again. You get pneumonia as a complication of the influenza and are admitted to the hospital where you get an infection and die."

He looked at her dumbfounded. "Whoever told you that?"

"Aunt Pearl."

"The font of all wisdom," he murmured.

"She's survived very nicely so far, Rudley. She hasn't fallen into the lake or been hit by a car."

"Or murdered."

"Bite your tongue, Rudley."

Chapter Eight

"Rudley"—Margaret hurried up to the desk—"I want you to get some lunch. It's going to be a hectic afternoon."

He folded his newspaper and tucked it under his arm. "If you insist, Margaret."

"Have the scallops. They're especially nice today."

"What's for dessert?"

"Coconut cream pie, mocha cake with butter cream frosting, peach Melba, and Jell-O with whipped cream."

"I think I'll forgo the Jell-O." Rudley took off for the dining room.

Margaret was about to review the linen inventory when the door opened and a young man entered, carrying a suitcase and duffel bag. He slammed the door, causing Margaret to utter a startled yip and drop her papers. He approached the desk, apparently oblivious to her reaction.

"May I help you?" Margaret asked, picking up the papers.

He smiled. "Yeah, I'm Eric Turnbull. I'm taking the canoe trip."

"Oh, yes." She turned the register toward him.

He scribbled his name. "Nice place."

"I'm glad you like it." She took note of the room number and reached for the key. "Did you bring a car?"

"It's out front."

"Do you happen to know the plate number?"

"Uh?" He looked at her blankly, then recovered quickly. "HRR... something." He sighed. "It's my girlfriend's car. I'll have to get it for you."

"You're in room 306. You can park your car in the lot at that number. It's just as you come in." She handed him the room key. "And we're asking our canoeists if they'll leave their car keys at the desk while we're away. Just in case the car has to be moved."

He flipped the room key into the air and caught it. "Great. I'll just stow my gear, then I'll move the car." He looked around. "Where's the elevator?"

She pointed to the stairs. "We have just two flights up, Mr. Turnbull."

He shrugged and headed for the stairs.

Margaret paused in thought. She and Rudley had never considered an elevator. The cottages were completely accessible and they had a ramp available if one were needed for access to the main inn.

She didn't have long to contemplate the merits of an elevator because Mr. Turnbull pounded back down the stairs and out the front door, nearly bowling over Norman and Geraldine who were on their way in.

"That young man seems to be in a hurry," said Geraldine.

"That was Mr. Turnbull," said Margaret. "He's one of our adventurers."

"He seems energetic," said Norman. He and Geraldine went on into the dining room.

A few minutes later, Rudley returned to the desk, carrying a plate of scallops and a piece of cake.

"You just missed Mr. Turnbull," said Margaret. "He's gone to park his car."

"I expect I'll catch him later," Rudley said, adding, "or perhaps now," as Turnbull zipped up the steps and into the lobby.

"Lunch is being served in the dining room," Margaret called out as Turnbull stopped in front of the dining room door and peered in.

"Great." He took off into the dining room.

After a moment of silence, Rudley said, "It seems the young people we've had to date have been more of the mature, sober types."

"I rather like his youthful energy," said Margaret.

"I never had an ounce of youthful energy."

She looked at him, bewildered.

"What I mean to say is I've always had a good metabolism. My energy level has always been most satisfactory." He smiled a jaunty smile. "Consider, Margaret, a mature man, up at the crack of dawn, working tirelessly throughout the day, seldom in bed before midnight."

She smiled back. "Oh, Rudley, I remember the days you could go day and night. My father thought you were taking amphetamines."

By moving rapidly room to room, I was able to avoid lengthy conversations with him, Rudley thought. "As I matured, Margaret, I harnessed my youthful energy to purposeful tasks."

Before she could challenge this, the door opened and a young couple, laden with luggage, entered.

"Mr. Rudley, Mrs. Rudley."

"Elizabeth, Edward." Margaret went around the desk and exchanged hugs with the new arrivals.

"Miss Miller, Mr. Simpson," said Rudley. "How refreshing to see someone normal."

Simpson's forehead crimped. Miss Miller didn't miss a beat. She pulled the register toward her and signed in. "We would have been here earlier but we had a flat tire."

"Elizabeth changed it," said Edward, "but we had to find a garage to get a regular tire."

"I don't know why they don't include a decent spare," said Miss Miller. "It's one more example of forces conspiring to make us less independent."

"Yes, wonderful clunky things, those old spares, taking up half the trunk," said Rudley. "People were always removing them and leaving them at home so they could fit in their luggage."

"I imagine one could write a rather fascinating travel article about that," said Simpson.

"Oh, the good old days," said Rudley, "when all we needed was a patch and a pump."

Miss Miller smiled. "You should enjoy this adventure, then, Mr. Rudley. Seven days of living without modern clutter."

"He's really looking forward to it," said Margaret.

"I can't tell you how I'm looking forward to it."

"We'll take our luggage to our room and be right back down," Miss Miller said.

"Can we help with the luggage?" Margaret noted how Edward was sagging under the weight.

"Oh, Edward will be fine. Room 206?"

Rudley handed her the key. "As always."

He sighed. Miss Miller and Mr. Simpson—a lovely young couple, he thought. Refreshing after the last two boobs who had signed in. He'd known them for three years, since they had arrived separately, he a graduate student at the University of Toronto, via London, England, and she a young librarian. They had been inseparable since. Miss Miller was brave, cool-headed, and imaginative. Mr. Simpson was a lovely, kind-hearted young man who had been besotted with Miss Miller at first sight. Having Miss Miller on the trip would ensure, at least, that any emergency would be well in hand.

Miss Miller had developed into a freelance writer who travelled the world in search of unique stories for *The Star*. She had had some fascinating experiences—he reminded himself to ask her about her trip to Baja, California. Mr. Simpson taught at the university and wrote learned tomes. In spite of their life of adventure, the couple continued to find their way back to the Pleasant on a regular basis. Of course, no experience could hold a candle to those at the Pleasant. More murders per square foot than any place on earth—a fact Rudley would prefer to ignore, but Miss Miller showed quite an instinct for solving homicide cases. Better than that twit of a detective, Brisbois, he considered, or that dandy, Detective Creighton, neither of whom could recognize a clue if they fell over one. He smiled. Here was one bright spot about being away. He could be sure that for seven days he wouldn't see either of them.

"Wonderful young couple," Rudley remarked to Margaret.

"Yes," she said. "I can't wait to hear about their trip to Baja, California. It looks so dusty on the maps."

"Indeed," Rudley murmured.

Margaret uttered a sigh of contentment. "Rudley, at four o'clock tomorrow morning we'll be off. Our gear is packed. Our itinerary is set. The van is topped up and tuned up. Our guide has confirmed our meeting place, the canoes, and equipment. Mrs. Millotte will be here at the crack of dawn to relieve you. The extended forecast suggests we'll have prefect conditions. Pleasant temperatures, minimal cloud cover, no precipitation."

"Sounds like a walk in the park, Margaret."

"The terrain will be sufficiently challenging for those who desire such and pleasant for those who prefer something more relaxing."

Like myself, he thought. He let Margaret rattle on about the preparations. Why did people feel they had to go out into the wilderness to be challenged? Life was challenging enough where you found it. It was a challenge, for instance, to hold reality together every day for a group of ninnies fighting to let go of it. He had no desire for a vacation, which always made him feel at loose ends. He loved the Pleasant—sixty acres of Eden, beautiful lake, splendid woods, thriving collection of anurans. He paused. Anurans. He'd have to remind Tim about the frogs.

When he and Margaret took the key from Mr. MacIntyre almost thirty years ago, he felt as if he'd at last arrived, the way a nursery sapling might when finally tipped out of its pot and planted firmly in its permanent home. Like that sapling, his roots were now sunk deep in the soil and stretched out the width of the tree canopy.

His reverie was broken by Miss Miller and Mr. Simpson coming back down the stairs and turning toward the dining room.

Miss Miller waved to Rudley and Margaret. "Join us when you can," she called out.

Margaret was about to look for Tiffany to take the desk when the door opened and a young man with a bag and a backpack entered. He looked around uncertainly. Margaret smiled. "You must be Mr. Peters."

He approached the desk. "Yes, Vern Peters."

She offered him the register. "If you'll sign here please. You're in room 309."

He signed carefully and turned the register back toward her.

"Do you have a car here?"

He frowned. "I parked it where it said 'visitors.'"

"Oh, that's all right. You can move it to its assigned space later."

"Fine."

"Do you happen to know the plate number?"

He recited it. "I'll move the car now."

"Why don't you leave it where it is for now? If you leave your keys, the staff can move it, if needed, while we're away."

"I'm taking the car with me."

Margaret hesitated. "You can, of course. But we've rented a large van. There'll be plenty of room."

"I get sick on buses and vans."

Rudley crossed his eyes. Margaret said, "I understand completely. I had that problem when I was a child."

Peters didn't respond; he just stared at the key in his hand.

"Would you like some help with your luggage?" Margaret continued.

Before he could answer, Turnbull came out of the dining room, carrying a large piece of cake. "No rule against taking food out of the dining room?" he asked as they glanced his way.

"Not at all," Margaret responded. "Mr. Turnbull, this is Mr. Peters. He'll be with us on our adventure."

Turnbull smiled. "Sure. Eric Turnbull."

Peters nodded vaguely.

"Lunch is being served in the dining room," Rudley said to Peters whose eyes sought the floor.

"Oh?" Peters seemed to come out of his trance. He looked at his key and headed up the stairs.

Turnbull took a bite of his cake. "Now that is one seriously weird dude. He looks as if he escaped from a freak show. You could drive a train through those nostrils."

"Well…" Rudley began.

"Mr. Turnbull," Margaret broke in, "why don't you finish your cake on the veranda?"

Turnbull shrugged and ambled out as suggested.

"Mr. Turnbull's remarks were uncalled for," Margaret said when the man was out of earshot.

"You have to admit, Margaret, Peters does have large nostrils."

"He has a slightly upturned nose."

"And his ears, they're almost at the same level as his mouth."

"Nonsense, Rudley, it's an illusion. He has a high forehead."

"Yes, it does go on and on. If he had any hair it would help."

"Rudley," Margaret said impatiently, "he has hair. It's just very fine and pale."

"And thin. Perhaps he could grow a beard. It would even things out."

"It's cruel to make fun of someone's appearance."

"You're right, Margaret, it is." Rudley gestured toward the veranda. "I don't think we've ever had two such disparate types check in on the same day."

"It was bound to happen, Rudley. Statistically speaking." Margaret smiled. "I think it's a good omen for our adventure."

"How so?"

"A variety of personalities creates a stimulating environment."

Rudley crossed his eyes. "Yes, that's what I was hoping for."

Margaret paused in thought. "That cake looks so good I think I'll have a piece after all." She took off toward the kitchen, humming.

Chapter Nine

Mrs. Millotte looked up as Tiffany approached the desk, her chin set. She was clutching a roll of toilet paper.

"What's the matter?"

Tiffany shook her head, suppressing a sob.

Mrs. Millotte regarded her over the top of her glasses. "Want to talk about it?"

Tiffany's jaw trembled. She nodded and after a moment squeaked out, "Yes."

"I'm not used to getting a 'yes' to that question," said Mrs. Millotte. "But then I'm usually talking to my husband or the boys."

"Mr. Bostock insulted me," Tiffany managed. "He called me a snoop."

"Why on earth would he call you a snoop?"

Tiffany pressed her lips together, gathering her thoughts. "I was cleaning his bathroom sink when he returned to his cabin. I heard him come in. It was quiet for a minute, then he slammed the door and charged into the bathroom, screaming, 'What are you doing in my cabin?' I explained that he hadn't left out a DND sign so I assumed he wanted his cabin cleaned. He blustered and blundered about, then said that he had put the sign out and accused me of taking it in. I had no way of proving I hadn't. Then he ordered me out of the cabin. I didn't even get a chance to restock his toilet tissue."

"I hope he needs it right away."

"I tried to apologize for any misunderstanding, but he continued to scream at me. 'Out, out, out,' he yelled, then he grabbed me by the arm and practically threw me out the door."

Mrs. Millotte centred her pen on the ink blotter. "Tiffany, if you would watch the desk, I'll have a word with Mr. Bostock."

Mrs. Millotte took the roll of toilet paper from Tiffany and proceeded toward the Pines. She didn't march, she didn't rush forward, bellowing and throwing rocks, although that is what she fantasized. She travelled at a brisk, purposeful pace, and when she reached the Pines, she knocked firmly but politely.

After a minute, Mr. Bostock answered. "Yes?"

"I'm Mrs. Millotte. I'm in charge of the inn while Mr. and Mrs. Rudley are away."

He stared at her.

"Let me get to the point. I hear you were rude to Tiffany, our housekeeper. I won't have that."

He blinked. "So what?"

"Tiffany entered your cabin to perform her usual duties. She did not see a 'Do Not Disturb' sign. She's been doing her job for quite some time and is always careful to look for the sign. But even if on this rare occasion she did make a mistake, there was no reason to get nasty with her. It's not as if she caught you in a compromising situation."

He frowned.

"There was no reason to abuse the girl, Mr. Bostock. She works hard and, frankly, you had no right to grab her and throw her out of the cabin."

"I just took her arm to escort her out."

"I don't believe you had any reason to touch her at all. Not without her consent. I believe that could be construed as an assault."

His jaw dropped. "Now, see here, that's ridiculous. She was in my cabin, uninvited. I don't like people going through my things."

Mrs. Millotte gave him a stern look. "She was cleaning your bathroom."

He continued to regard her with suspicious eyes. "I don't want her in here when I'm not here. I don't want anybody in my cabin when I'm not here."

"Then perhaps you should leave your DND sign out at all times."

"Then how do I get my cabin cleaned?"

"Call the desk when you want your cabin attended to and we'll work out a time."

He considered a moment. "I guess that's okay, as long as you stick to it."

"And I'll let Tiffany know you regret your outburst."

"I didn't say that."

"You were going to." Mrs. Millotte thrust the roll of toilet paper at him and turned back to the inn.

What a queer lot people were, she thought as she walked along. She had worked at the Pleasant since Mr. Bostock was a mere glimmer in his father's eye and had never known a staff member to pilfer from a guest. Aunt Pearl had a penchant for borrowing small shiny items but only if she were on the owner's premises at their invitation, and only if the item was in full view. She was like a crow, fascinated by baubles and trinkets. Even then no harm was done. Everyone knew where to look if something went missing. In fact, "lost and found" had become a euphemism for Aunt Pearl's quarters. Mrs. Millotte told herself to be charitable. Mr. Bostock was probably either naturally mistrustful—which he couldn't help—or had been taken advantage of once too often. Of course, too, he didn't know the staff as well as the regular guests did.

Tiffany was sweeping the lobby when Mrs. Millotte returned. She stopped, clutching the broom handle expectantly.

"Mr. Bostock offers his apologies," said Mrs. Millotte. "He was contrite. He didn't understand the rules here. He wishes, however, to be in his cabin when any staff are there working. We agreed he would let us know when he wants his room cleaned. Then the two of you can work out whatever's convenient." She paused. "I think the man is paranoid."

"What a terrible way to be."

"Yes, it's a pain in the butt. Fortunately, he's just signed in for two weeks and, if we're lucky, he'll never come back."

Tiffany beamed. "Mrs. Millotte, it was so good of you to stand up for me."

"That's what I'm here for," Mrs. Millotte responded briskly. She slipped in behind the desk before Tiffany could hug her.

Displays of gratitude made Mrs. Millotte uncomfortable. And she didn't expect gratitude anyway. Her parents had taught her to speak up if she saw anyone being bullied or treated unfairly, no matter what the consequences. Even if it meant losing her job. She knew Rudley would back her up. He had no patience with anyone being rude to the staff, except himself.

"I'm not surprised Peters elected to drive his own car," Rudley remarked.

They were on a two-lane highway headed north, bobbing along in a sea of cars, vans, and RVs towing boats and piled high with luggage, bicycles, canoes, and kayaks.

"Nonsense, Rudley, he's missing the fun." Margaret cast a bright eye out the window of their van. "Isn't it exciting? You can sense the anticipation from every seat."

"I'm anticipating running up the rear end of one of those ludicrous RVs with the bicycles on top and the car in tow if Miss Miller continues to dart in and out of traffic. It's not as if she were driving a Jag."

"If she were driving a Jag, we'd be there by now," Norman piped up.

Miss Miller smiled into the rearview mirror. "Don't worry. I have excellent vision and reflexes."

"I thought you couldn't see a thing without your glasses," Geraldine ventured.

Miss Miller tapped the rim of her eyeglasses in reply.

"Elizabeth was a Girl Scout," said Edward. He winced as Elizabeth surged past an eighteen-wheeler and popped back into the driving lane with barely ten feet to spare.

"Got your badge in demolition derby, eh?" Turnbull remarked from the back of the van. He tipped his hat over his eyes.

"You seem very calm," said Geraldine.

Turnbull smiled. "That's because I can't see."

"That's probably for the best," said Rudley.

"No need to worry," said Miss Miller.

"Elizabeth has excellent eye-hand coordination," Edward explained.

"I think Miss Miller manages a van as well as she manages a motorboat," said Norman. "I've always admired the way you flirt with the shoal markers."

"You wouldn't if you held the insurance," said Rudley.

Margaret patted his shoulder. "Be nice, Rudley."

Rudley slumped in his seat. If Miss Miller was going to kill everyone, crashing into an eighteen-wheeler, he could at least take comfort knowing he had left Mrs. Millotte in charge of the Pleasant. She would take news of their demise in a measured way—grieve in the traditional manner, take a half-day to attend the funeral, dress properly in black, then return to the inn and resume her efforts toward its smooth functioning. Though he could trust the others to hold the fort and do their best, he suspected they would close the inn down for at least three days, not only out of propriety, but out of fear they couldn't maintain the reputation of the Pleasant in their grief.

Except perhaps Lloyd. He would continue to tend the garden while speculating about body parts strewn over the road and sticking to trees and the McDonalds, Next Exit sign. Looking like an axe murderer and fascinated with the macabre, Lloyd seemed ill equipped to run an establishment as sophisticated as the Pleasant. On the other hand, Rudley thought, Lloyd took in everything that went on around the inn, including the intricacies of running the front desk. Still, he preferred Melba as the front man. So he could relax in the knowledge he had left the Pleasant in good hands.

"Rudley, it's so good to see you enjoying yourself. I knew you would warm up to the adventure."

"Yes, Margaret."

A sign for a fast food restaurant and gas station loomed ahead. Miss Miller bounced off the highway and into the parking lot to a collective sigh of relief.

Miss Miller parked the van and pulled out her map. "Eighty kilometres from here, we board the train at Trillium Station," she announced. "We leave the train here." She indicated the location on the map.

"At the spot marked X," Simpson murmured.

"We walk approximately three miles to the confluence of the Swine and Little Beaver, where we meet our guide, who should be there ahead of us with the canoes, tents, etcetera."

Miss Miller folded the map and handed it to Simpson, who returned it to the glove compartment. She checked her watch. "We're forty minutes ahead of schedule. Would anyone care for a cup of coffee?"

"We could have some of the scones Gregoire packed for us," said Margaret.

Turnbull scanned the road and grinned. "I guess we lost Peters. Good move."

"He knows where we were turning off. He knows what time we'll be leaving here."

"If he were travelling the speed limit, he should be along in about twenty minutes," said Rudley.

Miss Miller smiled sweetly. "Coffee or tea?"

Gregoire took the soufflé from the counter and placed it carefully at the centre of the oven, closing the door with a sigh of satisfaction. He turned back to the counter, took out his cutting board, and began to slice an English cucumber. Mr. Bole was performing *Lady Chatterley's Lover* with finger puppets for the Benson sisters. The cucumber and watercress sandwiches were meant to set the mood, with a tray of Stilton cheese and crackers, strawberry scones with Devon cream, and Earl Grey tea to enhance it.

The back porch door slammed to the tune of pounding feet. Ned raced into the kitchen followed by Nora with a water pistol.

Gregoire turned white. "My soufflé!"

Ned ducked into the pantry just as Nora let loose with a spray of water, which hit Gregoire. Water dripping off his wilted cap, he turned just as Ned ducked out of the pantry and aimed his gun at Nora. Once again, Gregoire got caught in the crossfire.

It was this scene Tim came upon, tripping lightly into the kitchen carrying a tray of glasses for the dishwasher. Nora turned her water pistol toward Tim.

"I wouldn't do that if I were you," Tim warned.

Nora grinned, her finger on the trigger.

"I'd just like to remind you that I serve your food. A lot can happen to your food between the kitchen and your table."

Nora's eyes narrowed. "You wouldn't dare. We'll tell Grandma and Grandpa on you."

Tim shrugged. "Grandpa and Grandma love me. Now, get out of the kitchen. It's against public health regulations to have little pigs in a place where food is prepared."

Nora looked to Ned. "Let's go." She stroked the barrel of the gun. "We'll get you later."

"They'll get us later," Tim mimicked. He flipped a lock of hair off his forehead, then adjusted his tie. "No wonder their parents ran off to Europe with only the vaguest directions on how they might be located." He took a new tray and placed four old-fashioned glasses on it. "They're probably not coming back. They never intended to come back. They saw a chance to escape and they took it."

Gregoire looked through the oven window. "They are lucky they didn't make my soufflé lopsided. I would have killed them for that."

Tim searched for a bottle of Glenlivet and a bottle of soda. "You know what will happen if their parents have taken a permanent vacation?"

"I suppose they would go to live with one of their aunts or uncles." Gregoire opened a bin of flour.

"Wrong." Tim filled a bowl with ice cubes. "The little dears would come to live with their grandparents—Walter and Doreen Sawchuck, the only relatives who can stand them and the only reason they can stand them is they are so good at ignoring what the kids are doing."

Gregoire looked at him askance.

"The Sawchucks spend half their time here," Tim prompted.

Gregoire's eyes widened. "That will not happen. If the parents are not back as planned, I will go looking for them myself." He took a pastry board, rolled out the dough he had set aside for his pinwheels, spread the dough with butter, then removed a container of fruit and nut filling from the refrigerator. Halfway through spreading the filling onto the dough, he stopped and peered at his handiwork. "What is that?"

Tim looked over his shoulder. "It looks like gravel."

Gregoire balled up the mess and tossed it into the garbage. "If I hear one chuckle out of you, you will eat that!"

"Not as much as a smile." Tim took his tray and backed out of the kitchen. He strode out onto the veranda, put the tray down on Aunt Pearl's table, sank down in the chair beside her, and exploded in laughter.

Once he stopped laughing, he told her what had happened.

"I know it isn't funny, but those kids put gravel into Gregoire's fruit and nut filling. They ruined his pinwheels. But you should have seen the expression on his face!"

Aunt Pearl picked up one of the glasses from the tray and took a slug. "If I were him I would have served it up to them for supper. Anyone else would. Gregoire is too ethical to do that, too proud of his culinary accomplishments. If Mr. Cadeau were here, he would have taken them out to the garden and stood over them while they ate their fill."

Tim nodded. "They're brats. And there's no point in complaining to the Sawchucks. They apologize for the kids and ask that the damages be added to their bill. I have the feeling they have a special fund set aside to pay off people the kids have offended."

"There's a lot to be said for not having children. Winnie and I had Margaret. We agreed that a niece was plenty and she has been just like a daughter. She was a spirited kid, but never like those two."

"They're sadistic," Tim said, watching Pearl take a pack of cards from her purse. "Who are the unlucky marks this afternoon?"

"Whoever wanders by. My regulars all have other business to attend to at the moment."

"Meaning they're all tired of getting fleeced."

Pearl smiled. "Fortunately, there's always a few innocents."

Tim gave her a long look. "Are you cheating again?"

"Not so you'd notice." Pearl began to arrange the cards on the table. "I'll just play a few hands of solitaire until someone shows up."

"What about all this whisky?"

She gave him a smile. "Don't worry, dear, I think I can handle that."

"When the cat's away, the mice will play."

Pearl patted her lips with a tissue, leaving a smear of Sweet Conquest. "Rudley is such a killjoy."

"Has he figured out that when he dilutes the whisky you switch bottles on him?"

She patted his arm. "Not yet, dear."

A sudden shriek turned their attention to the lawn where Ned was chasing Nora, waving a bullfrog. Tim jumped up and ran down the steps. He cut in front of Ned, sending him sprawling. The bullfrog flew off in the direction of the marsh.

Ned glared at Tim. "You knocked me down."

"I didn't lay a hand on you. You tripped." Tim gestured toward Aunt Pearl on the veranda. "I have a witness."

Ned screwed up his face. "That old bat couldn't see an elephant if it sat on her."

Tim hunkered down so he was eye to eye with Ned. "I don't want to hear you refer to Miss Dutton that way again."

"I'll tell Grandpa you were rude to me."

Tim lowered his voice. "You can tell Grandpa anything you want. One other thing, if I catch you pestering the frogs or any other living creature around here, you don't want to know what could happen to you."

Ned gave him an uncertain look.

"Any problem here?" Mr. Bole came down the path.

"No, Mr. Bole, everything is quite copacetic," Tim replied, standing and straightening his vest. He marched back to the inn.

"He threatened me," Ned said.

"Good for him." Mr. Bole smiled and headed toward the dock.

Turnbull took the coffee Miss Miller passed around. "May I have the keys?" he said to her.

"Planning to leave?"

"No, I just want to catch the sports news. I have a running bet with one of my law school buddies: How many errors did the Blue Jays make last night."

She handed him the keys. With his other hand, Mr. Turnbull took the scone Margaret offered and climbed into the van.

They were standing around the van, enjoying the coffee and scones when Peters pulled his car in and started fussing with a road map. Margaret waved him over.

Turnbull climbed out of the van as Peters approached. "What kept you?" he asked.

"Nothing. I was travelling the speed limit."

Turnbull turned to the others. "Were we speeding?"

Margaret interrupted. "Did you get your sports, Mr. Turnbull?"

"Yeah." Turnbull helped himself to another scone. "Oh, there was something about a body in a ditch near your place."

Rudley started. "How near?"

"Not far from the Quebec border."

Rudley relaxed. "That's not too near."

"Usually they're right on the property." Norman grinned.

Peters looked at his watch. "Shouldn't we be going?"

"We have fifteen minutes to kill," Norman said. "Are you calculating the legal speed limit in catching the train, Miss Miller?"

"Yes, Norman."

Simpson nodded. "I think that would be wise. I noticed two patrol cars on the highway a few minutes after we pulled off."

"There's no need to rush," said Norman. "The train won't leave without us if we're a few minutes late."

"We won't be late, Norman."

Margaret clapped her hands. "Isn't this exciting, Rudley? Boarding a train and riding off into the unknown."

He smiled. "I'm tickled pink, Margaret."

Gregoire lifted the lid of a pot, standing well to one side.

"What's the matter?" Tim said. "Are you afraid you might find a rat?"

Gregoire stared at the pot. "That would not be a surprise." He stepped forward cautiously, looked into the pot, and sighed. "It is those children. What they did to my pinwheels is the last straw. I told you this morning a snake jumped out of my flour bin just after I arrived. They must have snuck down during the night to put it there." He brought the pot over to the stove, reached for a canister, recoiled. "My whole kitchen is probably booby trapped."

Tim chose a pear from the fruit bowl and examined it. "You have to admit, they liven up the place," he said, biting into the fruit.

"The place is lively enough for me as it is."

"And they were so well behaved when they first arrived."

Gregoire picked up a spatula and opened the cupboard doors. "That is because the parents were trying to give the impression they would be no trouble. They probably bribed them to behave until they had made their escape."

"I'm surprised Rudley agreed to have them in the first place."

"He agreed because he thought they were older and because he knew he would not be here."

Deciding the cupboards were safe, Gregoire took down a set of mixing bowls and placed them on the counter. "And to imagine I have been working my fingers to the bone, preparing the kinds of things kids like. My special macaroni and cheese, rice pudding the way kids like it, fruit bowls carved out of grapefruit and cantaloupe with trail-mix sprinkles and my special secret strawberry dressing, hot dogs with all the trimmings, chocolate pudding with whipped cream and three maraschino cherries."

Tim shrugged. "I agree you've knocked yourself out for the little wretches. Maybe they'd behave better if you fed them gruel and turnip soup."

Gregoire glowered. "That is disgusting. I would not stoop to insulting my kitchen. And they are guests."

"More like an invasion of locusts."

Gregoire eased open a drawer. "Where are they now?"

"Gone. I told Lloyd to take them up to the woods to show them the wild zebras."

"What zebras?"

Tim smiled. "There aren't any zebras. But it will take them an hour to find out."

"At least I can prepare lunch in peace."

"We have four reservations," Tim said. "Mr. and Mrs. Mishtook are in town with their boat. They phoned ahead to say they are bringing their own catfish."

"Which they will want rolled in Shake 'n Bake." Gregoire sighed. "I could do so much more for their catfish if they would let me."

"And the Clows," Tim continued. "He's dyspeptic. No onions, garlic, or hot spices."

"Their palates must be dying of boredom."

"And the Stevenses. They're new people on the lake. Vegan."

"I will prepare them a black bean soup and tofu loaf that will have their taste buds giving standing ovations."

"And the Noonans."

"Are they still dressing identically?"

"We'll have to wait to see. I would guess yes. And they will order the same thing."

"They are a very strange couple."

"And we'll probably have a few walk-ins. I've heard a rumour that the guests at the West Wind aren't crazy about their chef."

"I have heard he is trying to break his contract."

"When his cooking reaches the level of Mr. Cadeau's, he'll probably get his wish," Tim remarked.

"Mr. Cadeau should not insist on making a specialty of wild game in an area where people come to see Bambi skipping through the forest."

"Just to say, we'll probably be inundated for the next week or so."

Gregoire shrugged. "No need to worry. I have everything under control." He reached into the cupboard and took down the asparagus cooker.

Tim exploded with laughter as Gregoire removed the lid and a polka dot snake spiraled across the kitchen.

Detective Michel Brisbois got out of the car and started up the path toward the Pleasant.

"Here we are again." Detective Chester Creighton paused to adjust his fedora.

"Yes, here we are again."

"At least there are no dead bodies around here this time. As far as we know."

Brisbois pointed out a shrub to Creighton. "That's a new one Lloyd's put in. Mock orange. Nice fragrance when it's in bloom. The flowers look and smell like real orange blossoms."

"Looks good," said Creighton, who wouldn't know a Douglas fir from a rock.

Brisbois tramped up the steps to the veranda, pausing to turn and look back at the lake. "Seems odd not to see Norman or the Sawchucks out on the lake." He opened the door and stepped into the lobby. "Where in hell is everybody?" He peeked into the drawing room, then the ballroom. "Anybody home?" he called.

"Maybe this will work." Creighton gave the bell on the front desk a smack.

A tall, thin woman in a blue blouse and grey slacks appeared. "Detective Brisbois, Detective Creighton." She didn't seem surprised to see them.

Brisbois removed his porkpie. "Mrs. Millotte." He surveyed the room. "Where is everybody?"

"Communing with nature."

"Come again?"

"Mr. and Mrs. Rudley and a select group of guests are off on a week's jaunt in northern Ontario. A canoe trip into the wilderness."

"Which guests?"

"Miss Miller, Mr. Simpson, the Phipps-Walkers, and a pair of young fellows, a Mr. Peters and Mr. Turnbull, who are new to us."

"Canoe trip." Brisbois smiled. "I have a hard time seeing Rudley doing that kind of thing."

"He can do that sort of thing. He just doesn't like to."

"So you're holding the fort."

"Along with the rest of the staff."

"Any of the usual guests?"

"The Benson sisters."

"How are they getting along?"

"They don't look a day over eighty-five." Mrs. Millotte paused. "Mr. Bole is here and the Sawchucks. Plus their adorable grandchildren."

"I didn't know Rudley took children."

"If they didn't belong to one of our charter guests, I don't think he would."

Brisbois nodded. "I'm sure you're wondering why we're here."

Mrs. Millotte didn't skip a beat. "I suppose you were driving by and noticed a dead body on the premises."

Brisbois shook his head. "Not this time. We found a John Doe in the ditch just over the border from Quebec. We're making general inquiries in our jurisdiction. Just in case anyone's seen anything unusual."

Mrs. Millotte gave him an are-you-kidding look. "I can't remember when I last saw anything usual around here," she said.

"We're asking people to let us know if they notice anyone who doesn't seem to belong, anyone who's acting suspiciously."

"We'll do that."

"And we're asking people to be a little extra careful. Keep your windows and doors locked at night or if you're out during the day. Ask your guests to be aware. Just in case."

"I don't think anyone would want to tangle with me. Besides—" Mrs. Millotte pointed to the large dog stretched out on the rug in the middle of the lobby "—we have protection."

Albert stirred and rolled onto his back, leaving a puddle of drool. Brisbois gave him a long look. "Lock your windows and doors."

The two detectives headed back to the car. Brisbois stopped to light a cigarette.

"What do you think?" Creighton asked.

A pair of bluejays erupted from the pine grove. Brisbois watched them settle into a spruce near the dock. "I'd feel better if more of the regulars were around. They'd be more apt to notice something out of place."

Creighton watched a sailboat skimming toward the opposite shore. "Don't tell me you miss Rudley."

Brisbois flicked away an ash and sank down onto a bench near the parking lot. "I can do without him this trip," he responded, fixing his gaze on the lawn running down to the lake.

Everything in perfect condition as always, he thought. But without the regular crowd it had a lonely feel. He stared out into the lake, hoping Norman Phipps-Walker might materialize, dozing in his boat, waking just in time to retrieve his pole before it slid into the water. Or Miss Miller appear at his shoulder to give him her version of what was happening on the case. Or Rudley butt in to give him hell. Or Margaret...

He caught sight of Tiffany trundling her linen cart down the path toward the cottages. Funny that a young woman with a master's degree would stay on as housekeeper at the inn year after year. She'd had some success with her short stories, and the last time he'd seen her, she told him she was working on a novel. He wondered if he might turn up as a character in the book and how she might portray him. He liked to think he was a decent, hard-working guy, ethical, a good father, a faithful husband. He sighed. He hadn't always been there for his family when he wanted to be. He'd missed his youngest son's clarinet recital because one drunk had clobbered another. He'd missed his oldest daughter's first hockey game to stand at a riverbank while the divers brought up a weighted body. The kids' lives were a blur as he got busier and busier. They'd all turned out well—thanks to Mary. And now that the kids were out of the house, Mary was progressing in her career at the bank. He'd aimed to retire at sixty, buy that cottage, spend whole days with his wife, every day. Now he wasn't sure if she'd be available to spend all of her time with him.

Maybe Tiffany would make him a hero, the conscientious, slightly overweight, somewhat melancholy investigator who did his job without drama—an everyman hero.

Creighton interrupted his thoughts. "Chances are the killer's already left the jurisdiction."

"He starts out in Fredericton," Brisbois mused. "He kills an eighty-five-year-old man. Belts him on the head. Strangles him. A few days later, he ends up in Ottawa where he kills three people for next to nothing. He incapacitates them, then smothers them."

"Unimaginative but effective."

"Why would he stop in Ottawa to kill three innocent people for peanuts?"

"Maybe he hitchhiked and that's as far as the ride took him. Maybe he blew the take from the jewellery store and couldn't get any further."

Brisbois shook his head. "The old couple and the cabbie were just unlucky."

"Yup."

"They thought he took the bus," Brisbois said, "because that's what the old lady told the cab company." He took a drag of his cigarette. "This guy's smart. He went to the train station instead. Bought himself some time. Muddied the waters."

"But maybe he didn't get on the train," Creighton said. "Or maybe he did."

"Somehow he encountered the young couple in the RV. He cranked the guy's neck, smothered the woman."

"The last guy," said Creighton. "Our John Doe. He was shot. That suggests a different operator."

Brisbois stared over the lake. "He used the gun because he didn't have the opportunity to use his preferred method. Or he didn't have a gun to use before. Maybe it was the John Doe's gun."

"Okay."

"It's got to be the same guy. The RV victims and our John Doe died within hours of each other, two miles apart. That links them. And the preferred MO links the whole kit and caboodle. Mel Turk"—

he named the lead detective on the murder in Fredericton—"when he heard about the murders in Ottawa, he glommed onto that right away. Some guy who kills for next to nothing, whose preferred method is suffocation or strangulation."

"He'd have to be one cool customer."

"One dangerous customer."

"He could be miles away from here," Creighton said. "I don't think the folks out here are at any particular risk."

"What about last night—that guy who ate and ran at the bus station in Lowerton? That's only eight miles from here, maybe twelve miles from the last murder scene."

"You think that's the same guy? Maybe he was just some guy couldn't afford to pay for his meal."

Brisbois shifted restlessly. "Or maybe a serial murderer who got spooked when the security officer wandered through." He shook his head. "There was a lot going on in a relatively small rural area for one twenty-four-hour period."

"No fingerprint hits," said Creighton. "Not even the same unidentified prints at any two scenes."

"Gloves," said Brisbois.

"The RV was a rental. They probably don't clean them that thoroughly between customers." Creighton stretched his legs. "Maybe our John Doe was a mob hit."

"One shot between the eyes at close range," Brisbois murmured. "They're guessing something like a .32. Nothing more definite until later today."

"Our John Doe was stripped down to his shorts," said Creighton. "Maybe to make it hard to identify him. Buy some time."

"Or assume his identity," Brisbois stubbed out his cigarette, tore off a piece of foil, wrapped the butt in it, and stuffed the foil into his pocket. "Anyway, the guy who killed the couple in the RV is the same one who killed our John Doe."

"Yup." Creighton wasn't sure Brisbois was right, although he was a lot of the time. He didn't say anything more.

Rudley peered out the window as the train slowed. "I don't know why in hell we're getting off here, Margaret."

She looked past him at the spotty mix of conifers and deciduous trees alongside the track. "Where would you like to get off, Rudley?"

"Anywhere, Margaret, with a suggestion that a human being had, at some point, set foot on it."

Norman leaned over his shoulder. "I'm sure that thousands of human feet have trod this soil. Our Cree friends were widespread. And prior to that, whatever group crossed that isthmus that used to connect Russia and Alaska."

Rudley shot him an irritated look. "A simple sign would be reassuring, Norman. Even something of the 'You Are Here' variety."

Margaret turned to Miss Miller, who was studying her map. "Rudley is worried we're in the wrong place."

Miss Miller looked from the map to the train window. The train was slowing. "I believe we're as close to our destination as the train takes us. From here it rounds a curve and loops south to Terrel's before turning north again."

Geraldine trained her binoculars on the tree line. "Is this the confluence of the Little Beaver and the Swine?"

"It's the confluence of Outer Hell and East Outhouse, Geraldine."

Geraldine swatted him on the back. "You have such a sense of humour, Rudley." She wrenched her binoculars skyward. "Is that a bald eagle I see, Norman?"

He grabbed his own binoculars. "Why, I believe it is, Geraldine."

"Beautiful specimen," she murmured.

The train lurched to a stop. Norman fell into Simpson's lap. Geraldine tumbled on top of them. Norman chortled.

"This reminds me of the train we took in India," Geraldine said. "We were packed in like sardines and ended up stacked in the lap of a former Gurkha soldier. Fortunately, he was a large man."

"I'm not," Simpson squeaked.

"Oh." Geraldine wriggled up, "Norman, let's get you off before you squash Edward."

"I'm sure he's already relieved," Rudley murmured to his wife. "Geraldine could make a whale say 'uncle.'"

"Be nice, Rudley."

Turnbull paused to look out the window then began to gather his gear. Peters's gaze swept the landscape. "Is this it?" He stood up and likewise started to collect his things.

"Would you like a hand with that?" Simpson offered, reaching toward Peters's bag.

Peters snatched the bag away. "I can do it."

Simpson recoiled. "Of course."

Peters climbed down from the train to join those who had already assembled. "So this is it," he repeated. "Nothing around."

"Not for many miles," said Miss Miller. She put down her bag to strap Edward into the frame of his backpack.

"Just us and white water," said Turnbull.

Rudley helped Margaret down.

"The trip doesn't call for white water, Mr. Turnbull," Margaret said. "I understand there's just one stretch where we'll be compelled to portage. We chose the route partly because of that and partly because it promises an intimate experience."

"Intimate?"

"Without crowds of strangers flitting about on Jet Skis."

Turnbull shrugged. "We'll probably run into a lot of people with the same idea."

"Our guide reports from his experience that the area should be deserted. It's early in the season and not the sort of area white water canoeists favour."

"Like Miss Miller and Mr. Simpson," Norman chuckled.

"Like Miss Miller," Edward corrected.

Miss Miller smiled. "I'm quite happy with a more leisurely pace on this excursion."

"Elizabeth and I had several challenging white water experiences last fall," said Edward.

"Colorado River?" asked Norman.

"Northern British Columbia."

"The scenery must have been spectacular," Geraldine remarked.

"Huge boulders," Edward countered. "Which seemed to come at us every few seconds. We were in a raft with several others. One man ended up with a broken leg. It took hours to get him out."

"We should be fine," said Margaret. "Almost everyone here has had some sort of emergency training." She nodded toward Elizabeth. "I know Miss Miller has advanced training, as I imagine our guide will as well. He also has a satellite telephone."

"You'll never know you aren't in Toronto," said Norman with a grin.

"The phone's only for emergencies, Norman," Geraldine trilled. "I don't think we'll be using it to call the grandchildren or anything like that."

The grandchildren. Rudley smiled, whistled a few bars, then murmured under his breath, "Mrs. Millotte has things well in hand."

Margaret squeezed his arm. "You're such a trouper, Rudley.

"If we're all together, let's set out," said Miss Miller. She checked her compass. "This way."

They set out across the countryside as the train chuffed away behind them.

Chapter Ten

"That does it." Rudley yanked off his backpack and sank down onto a rock. "We're clearly lost."

Norman stopped and sat down beside him. "Why would you say that, Rudley?"

Rudley searched furtively in his pockets for a cigarette. "Do you know where we are?"

"I would say, according to our itinerary, we are at the confluence of the Little Beaver and Swine Rivers. Oh"— he motioned toward Rudley's vest—"your cigarettes are in the side pocket. Left side."

Rudley glared at Norman and pulled out the pack.

"Now you have to take care when you smoke in the forest," Norman went on. "Far too many forest fires are caused by human carelessness." He watched as Rudley lit up. "I don't know why you brought cigarettes. It's not as if you're a dedicated smoker."

Smoke spewed from Rudley's nostrils. "I brought them in case I found myself surrounded by ninnies." He looked over his shoulder. "I don't see a confluence, Norman. I see patches of rock and an impenetrable forest."

Norman squinted at the map. "According to this, we have reached the confluence."

"I don't think you could tell a confluence from a cesspool, Norman."

Norman smiled. "Now, Rudley, I am not a stranger to the wilderness. I know you're feeling anxious and frustrated because you think we're lost."

"We are lost, Norman. We never should have agreed to let Miss Miller and the others go ahead—especially Miss Miller."

Norman nodded. "I agree that it is always wise to stay close to Miss Miller."

Rudley drew hard on his cigarette. "You know we would have been further ahead if we'd driven in the van all the way to Campbell's Landing, met up with the guide, and started the expedition from there."

"There's no road into Campbell's Landing, Rudley. As Miss Miller explained, our guide and some pals were to bring the canoes down to the confluence of the Little Beaver and the Swine."

"Then his friends walked home?"

Norman stared at him. "I must say, Rudley, the details of our preparation seem to have gone over your head."

Rudley savaged the filter of his cigarette.

"Our guide's pals were picked up by a float plane returning from dropping another party at Salinger's Bay. Our guide will be waiting for us with the canoes and supplies at the confluence the of the Little Beaver and Swine."

Rudley's eyes crossed. "I have to say, Norman, this is the most convoluted travel arrangement I can recall. It would have made more sense to catch a plane at the local airport, fly to the confluence, marvel at how dismal it is, then fly home again."

Norman looked bewildered. "But then it wouldn't have been a canoe trip. It would have been a plane trip."

"But at least we wouldn't have gotten lost."

Norman looked around. "I don't believe we're lost, Rudley. We're merely detained. We probably should have asked the others to wait while you went into the bushes to change your shorts."

Rudley glowered. "I didn't want the entire country to know my shorts were chafing, Norman, and I'll thank you not to broadcast the fact."

"You should always wash your shorts prior to wearing them, Rudley. I have found it's always wise to wash shorts the first time."

"They were washed, Norman. The cut is something I'm not used to."

Norman took off his hat, smoothed the sweatband. "I've always found the traditional boxer the most comfortable."

"I'm glad to hear that, Norman."

"I take it Mrs. Rudley picked them out. A man should never let his wife choose his shorts. Women are inclined to choose style over comfort, you know."

Rudley took a deep drag from his cigarette. "I imagine women lack an intuitive feel for what might be comfortable in men's under apparel."

"I think you might be right, Rudley."

Voices interrupted: "Norman! Rudley!"

They turned to see Miss Miller and Geraldine.

"We thought you'd fallen down a rabbit hole," Geraldine trilled.

Rudley stubbed out his cigarette, dug a hole, and buried the butt as Norman nodded his approval.

"And here you are, just slacking off," Geraldine continued. She turned to Miss Miller. "I knew we should have waited for them. Norman couldn't find his way out of an elevator without me."

Norman smiled a buck-toothed smile.

Rudley struggled up and strapped on his backpack. "I gather this is supposed to be the confluence. I don't see a confluence, Miss Miller."

"We're three hundred yards from the confluence," said Miss Miller. She took out her map and indicated the area to Rudley.

Rudley peered at the map. "Yes, we're here at the confluence, which is two hundred yards from the falls." He stabbed his finger at a spot on the map.

Miss Miller shook her head. "Mr. Rudley, what you're pointing at is the orienteering symbol for a marsh."

"Come along," Geraldine beckoned.

"The others are waiting at the confluence," said Miss Miller. "Our guide, Gil Jackson, was waiting there when we arrived. He has the canoes and provisions and is right on schedule."

"I hope he's competent," Rudley grumbled.

Miss Miller smiled. "I think you will find him satisfactory."

They covered the remaining three hundred yards without incident. The rest of the party sat on the ground, chatting. Five red canoes snoozed on the shore edge.

"Norman, Mr. Rudley"—Simpson saw them arrive and jumped up—"I'd like you to meet our guide, Gil Jackson."

The man hunkered down over one of the bags lifted his head, turned, and smiled.

"I'm pleased to meet you," Rudley said. As Norman went over to talk to Gil, he turned to Margaret and muttered, "Christ, Margaret, he's a teenager."

"Now, Rudley, I'm sure he's in his twenties."

"I would have thought Clifton would have at least sent his son, not his grandson."

"Clifton's son is an insurance agent. I'm sure Gil is much more qualified."

"He looks like a Boy Scout."

"Well, then Rudley, at least we know he'll be clean."

The sun hung heavy in the west, casting a brazen sheen downstream as the paddlers pulled up for the night. Once the canoes were secured, Miss Miller set about preparing a campfire.

"Wouldn't it be easier if you had a propane cooker?" Turnbull asked, as Miss Miller dug a pit and arranged the rocks Simpson had collected.

Miss Miller looked at Turnbull over her glasses. Her hair had escaped its bobby pins and trailed across her face. Her cheek was scratched from a branch that had whipped back on her. Edward, positioning the last stone, thought she had never looked lovelier. "Whatever for?" she asked.

"It would be easier than what you're doing."

Miss Miller arranged a handful of twigs in the bottom of the pit. "I would prefer not to drag around a Coleman camper and dozens of propane tanks."

"You could have had one of the staff cart around that crap."

Miss Miller smiled. "This is an equal opportunity venture, Mr. Turnbull."

Turnbull shrugged. "Sure. So you're doing the cooking?"

"I imagine each of us will contribute to the effort, Mr. Turnbull," Simpson replied.

Peters lingered near the pit, watching Miss Miller intently as she coaxed a flame from the twigs.

"You're kind of like a kitten watching a fire," Turnbull remarked to Peters as he bent to pick up a few pebbles.

Peters gave him a quick look.

"Never see anyone make a fire before?" Turnbull tossed the pebbles from hand to hand.

When Peters didn't respond, Turnbull's attention drifted to the shoreline where Gil was bent over a satellite phone.

When Gil finished his call and joined the others, Turnbull gave him a smile. "Calling home?"

Gil shook his head. "Just checking to make sure everything was working properly."

"Is the equipment so bad it couldn't survive a short trip?"

"The equipment is good. But if there's going to be a malfunction, better to find out earlier than later."

"Sounds sensible to me," said Miss Miller.

Norman held out a jug. "I'll prepare some water, Miss Miller."

"Are you taking charge of water purification, Mr. Phipps-Walker?"

"Norman specializes in making potable water," said Geraldine.

"I can look after that," said Gil. "It's really my job."

"Oh, your job is to get us safely down the river and keep the bears away," said Margaret, "and supervise the overall operation. We're all prepared to do our share of the day-to-day tasks."

Gil smiled. "And to wake you up with coffee every morning and to make sure the water is safe."

"Yes, it would be embarrassing if we were found sprawled out, dead from cholera," Rudley murmured.

"Be nice, Rudley," Margaret murmured in return.

"What do you do to make the water safe?" Turnbull asked.

Norman described the procedure. Gil nodded his approval.

"Oh, I thought you just muttered an incantation—" Turnbull began.

Margaret interrupted. "Would anyone care for a trail cookie?"

"It was clever of Gregoire to put those trail cookies together," Norman remarked. "Tasty. Light to carry and if we get lost, we could probably live on them for days."

Gil looked hurt. "I won't get us lost," he said.

"Of course you won't," said Norman. "But we can feel secure in the knowledge that no matter what might happen, we won't starve."

"I doubt if we would starve," Rudley grumbled. "The rivers up here are teeming with fish…although…"

Margaret nudged him in the ribs before he could comment on Norman's fishing skills.

"Even if there were no fish we could always snare a rabbit or a bird," he added.

Norman started to splutter.

Margaret made a soothing sound. "Rudley's joking, Norman. We certainly won't get to a point where we need to sacrifice birds and bunnies. I couldn't eat a robin or a little bunny even if I were starving."

"We'll resort to cannibalism before we stoop to that," said Rudley.

"Now that's a terrible idea," said Margaret. "Selecting someone to kill so the others can survive."

Turnbull appeared bored. "I think they wait until somebody dies. Usually the weakest member of the group." He flipped a pebble in Peters's direction, hitting him in the shoulder. "Sorry."

"Or maybe the most annoying," Peters muttered. "After he's had some kind of accident."

Turnbull rolled his eyes. Gil watched the proceedings with an anxious look.

Norman turned to Rudley and said in a low voice. "I don't think those two like each other."

"Probably not," Rudley muttered. "I can't say I like either one of them."

"I hope everybody's hungry," Miss Miller said. "We're having sausage dogs, hash browns, and skillet blueberry pie."

Simpson started to gather kindling. Peters joined him, saying, "I saw a big piece down by the river," he said.

"I'll bet it's kind of waterlogged," Turnbull drawled.

Peters's jaw tightened.

"Let's have a look at it, shall we?" Simpson said to Peters.

Turnbull sighed and grabbed his backpack. He stuck it under his head for a pillow and stretched out.

Gil went down to the canoes and returned with his personal gear and the satellite phone. "I think we did well today," he announced. "Made good progress."

Turnbull peeled a callous from his palm. "I think we'd do better without him." He gestured toward Peters, who was climbing the rise laden with branches.

Gil looked at him, surprised. "I think he's doing all right."

"I could go faster by myself. I'm a pretty experienced canoeist."

Gil shrugged. "I'll take Mr. Peters with me if you want to carry the extra gear."

Turnbull shrugged. "Sure."

Rudley had been studying Turnbull and Peters. "At the risk of repeating myself, Margaret," he began, "where do you find these people?"

"They both seemed quite pleasant on the phone, Rudley."

"I find Turnbull twitchy, Margaret, and an ass to boot."

"Perhaps he's one of those people who suffer from what they call adult attention deficit disorder." She shook her head. "I do think he could show more enthusiasm for the camp work. Mr. Peters seems willing."

"I find him edgy, too, although in a quieter way."

"I get the feeling he thinks everyone is watching him and judging him."

"He has an unusual head, Margaret."

"Mr. Turnbull seems to enjoy making fun of him. I suspect he's a bit of a bully."

"He said he was a law student, Margaret. I believe they're trained to be bullies."

"Well, then we need to support Mr. Peters…in an inconspicuous way."

"I don't know. I've never had the desire to be a nursemaid."

"He's young. I'm sure he could benefit from the support of a mature man."

Rudley looked toward Norman, who was gazing into a tree, making chirping noises. "I guess that would have to be me."

"We'd better get the tents pitched," Geraldine interrupted them. "Best to get at it while Miss Miller's getting the supper going."

"Before it gets dark," Gil added with a smile. "Or you could find yourselves sleeping on a rock."

"That does it for me," Rudley muttered. He grabbed a tent and followed Geraldine up the rise.

Mrs. Millotte took the flashlight from the desk drawer. "I'm going to check the Elm Pavilion," she told Lloyd. "Stay near the phone."

Lloyd's gaze wandered to the gathering gloom outside the windows. "Want me to go with you?"

"No, someone needs to stay by the phone."

"Want me to go instead?"

"I'll be fine."

"Detective Brisbois said we was to be careful. Maybe we shouldn't be out at night alone."

"I'll take Albert with me." Mrs. Millotte removed the leash from the hook by the door and called to the dog.

Albert stretched, yawned, and rolled onto his back, regarding her affectionately.

Mrs. Millotte jiggled the leash. "Come on, Rin Tin Tin, you're riding shotgun." She opened the door. "Lock this after me," she said to Lloyd.

"Yes'm." Lloyd reached under the desk and pulled out a comic book.

Mrs. Millotte paused on the veranda. The water lapped the dock, the sound amplified in the silence. A light moved along the opposite shore, the boat too far away for her to hear the engine.

Mrs. Millotte had grown up on the lake. Her father and grandfather had been fishing guides and boat builders. Her mother took in summer guests, mainly fishermen. Nothing like the fancy people who frequented places like the Pleasant. The sounds of the lake were stored deep in her memory. She headed down the path toward the Elm Pavilion, Albert padding along beside her.

She liked Albert but thought him a poor excuse for a dog. He couldn't help being what he was. He was a city dog. Sure, he sniffed things and chased everything in sight, but his activity wasn't particularly purposeful. He had a lot of spunk but few brains, in her estimation. Skunks had sprayed him more times than she cared to remember. He'd been sprayed twice by the same skunk, no less, the one who liked to hang out under the back steps and didn't bother anyone who wasn't foolish enough to bother her. He'd tangled with a porcupine twice. Albert didn't want to kill anything. He wanted to make friends.

She arrived at the Elm Pavilion, circling it before knocking. She had her master keys out but when she tried the door it was unlocked. Pushing it open a crack, she saw the Benson sisters, Louise, Emma, and Kate, huddled on the sofa watching *Bringing up Baby*.

Mrs. Millotte hesitated. If she startled them, one of them might have a heart attack. She was considering the best way to get their attention when Albert barked. The ladies turned in unison, unalarmed. Mrs. Millotte moved to the front of the sofa while Albert frisked among the sisters, soliciting pats.

"You didn't lock your door," Mrs. Millotte said.

The sisters exchanged glances.

"No, we didn't," Emma replied. "We didn't want to have to get up in the middle of our Cary Grant marathon to answer the door. We thought if anyone needed us, they could let themselves in."

"Detective Brisbois strongly advises us to keep our windows and doors locked at all times."

Emma made a dismissive gesture with her right hand. "The detective is a nice man, but as you know, he's an alarmist."

"He's asking us to take precautions because there may be a multiple murderer on the lam in our area."

Louise's attention drifted back to Cary Grant. "We've had murderers around here for years. None of them ever bothered us."

"No one has a motive to dispose of us," Kate added.

"Except me at this moment," said Mrs. Millotte.

Louise tittered.

"Perhaps this man doesn't need a motive," Mrs. Millotte continued. "Perhaps he just enjoys killing people."

Emma shook Kate's arm to get her attention. "Mrs. Millotte says this man derives sexual satisfaction from killing people."

"That's not exactly what I said."

"All of these people on *Criminal Minds* who don't have legitimate motives kill because they derive sexual satisfaction from particularly gruesome, horrific crimes."

"Usually after hours, perhaps days, of torture," Kate added.

The sisters looked at each other. "We'll keep the doors locked."

"And don't open the door unless you know who's on the other side," Mrs. Millotte added.

"Seventy percent of murders are committed by someone the victim knows," said Louise.

"Well, figure out who around here is most likely to murder you and don't let them in."

"What if we all died during the night," Kate piped up, "and no one knew because they can't get in?"

"We'd notice if you didn't call for breakfast."

Louise shuddered. "My greatest fear is having someone find me dead on the toilet."

"I'll make sure they don't include that in your obituary," Mrs. Millotte said. "Now, is there anything I can do for you ladies?"

They glanced at each other and shook their heads.

"No, thank you," said Kate.

"All right. Good night." Mrs. Millotte peeped through the window, then slipped out the door, urging Albert ahead of her. She locked the door behind her and paused, gauging the sounds of the night.

Mr. Peters sat beside the fire, his marshmallow skewer over his knees, gazing into the flames.

"Like a kitten," Turnbull murmured again.

Gil had gone to an open area to use the satellite phone. He came back to the group, loaded his skewer with marshmallows, and dropped down beside Simpson.

"Are you going to call home every five minutes?" Turnbull fixed Gil with a mocking smile.

Gil flushed. "No."

"Makes a person wonder if you know where we're headed."

"Any news?" Miss Miller asked when Gil didn't respond to Turnbull's provocation.

"I was talking to my fifteen-year-old cousin. He's not big on news."

"I wonder if the police have found out anything about that poor man in the ditch?" Margaret worried.

"At least he wasn't found on our property," said Rudley.

"The murders that take place on our property are usually committed by our guests or their associates," said Margaret.

Turnbull turned to stare at the Rudleys.

"They are usually in-house," Simpson agreed.

"And usually with a well-defined motive," Norman added. He looked to Miss Miller. "I don't recall a murder at the Pleasant that was committed purely for pleasure."

Miss Miller thought a moment. "I agree, Norman. In each case the motives were clear."

Turnbull looked into the trees. "Did they catch the perps?"

"Oh, yes," said Geraldine. "Every single one of them."

"We have Miss Miller to thank for much of that," said Margaret.

Turnbull looked at Miss Miller and shook his head dismissively.

"Really," said Norman. "Miss Miller is a capable sleuth."

"Nothing escapes her attention," Geraldine added.

Miss Miller tilted her head in a self-deprecating gesture. "I believe we should give Detectives Brisbois and Creighton appropriate credit."

"Which would be almost none," said Rudley. "The two of them couldn't find their own car in a parking lot."

"Maybe someone else is on the case," said Gil.

Norman frowned. "Oh, I don't think so. They seem to look after most of the goings-on in the district."

Rudley crossed his eyes.

"Well, we have nothing to worry about here." Geraldine turned a fond eye toward the guide. "We have Gil to protect us."

"I'll do my best, Mrs. Phipps-Walker."

A sudden footfall interrupted the conversation.

Peters jumped. "What was that?"

Norman speared two marshmallows. "Given our location in the boreal forest, I believe it could be a deer, possibly a moose." He held his skewer over the embers. "Nothing to worry about. A moose can be formidable, especially in mating season, but..."

"I think the steps were too light to be a moose," Geraldine said. "It was probably just a raccoon."

"Or a mad trapper," said Turnbull, grinning.

"Yes," Margaret wondered, "what would we do if a mad trapper materialized out of the darkness pointing a high-powered rifle at us?"

"Why, I would throw myself on him," Rudley said with a jaunty smile. "Take one for the team."

Margaret beamed. "Why, Rudley, how gallant of you."

Turnbull smiled smugly. He picked up a marshmallow, started to skewer it, changed his mind, and popped it into his mouth. He poked the skewer into the embers and watched it catch fire before thrusting it the rest of the way in. "If someone showed up with a high-powered rifle, he'd just pick us off one by one and we couldn't do a thing about it."

Miss Miller gave him a cool smile. "You might choose to do nothing, Mr. Turnbull, but Mr. Rudley is prepared to be heroic." She turned to Simpson. "And Edward would also challenge the gunman. Wouldn't you, Edward?"

"Of course, Elizabeth." Simpson had just swallowed a marshmallow. The words came out in a high-pitched squeak.

"And Norman too," said Geraldine.

"I would certainly challenge anyone with the audacity to point a weapon at us," Norman declared.

"We would rush the intruder simultaneously," said Miss Miller.

Turnbull picked up a handful of pebbles and began tossing them into the fire. "What about you, Peters? Maybe you'd just freeze."

Peters had been eating a marshmallow. He looked up quickly.

"I think you'd all just freeze," Turnbull added.

Margaret frowned. "Oh, I don't think we would. We could have some sort of password worked out in advance. And at the password we would rush the intruder. The element of surprise would work in our favour."

Turnbull smirked. "What kind of password? Like 'that's all, folks?'" He tossed another pebble, this time nicking Peters's knee.

"How about 'shoot Turnbull first,'" Peters muttered.

Turnbull's smirk faded.

"I'm sure Mr. Peters doesn't want you to be shot," Margaret hastened to say. "After all, our mad trapper wouldn't know who you were, so he wouldn't know to shoot you first."

"Couldn't we simply scream 'attack?'" Geraldine suggested.

"All of us at once?" Norman asked.

Geraldine looked at him, befuddled.

"May I suggest," said Norman, "that since Miss Miller has always proven perspicacious in her assessments and the execution of any action that might be suggested by those assessments, that Miss Miller be nominated to shout 'shoot Turnbull first'? And in her absence, this duty would fall to her delegate."

Rudley's eyes crossed. "Have you recently chaired some sort of meeting, Norman?"

"The semiannual Sparrow Society meeting," Geraldine replied for her husband. "In Ottawa."

"The sparrow is a much maligned and underappreciated member of our avian family," said Norman.

"Plucky little chaps," said Simpson.

"So it's agreed, then," Norman said, "that Miss Miller or her delegate will shout 'shoot Turnbull first.'"

Turnbull looked at him, a faint smile playing about his lips.

Rudley encouraged a moth from his breast pocket. "Splendid plan. I doubt if a mad trapper will wander into our camp. But in the event one does, I am confident we will act in an effective and coordinated manner."

Norman regarded him blankly.

"We'll all turn and run like hell," said Rudley.

Turnbull shook his head and laughed.

Lloyd was immersed in his comic book when Mr. Bole came out of the drawing room.

"I'm headed back to my cabin," Mr. Bole announced. "If I don't show up for breakfast, you'll know I've been done in."

"Yes'm," said Lloyd without looking up.

Mr. Bole hesitated. "Lloyd, I'm going upstairs to hack the Sawchucks up with the fire axe."

"Yes'm."

Mr. Bole gave up and came around behind the desk. "What's so interesting, Lloyd?"

Lloyd pointed to a cartoon panel. "The mayor just found out the guys he gave the keys to the city to were from outer space."

"That would certainly throw a wrench into one's day."

"Yup."

"Goodnight, then, Lloyd. Don't forget to lock the door behind me."

Lloyd locked the door.

Mrs. Millotte had let go of Albert's leash for a second to make sure the Benson sisters' door was locked. But a fox flashed past the inn and Albert took off into the woods in hot pursuit. She called the dog in vain. Albert was such a dummy, she thought. She checked her flashlight. The batteries were failing. Well, if she were going into the woods, she'd need the big light from the basement. She took her master key and set out up the path.

"Lloyd." Tiffany ran up to the desk.

"Yes'm," he said without looking up.

Tiffany grabbed the comic book and closed it. "Lloyd, I need you to help me with the Sawchucks. Doreen sat down in the occasional chair and she's wedged in so tightly I can't get her out. I need you to support her weight while I wriggle the chair free."

Lloyd came out from behind the desk. "Mr. Rudley says she's well-upholstered."

"Lloyd, if you must make any comments in her presence, make sure it's about the chair being terribly small."

"Can do."

"There are some bigger chairs in storage. We'll pretend the little chair is broken and must be replaced."

"Probably does now."

Tiffany urged him up the stairs. "Lloyd, don't say anything except perhaps 'good evening' and 'yes, Mrs. Sawchuck' or 'no, Mrs. Sawchuck.'"

"Can do." He paused. "There won't be nobody at the desk."

"It's all right, Lloyd, I saw Mrs. Millotte come in the back door while I was checking the window locks in 206."

"Could have been a robber."

"It was Mrs. Millotte. I waved to her and she waved back."

Tiffany quickly scribbled a note: Lloyd's helping me in 209. She put the note on the desk and hurried up the stairs.

Mrs. Millotte had come through the back door to get the high-powered flashlight that was usually kept in the storage closet across from Rudley's basement office. She searched high and low, with no results. Finally, she gave up, climbed the stairs to the first floor, and checked the closet in the hallway. There it was—perched on a box of toilet tissue. She cursed whoever was in the habit of taking things and not returning them to their appointed places. She removed the flashlight and proceeded to the desk, intending to let Lloyd know she was going out again.

No Lloyd.

She was about to give the bell a smack when she saw Tiffany's note. She shook her head. Don't tell me there's a bat in the Sawchucks' room, she thought. If that was the case, Lloyd and Tiffany were welcome to the task of removing it. She wrote a note of her own: Lloyd, I'm going out to look for Albert. He slipped the leash. Have master keys.

Mrs. Millotte considered that she should have asked someone to accompany her. She thought about tapping on the door to the bunkhouse, but Gregoire had just closed down the kitchen and she knew he and Tim had had a long day. Besides, she felt embarrassed about the lapse that had allowed Albert to escape in the first place.

She was also worried. Albert was a good dog in many ways but the only one he paid much attention to was Edward Simpson. Must be the British accent, she thought. She'd grown up with dogs, all of which roamed the country freely. They were quite capable of finding their way home. She wasn't sure if Albert had that capacity. What worried her more was that he had run off with his leash attached. He could get snagged and hang himself or become easy prey for a coyote. Mrs. Rudley said he was an innocent dog, full of good will, believing all the forest creatures wanted to play with him. Innocent dogs usually learned after one or two unfortunate encounters. Stupid dogs never learned.

Mrs. Millotte took the usual path into the forest, calling Albert's name as she went. She was glad she had the powerful flashlight. The quarter moon was a useless sliver.

She wasn't afraid of wild animals. None of them gave her cause for concern. She was more concerned about being shot by some local yokel who'd had too much to drink and decided he was Rambo on a night mission. She realized, with a chuckle, that after warning everyone to lock their windows and doors and exercise caution, she was out in the woods, armed only with a flashlight.

Mrs. Sawchuck was in a dither. Walter was pretending to be in a dither but was actually weary of the situation. He had warned Doreen not to sit on that occasional chair, telling her he thought the leg was wobbly. He'd been meaning to ask Rudley to replace it with a wider chair, but wasn't sure how to explain his request to Doreen. She liked the pretty little antique chair and, before tonight, had been able to squeeze into it and get herself out. The straw that broke the camel's back, he surmised, was the bulky nightgown Doreen had chosen that evening. Although the weather was seasonable, Doreen, because of her arthritis, felt a chill in the air. Besides, as she told him, she liked being extra warm. She could have been extra warm in a bigger chair, he thought, instead of being wedged into that dainty little thing while Lloyd pulled and Tiffany wriggled it, trying to pry her out.

"You're hurting me!" Doreen shrieked.

Lloyd released Mrs. Sawchuck. Tiffany stepped back before the chair leg landed on her foot.

Tiffany patted Doreen on the shoulder. "We'll take a rest while we decide what to do next."

"Maybe grease," said Lloyd.

"You're not going to ruin my lovely new nightgown with grease!"

"I think the nightgown's caught in the arm," Tiffany said.

"Guess we have to take it off then," said Lloyd.

"Well, I never!" Doreen spluttered.

"I can pry it off and fix it good as new," said Lloyd.

"He means the arm of the chair, Doreen," Walter yelled from the bed as Doreen continued to splutter.

Tiffany sighed with relief. "That's a wonderful idea. Mrs. Sawchuck, your nightgown won't be damaged and we'll get you another chair until Lloyd can fix this one."

By the time Lloyd had run down to the basement, got his toolbox, and returned, Mrs. Sawchuck had calmed somewhat. Lloyd employed a thin wedge and a rubber mallet to remove the arm. He and Tiffany then hauled Mrs. Sawchuck up and into bed.

Tiffany tucked Mrs. Sawchuck in. Lloyd picked up the chair and headed for the door.

"Take your time fixing that chair," Walter called after him.

Mrs. Millotte was off the property, a good mile into Crown land. She had a number of things on her mind besides finding Albert: Being away from her post so long, rechecking the linen inventory for the laundryman, who appeared not long after sunup, getting a decent night's sleep. Her concerns about the most recent psychopath were shoved to the back burner.

She sat down on a stump, took out her cigarettes, and lit up. Clamping the cigarette between her teeth, she shone the flashlight at her wrist. It was already after eleven. She finished her cigarette, buried the butt in the damp forest floor, and moved on.

Lloyd took the chair to the basement, repaired the arm, and left it in clamps to dry. Then he went into the storage room and checked the spare chairs. He finally decided on a nice upholstered armchair with embroidered cushions. It was like the little one Mrs. Sawchuck favoured but it was three inches wider. He made some quick calculations and decided three inches would be enough allowance for Mrs. Sawchuck's girth. This year at least.

Mrs. Millotte estimated she was about two miles from home, deep in the forest. She wasn't tired but she was getting desperate. If Albert had caught his leash on a limb and hung himself she would never forgive herself.

She stopped, shone the flashlight around, and called his name. She noted with alarm the hesitancy in her voice.

Was it her imagination? She was sure she heard an excited yip. She headed in the direction of the sound, calling the dog's name, stopping periodically to listen.

The yip seemed closer.

She broke through a dense stand of undergrowth and there he was. Albert leapt up when he saw her, then fell back.

"Do you know how long I've been looking for you?" Mrs. Millotte tried to sound gruff. She checked her watch again in the beam of the light. It was after midnight. "Two and a half hours!" She freed Albert's leash from the fallen log and wrapped it firmly around her wrist. "It's a good thing you got caught up on that. God knows where you might have ended up." They set off toward the Pleasant, Albert leading the way, tail wagging.

Lloyd went back upstairs. He met Tiffany on her way down from the second floor.

"Want me to bring that big chair up now?"

Tiffany shook her head. "Better wait until tomorrow. I've just got Mrs. Sawchuck settled." She yawned. "I'm going to bed. Are all the doors locked?"

"Yes'm. I'll check them all again."

"Don't forget to throw the bolts."

"Can do."

Lloyd made his rounds, checked and bolted the front door, the side door, and the back kitchen door, then went down to the basement where he ususally slept. He checked the back door and threw the bolt.

"Rudley."

"Hmm?"

"Rudley."

Rudley opened one eye. Margaret was shaking him by the shoulder. He opened the other eye. "What's wrong, Margaret?"

"I couldn't sleep." She sighed. "Rudley, I think we should ask Gil if we can use the satellite phone tomorrow. I want to call home."

"Why?"

"I'm worried about the staff."

"I worry about those ninnies all the time, Margaret."

"Rudley"— she propped herself up on one elbow, leaned over him—"I'm serious."

"So am I."

"With that murderer so close, I just want to be assured that everyone is all right."

"They've had murderers close by before and they've been all right."

"Yes, but we've always been there." She paused. "I suppose that didn't help much before, us being there."

"I like to think we had some positive influence."

"Do you think they're all right?"

He groaned. "I'm sure they are, Margaret. If not, we'll probably read about it in a two-inch headline. Perhaps a plane will fly over trailing an announcement: Another Murder at the Pleasant."

"Rudley, don't be facetious."

"Margaret, Mrs. Millotte is in charge. What could possibly go wrong with Mrs. Millotte in charge?"

"I suppose you're right."

"Of course I'm right, Margaret." With that Rudley rolled over and went back to sleep.

Lloyd was sleeping soundly on the couch in Rudley's office, dreaming. In his dream, he was in the tool shed behind the Pleasant with the transom open wide, enjoying the music of the night birds and the soft rustling of nocturnal creatures. The air felt fresh and slightly moist. The breeze off the lake sighed through the evergreens and rustled the leaves in the maples and oaks. And in the background, a tap, tap, tap. Then closer, tap, tap, tap.

In his dream, he couldn't move a muscle. The tapping continued, joined now by shuffling. He wasn't frightened; in the dream, he simply couldn't figure out who or what was making the noise. Aunt Pearl? Sometimes she came downstairs for a snack in the middle of the night. But the tapping and shuffling came not from above. They seemed to come from down the hall.

Then the tapping stopped, replaced by the squeak of a door opening. Lloyd drifted up through REM sleep, waking with a jolt as something struck him in the ribs. He opened his eyes to see Doreen Sawchuck in a sliver of light. She was standing over him, trying to extricate her cane from his armpit. Walter hovered behind her.

"Lloyd," Mrs. Sawchuck said in a hoarse whisper.

Lloyd blinked into the flashlight Walter directed into his eyes. "Yes'm?"

Mrs. Sawchuck motioned him to keep his voice down. "Someone's trying to break in."

Lloyd raised himself on one elbow. "Think so?"

Walter glanced over his shoulder. "We know so," he whispered irritably. "We heard someone on the veranda, trying the front door."

"Maybe a raccoon."

"Why would a raccoon be trying the front door?" Walter's voice rose a notch.

"Don't know." Lloyd rubbed the sleep from his eyes. "You want me to look?"

"Yes. Then, if necessary, call the police."

"Mr. Rudley doesn't like the police around."

"Mr. Rudley isn't here."

"He'll know." Lloyd got up and pulled his jeans up over his pajamas. "You stay here and if I don't come back, you can call the police."

He turned to see the flashlight, but no Walter.

Taking the flashlight, he started down the hall. Mrs. Sawchuck hobbled after him. Behind them a toilet flushed.

"That was Walter," Mrs. Sawchuck whispered.

Lloyd slid the bolt across the back door and unlocked it.

Mrs. Sawchuck hovered at his shoulder and he pushed the door open. "Do you see anything?"

Lloyd's gaze shifted left to right. "Nope."

"Are you going out to look around?"

Lloyd turned and grinned. "Was thinking about going back to bed."

"There could be a murderer out there."

"Probably better to go back to bed."

"Oh," Mrs. Sawchuck fretted, "I won't sleep a wink if you don't go out there."

"I'm going."

Mrs. Sawchuck closed the door once Lloyd was clear and slid the bolt across. A hand touched her shoulder. She shrieked.

Walter stumbled back. "Sorry, Doreen."

Lloyd stood, one hand against the clapboard side of the house, listening. There were lots of sounds at night at the Pleasant. He was used to them. Most were simply pleasant. But tonight he listened to each one of them. He heard the croak of frogs—bullfrogs, green frogs, leopard frogs—the hoot of owls—barn owls and screech owls—the chant of whippoorwills. He heard the water brush softly against the dock and the halyard ping against the flagpole. He wasn't afraid, but he could understand why the Sawchucks were nervous. A twig snapped. In spite of the Pleasant's history, he'd never worried much about being murdered. The Pleasant was home, a nice place with friendship and pie.

He let go of the clapboard and eased around the building. He couldn't imagine himself being dead. He knew if he died, Mrs. Rudley would be sad.

A plop sounded in the water. He walked to the end of the dock, bent to his knees, and looked over the edge. If the moon were full, he thought, he would be able to see his distorted reflection in the rippling water. It would be like looking into a funhouse mirror. The moon was only a sliver, but he lay down on his stomach anyway and let his head hang over the dock to see if he could see a hazy reflection in the pale light. He couldn't, but he enjoyed the music of the frogs, forgetting for a moment that he was supposed to be looking for Mrs. Sawchuck's "murderer."

And then he did remember. He scrambled back up and headed to the inn, glancing about as he went. A few yards from the building, out of the corner of his eye, he thought he glimpsed a shadow. He stopped, stood very still, and peered into the dark. The shadow seemed to dissolve into the trees. He skirted the veranda, plastered his back to the wall, and peeked around the corner.

Nothing.

A hand touched his shoulder. He spun around.

It was Mrs. Millotte. Her hands were on her hips and she was glaring at him. At her side, Albert gave him a dog smile. "What in hell are you doing out here?" she demanded.

Lloyd broke into a grin. Mrs. Millotte didn't usually swear. He guessed her spending so much time at the desk was driving her to it. Mr. Rudley was at the desk all the time and he swore a lot. "Mrs. Sawchuck said there was a murderer out here. She said she heard boots on the veranda."

Mrs. Millotte pointed to her Keds. "Do these look like boots?"

"Nope."

"It was me," she said.

He grinned. "Are you the murderer?"

"I could be." Mrs. Millotte looked at her watch. "I've been up in the woods the last two hours. Albert took off on me. Then when I tried to get back into the inn, I found someone had thrown all the bolts."

"Did do."

"How did you expect me to get in?"

"Thought you was in. Tiffany said she saw you at the back door."

"I came in to get the big flashlight to look for Albert, then I went back out. Didn't you see my note?"

"Nope."

Mrs. Millotte felt like saying the next time she would tack it to his forehead but she felt that would be unkind since Lloyd meant well. "How do we get in?" she asked.

"Basement door. Mrs. Sawchuck's waiting there."

"Good." She took him by the arm. "Now, we're going to go in there and tell Doreen that what she heard was just a sassy raccoon and that you shooed him away."

"That's telling a fib."

"Think of it as for the greater good. If you tell Doreen that I was locked out of the inn with a murderer around, her imagination, or what she has of it, will run wild. She'll start having doubts about our competence. She'll imagine we aren't capable of protecting her from the things that go bump in the night. She'll be on edge the rest of the summer. Which means, she'll be down every night, perhaps several times a night, waking you up because she thought she heard something." Mrs. Millotte stopped, put her hands on his shoulders, and have him a stern look. "Do you get my drift?"

Lloyd grinned. "Yes'm."

"Good."

She steered Lloyd around to the basement door and knocked.

"Who's there?" Doreen's voice came from the other side.

"Mrs. Millotte and Lloyd."

The bolt slid aside and the door opened.

"Everything is fine," Mrs. Millotte said. "Nothing but a raccoon. We can all go to bed now."

"Are you sure it was a raccoon?"

"Positive."

"There's lots of raccoons out there," said Lloyd.

They collected Walter from the bathroom and saw the Sawchucks back to bed.

"Now," said Mrs. Millotte when they'd returned downstairs, "I'm going to have a cup of coffee and you're going back to bed."

"Yes'm." Lloyd hesitated.

Mrs. Millotte read the disappointment on his face. "Wait here," she said. "I'll get you a piece of apple pie and a glass of milk."

That done, she handed the tray to Lloyd and shooed him off to the basement. Back in the kitchen, she heated the dregs of the coffee in the microwave and sat down at the counter. She knew she should have invited Lloyd to sit with her but she wanted to relax for a few minutes before going to bed and having coffee with Lloyd didn't fit the bill.

She had known Lloyd since he started working at the feed store in Middleton eight years before. Sam Henson, who ran the place, kept Lloyd at the rear of the store where he loaded seed or feed or other heavy items from the loading dock to customers' trucks. Sam had confided in her that Lloyd was not a good front man.

After Lloyd came to do some chores at the Pleasant he never went back to Henson's. Rudley didn't seem to care about having an eccentric like Lloyd out front. Of course, Rudley, in her opinion, was just as alarming and much more off-putting than Lloyd.

As for the fugitive murderer showing up at the Pleasant, she thought the odds were remote. And even if he did show up, they'd have nothing to worry about if they took the precautions Detective Brisbois suggested. She was more worried about the police constantly dropping by to give updates, which would alarm the guests, particularly Mrs. Sawchuck. As long as the police kept their presence to a minimum, everything would be copacetic.

Mrs. Millotte was determined that no one would be murdered at the Pleasant on her watch.

Chapter Eleven

Margaret snuggled deeper into her sleeping bag as a ray of sunlight penetrated the canopy. "I could swear Gregoire was making fresh bread next door."

"Were that it was so," Rudley murmured. "Gil's probably got the fire going and is making up breakfast."

"Oh!" She grabbed his arm. "Rudley, you were going to see if you could call home."

"Yes, Margaret." Rudley crawled out of the tent and stumbled off in bare feet and pajamas, cursing the pinecones and pebbles.

He borrowed the satellite phone from Gil, who obligingly showed him how to use it. When he returned, Margaret was up and dressed.

"Did you make your call, Rudley?"

"Yes," Rudley replied as he ducked into the tent and grabbed his trousers and shirt. "Apparently, everything is going smoothly."

"Whom did you speak to?"

"Melba." He sat down and yanked on his socks and shoes.

"What did she have to say?"

"Albert is getting plenty of exercise, Lloyd is keeping a careful eye on the grounds, the Sawchucks are active and alert, and Aunt Pearl is enjoying her time relaxing on the veranda." Rudley tied his laces with a double knot. "Which means she probably has a case of Johnny Walker stashed in the window box."

"It sounds as if they're coping well with your absence, although I'm sure everyone eagerly awaits your return."

Rudley smiled. "Of course, Margaret. I give their lives structure."

She returned his smile. "Come, Rudley, breakfast."

Tiffany came up the back steps and fetched her broom from the closet. Mrs. Millotte was at the desk.

"The boss phoned," Mrs. Millotte greeted her. "He sends his regards."

"Are they having a good time?"

"He didn't say. In fact, he avoided the question. He wanted to make sure we were all right, given the fugitive in the vicinity."

"How sweet of him."

"I told him everything was just fine. No point in putting his blood pressure through the roof."

"I'm sure that was best."

"And how are you getting along with Mr. Bostock?"

"All right." Tiffany commenced to sweep the area in front of the desk. "This morning, he drew up a chair and sat and watched my every move. When I went into the bathroom, he followed and stood at the door until I was finished."

"Perhaps his razor is encrusted with diamonds."

"You would think."

"He is an odd duck."

"Yesterday afternoon he took out a rowboat. He had a satchel with him."

"Perhaps it was his fishing gear."

"No, he was carrying that in the other hand. This morning he took the paddle boat and the bag."

"Maybe it's his lunch."

"I don't know. I do know he went off in the same direction."

"He must prefer the scenery that way."

"There's something disturbing about Mr. Bostock."

"If Miss Miller were here, you could make a case of it."

"I'm going to keep an eye on him."

Mrs. Millotte tapped her fingers along the guest register. "Good idea. That will keep you out of trouble and keep you from conspiring with Lloyd to wreck the antique chairs."

"You're making fun of me, Mrs. Millotte."

"Sorry." Mrs. Millotte went into the cupboard and brought out the invoices. "I agree that Mr. Bostock may have a screw or two loose. But he's probably not dangerous. He hasn't taken a hatchet to us yet."

"True." Tiffany went on with sweeping the lobby. Albert rolled over to the middle of the rug. She gave him a nudge with the broom but he didn't wake.

I should wake him up and make him take a brisk walk, Mrs. Millotte thought. Some of us had to be up at the crack of dawn after last night's fiasco.

Nora and Ned wandered into the kitchen. Gregoire turned and frowned at them. "I have said that you cannot come into the kitchen."

Nora gave him a cross look. "Why not?"

"Because you are guests."

"I've seen that skinny old man come in here and that old drunk," Ned said.

Gregoire pointed the spatula at him. "I will not have you call Miss Dutton an old drunk. And that skinny old man is named Mr. Bole." He gathered himself. "You cannot come into my kitchen because you are children. Children do not wash their hands. And that would be against public health regulations."

"You let Lloyd come in," Nora countered.

Gregoire didn't have a quick answer for that. "You must have more interesting things to do than pester me in my kitchen."

"No," said Ned. "We don't."

"We're bored," said Nora.

Gregoire raised the spatula and brought it down, stopping just before it hit the counter. "How can you be bored at the Pleasant?"

"Easy."

"Why don't you go swimming?"

"We've done that."

"You could go hiking."

"We've done that."

"And there weren't any zebras," said Ned.

"You could take the binoculars and look at the birds."

"We've done that."

"I suppose you've taken Albert for a walk in the woods."

"Millions of times."

"You could go out in the paddle boat."

"Paddle boats are boring."

Not if you forget your lifejackets and the thing springs a leak, Gregoire thought.

"Why can't we take the motorboat?" Ned asked.

"Because it is not legal for someone your age."

"We shouldn't have come to this stupid place," Nora pouted. "They said there'd be all kinds of arcade games and a midway. And they said we shouldn't bring any of our games because the place was full of them. Better ones."

"And you don't even have a computer," Ned concluded.

"And we don't have a charge card," Nora added. She began to pick at the cupboard door.

Gregoire raised the spatula again. It twitched in his hand like the tail of an angry cat. "Mr. Rudley does not like electronic devices. If you wash your hands, you can make fudge with me."

Nora rolled her eyes. "We can buy fudge in the store."

Tim entered the kitchen carrying a tray.

"The children are bored," Gregoire said.

"Perhaps you'd like to help me in the dining room." Tim placed the tray on the counter. "Or, if you'd rather, I'm sure Tiffany would like some help with the cleaning."

Nora made a face, while Ned climbed onto a stool and slumped over the counter. "That's no fun."

"But it is different," said Gregoire.

"Maybe you should see if Grandma and Grandpa would like to amuse you." Tim added.

Ned buried his head in his arms and uttered an anguished yowl.

"What he's saying," Nora said, "is Grandma and Grandpa aren't interested in anything except their bowels and joints and prostate glands."

Tim laughed. Gregoire blushed.

"I do not want to hear that language from children in my kitchen," Gregoire said. "Not to mention that it is disrespectful to your grandparents."

Ned raised his head. "Grandma and Grandpa aren't any fun."

"They're too old," said Nora.

"Perhaps you are too young," said Gregoire.

Tim began to load his tray with the canapés Gregoire had taken from the oven. "Lloyd's going into town to pick up some things. Maybe you could go with him."

Nora made a face. "He smells."

Tim shrugged. "Ask him to take the motorboat. That way, with the gasoline fumes and fishy smell, you won't notice Lloyd at all."

"You can make it an adventure," Gregoire declared. "Pretend you are in the middle of the ocean, looking for pirates. Or you are about to get shipwrecked."

"If only that were so," Tim murmured. He took the tray and whisked out to the dining room.

"He doesn't like us," said Nora.

Lloyd was in the garden when Gregoire appeared on the back porch. "Will you be going into town soon?"

"Ten minutes."

Gregoire looked off into the line of trees at the back of the lawn. "I need you to do me a favour."

"Can do."

"I wonder if you could take the boat instead of the truck."

"Could do." Lloyd tidied the mulch around the Labrador tea shrub.

"Do you have my list?"

Lloyd reached into his back pocket and pulled out a strip of white paper. "This is it." He shoved it back into his pocket.

"And then there is the favour."

"Said will do."

Expecting to do some wheedling, Gregoire paused, flummoxed. "You don't know what the favour is."

Lloyd finished his work and shook the mulch from his cultivator. "Don't matter."

"I want you to take the children into town in the motorboat."

"Okay."

Gregoire looked at him, round-eyed. "Is that all? Okay?"

Lloyd grinned. "Are you making pie?"

"What kind do you want?"

"One pecan, one lemon, and one apple."

Gregoire hesitated, then said, "It's a deal."

Tim was in the kitchen when he returned, noshing on a bowl of strawberries.

Gregoire whisked the bowl away. "These are for my shortcakes."

"I wouldn't have done it for three pies," said Tim.

Gregoire tucked the strawberries into the refrigerator. "If you keep eavesdropping all the time, you will get a reputation."

Chapter Twelve

Brisbois threw his pen onto the desk and shoved his chair back. "So we still don't have anything on our John Doe."

Creighton picked up the reports Brisbois had been reviewing and thumbed through them. "Nothing that's panned out. The only ones close are a couple of homeless guys who have gone missing."

Brisbois shifted restlessly in his seat. "This guy sure wasn't homeless. Clean toenails. Even his nose hairs were clipped."

Brisbois wheeled his chair back to the desk. "Let me see that sketch again."

Creighton handed it over.

Brisbois took a look and shook his head. "Kind of expressionless."

"It's hard to get a lively pose from a stiff."

Brisbois didn't like Creighton referring to the unfortunate John Doe as a stiff but let it go. He supposed Creighton talked that way to hide his feelings. "He was found close to the border crossing. He could be an American."

"He wasn't wearing a flag pin," Creighton said.

"Where would he have put it? On his jockey shorts?" Brisbois swiveled in his chair. "All we know for sure is somebody didn't want us to know who he was."

"Or somebody just wanted his clothes."

Brisbois thought for a moment. "Let's get the artist to do something different—like a sketch of him leaning out the window of a generic vehicle, smiling, handing his papers to the border guards. If he's American or a returning Canadian that might twig somebody's memory. Maybe something with him just sitting in a chair, smiling, or at least looking alive."

"Sounds good, Boss."

"And let's get them out on the air as soon as possible."

"Can't you go any faster?" Nora sat in the middle seat of the motorboat, arms folded over her chest.

"If we go too fast, we'll smash up on those rocks."

"You can go around them. Or jump over them. The way they do on television."

"They aren't driving Mr. Rudley's boat," said Lloyd. "You don't go fast unless you're running away from a thunderstorm." Lloyd navigated past a shoal marker. "You want to go slow to see the turtles and the birds and the muskrats and otters. Up where the river runs in, sometimes there's beavers."

"We've seen all that," Ned said.

Nora leaned over the side of the boat. "What would you do if I fell in?"

Lloyd grinned. "There's snakes in the water around here, some of them taller than me." He pointed toward a rock plate at the shoreline. "Like that one lying there."

Nora recoiled.

"They like to lie on the rocks and sun themselves," Lloyd went on. "And if they get scared they get into the water lickety-split. And sometimes, if you're just sitting quiet, they climb into the boat." A thought sobered him: "One got caught in the motor once. That was bad. It got all over Tiffany."

"All right," Nora said. "We get it."

"Sometimes you see the deer," said Lloyd. "If you watch out for where the trees get thinner."

"Big deal," Ned said.

"I guess you've seen everything."

"Yeah," said Ned. "Pretty much."

"Glad I haven't." He waved at a boat flying a fleur-de-lis. "That's Mr. and Mrs. Belanger. They have a place on one of the little islands."

"Why don't you have a big boat like that?"

"Don't have that many groceries."

Nora poked Ned in the arm and rolled her eyes.

"You're weird," Ned said.

Lloyd responded with a broad smile.

"Are we going to the ice-cream parlour?" Nora asked.

"We can get ice cream at the dock. Then we have to get the groceries and go home."

"Why?"

"Cause if we don't, everything will spoil and melt."

Ned flopped back in his seat.

"Why can't we go to the amusement park?" Ned whined as they left the dock and proceeded toward Main Street.

"They don't have one here."

"Not even a miniature golf course?"

"They got a real one but that's a ways away."

"Isn't there anything here?" Nora moaned.

"Here's all that's here."

Nora regarded him, incredulous.

"You got chocolate all around your mouth from the ice cream," Lloyd observed. He dug a few dollars from his pocket. "Here, you can get a drink."

"Big deal," Nora said, but she took the money.

Lloyd went to talk to the grocer while Ned and Nora wandered off to the cooler. Ned pulled out a Pepsi. Nora rejected lemon-lime and orange before settling on a Swiss Cream Soda.

"Let's lose him," Nora suggested.

Ned sighed. "We'll probably get in trouble. They'll lock us in our room until Mom and Dad come home."

"They can't do that," Nora said. "That would be forcible confinement."

"Okay. Let's go."

They were about to take off when Lloyd surprised them by appearing at the door. He was carrying a large box.

"You got the groceries already?"

"They get the groceries ready and I just have to check the list."

"Is that all you're getting?"

"All we need for right now."

"We want to go to the electronics store."

"There ain't one of those until you get to Brockton," said Lloyd, setting off toward the dock.

Ned and Nora minced along behind him, holding their noses and making exaggerated gestures in his direction.

Mrs. MacPherson, who ran the West Wind, was at the dock, dropping off two of her guests with a yacht in port. "Who are your little friends?" she asked Lloyd.

"Nora and Ned Danby. They're staying at the inn."

The children stared at her, sullen. Mrs. MacPherson gave Lloyd a sympathetic look. "I hear the Rudleys are away."

"We want to go home now," Nora interrupted with a shriek before Lloyd could respond to Mrs. MacPherson.

"We don't want to go on the boat," Ned cried.

"You gotta come with me," Lloyd said.

Nora commenced to jump up and down and scream. "I'm not going!"

"I'm driving home now," Mrs. MacPherson offered. "I can drop them off at the Pleasant."

"Right at the door?"

She took his meaning, nodded, and winked. "I'll hand them over at the desk."

Mrs. Millotte was at the desk when Mrs. MacPherson entered, nudging the children ahead of her.

"I'm returning Ned and Nora to you. They decided they preferred coming home by car rather than in the motorboat with Lloyd."

"That bad," Mrs. Millotte murmured as the children drifted toward the dining room.

"Who do those kids belong to?" Mrs. MacPherson asked.

"Their grandparents are our regular guests."

"What a pair of little snots. I couldn't believe the way they treated Lloyd." Mrs. MacPherson glanced toward the dining room to assure herself the children remained out of earshot. "Why do you put up with them? Are they extra rich or something?"

"We put up with them because we're not allowed to send them home COD."

"They were rude to me in the car, acted as if they were used to having a chauffeur, made rude gestures at other drivers." Her eyes widened at Ned and Nora rubbing spit into the panes of the French doors. "I can't believe Rudley would have them."

"I doubt if he will again."

Mrs. MacPherson glanced at her watch. "I'd better get going. You might want to check on what they're doing to those doors."

"Thank you for bringing them home," Mrs. Millotte said, thinking: I would have thanked you more if you'd dumped them a few hundred miles away.

Ned and Nora continued spitting on the French doors, oblivious to Mrs. MacPherson's departure, smearing the panes with their fingers. Mrs. Millotte took a can of Windex and a cloth from the closet and tiptoed up behind them.

"I think you might need this."

They turned, startled. Mrs. Millotte sprayed the windows and handed them the cloths. "Get cracking."

The children gave the panes a few half-hearted swipes.

"I don't think you deserve supper," Mrs. Millotte told them.

"We're going to the Elm Pavilion," Nora announced. "The Bensons will give us whatever we want."

"The Benson sisters are watching adult movies. Remember? They can't receive you today. I think you should go to your room until dinner."

The twins tossed the cloths onto the desk and flounced toward the stairs. Nora turned, one foot on the first step. "Did anybody ever tell you you look like the Wicked Witch of the West?"

"Yes," Mrs. Millotte replied, "but just once."

Nora thumped up the stairs after Ned.

Five minutes later, the phone rang at the desk. Mrs. Millotte picked up.

"It's room 207."

Mrs. Millotte rolled her eyes. "How may I help you?"

"We want to order supper."

"Of course." Mrs. Millotte reached for the order pad.

"We want spaghetti and meatballs."

"And what will you have to drink?"

"Coffee."

"Coffee for two. And what about dessert?"

"Chocolate cake and banana cream pie."

"I don't believe we have banana cream pie today. Yes? Lemon meringue pie with a side order of maraschino cherries. Very well." She finished the order off with a flourish. "And when would you like this to be delivered?"

"Five minutes ago."

Mrs. Millotte reviewed the order and beckoned to Tim who had just come in from the veranda. "Would you give this to Gregoire?"

Tim read the order. "Coffee? Won't that stunt their growth?"

"We can only hope," Mrs. Millotte replied. "They want room service and they want it right away."

"I'll let Gregoire know." Tim headed toward the kitchen.

Tim trotted down the stairs to the kitchen with the tray and emptied the dishes into the dishwasher.

Gregoire sniffed. "So what did they decide about their supper?"

"Fine," said Tim. "They said it was fine."

"Only fine?"

Tim decided not to mention the twins said the word in a grudging tone. "They ate every crumb."

"Of course! It was delicious, after all."

"And they gave me their breakfast order." Tim whipped a piece of paper out of his hip pocket. "They each want a stack of buckwheat pancakes with a pat of butter and syrup with fruit on top. Blueberries. And café au lait." He slid the paper onto the counter in front of Gregoire. "Maybe they're coming around to your way of thinking."

Gregoire glanced at the slip and slapped it onto his clipboard. "They will probably send the order back, saying they wanted three blueberries between each pancake and on the top they wanted them to form the shape of a pine tree."

"And they made it clear they don't want to be disturbed for breakfast until ten," Tim added. "I think they wrote that on the menu, too."

"They must plan to be up late drawing," Gregoire mused. "Or they're planning some diabolical thing to do to make my life miserable tomorrow."

Tim poured himself a cup of coffee and sat down at the counter. "Maybe they'll start another ant farm in your sugar bin."

"I don't think they like to do the same thing twice."

"Where do you think they got the plastic ice cubes with the flies in them?"

Gregoire stared morosely at the wall. "Those children have got to go."

Dusk fell softly on the Pleasant, teasing out the resins from the conifers and handing them off to the passing breeze. Dinner guests came early and stayed late. Many lingered on the veranda for coffee and liqueurs as new arrivals took their place in the dining room.

Mr. Bole had dinner in the Elm Pavilion with the Benson sisters. Gregoire had prepared a roast chicken stuffed with wild rice and almonds, with mashed potatoes and green beans and a side salad of tomato and cucumber in a light vinaigrette. For dessert, spice cake and angel food miniatures with raspberries and whipped cream accompanied by strong coffee (since the sisters were nighthawks) and a bottle of Harvey's Bristol Cream (since the sisters had strong faith in the redemptive powers of sherry). The sisters were hearty eaters and relished hosting an evening at the Elm Pavilion.

"It was lovely of you to join us for dinner," said Louise.

"My pleasure entirely," Mr. Bole responded.

"Terrible news about that murderer lurking about."

"He sounds like a bit of a rascal," said Mr. Bole, "but I don't think we need to worry unduly. I imagine he's miles away by now."

"Oh," said Emma in a disappointed tone.

"If I were a serial killer," Mr. Bole continued, "I wouldn't linger in one place too long. That's why these types are usually apprehended. They carry out their nefarious activities in a limited area, thus allowing the authorities to map their probable location."

"I suppose some of them have jobs," said Kate. "They're not free to flit about at will."

"Yes," Mr. Bole mused, "it would be hard to conduct a cross-country killing spree if you had to report for work in the morning."

Mr. Bole hadn't previously considered the killer might need to work. Independently wealthy, he had never worked a day in his life. His father, grandfather, and great-grandfather had been bankers with considerable business acumen, but Mr. Bole chose not to go into banking. He had no interest in business or money, except insofar as it allowed him freedom. He had taken a liberal arts education at the University of Toronto and studied an eclectic mix of subjects independently, including antiquities in the Middle East and the migration of Thomson's gazelle in Tanganyika. He had toured the galleries of Europe and spent a bohemian year on the Left Bank in Paris. He had taken part in ceremonies at Stonehenge, walked the Great Wall of China, climbed Kilimanjaro, lived with Lapp herders, tended cattle with the Masai, and crossed the Sahara with Berber nomads. He was no stranger at either pole. He was particularly keen on the Incas and had gone on a sailing trip around Cape Horn, hoping to approximate the experience of Richard Henry Dana, Jr. in *Two Years Before the Mast*.

At some point—perhaps after an Australian outback experience—someone asked Mr. Bole if he'd ever been to Newfoundland. Mr. Bole was embarrassed to say that he had not. Not to Cornerbrook or Come By Chance or St. John's or, really, anyplace in Canada outside of Toronto. This epiphany was the prod for his decision to explore Canada, an undertaking that eventually led him to the Pleasant.

As the years passed, he found himself spending more and more time at the Pleasant. He had developed a keen interest in finger puppets and found an appreciative audience at dinner theatre, in the drawing room, and at Music Hall. He enjoyed the nearby village of Middleton in the summer, frequently attending events at the library and jazz sessions in the public square. He enjoyed the waterfront and the leisurely stroll into town from the Pleasant. He loved the Pleasant, loved its constancy and loved its civility. He thought there was a place for everyone here. He enjoyed the people, the staff, and the guests who came year after year. Aunt Pearl was a card, Margaret Rudley was a doll, Trevor Rudley was…well, in spite of being impatient, rude, volatile, sarcastic, and thoughtless—a bit of a fly in the ointment of paradise—he was definitely not common. Mr. Bole had no interest in the common. He loved the Pleasant because it was a treasure trove of the uncommon.

Which is why he didn't enjoy dwelling on psychopaths. He realized many people found them fascinating. He found them banal, as banal as vandals. In each case, something common destroyed something beautiful. Accordingly, he turned the conversation away from the killer by telling the sisters about the time he ran into Katharine Hepburn while motoring in Connecticut. Since the sisters loved celebrity and enjoyed gossip, the misdirection was not difficult.

James Bole had known the sisters for twenty years, from the time since he started coming to the Pleasant. The sisters had transferred their patronage decades ago to the Pleasant from the Water's Edge when the owner refused to give them a seasonal rate and make their preferred accommodation available at all times.

Like Mr. Bole, the sisters were well-educated and independently wealthy. They had inherited a reasonable sum from their father, a career diplomat, and had increased their wealth through an investment strategy that involved putting up a list of investment options and throwing darts at it. Somehow, the darts always fell on General Electric.

Mr. Bole knew this, although he had trouble reconciling business acumen with the trio who sat across from him. The sisters lived largely in their own world, he believed, and were subject to flights of fancy. He enjoyed the sisters' company, but society was not his main motive this evening. He had proposed to Mrs. Millotte that he check in on the elderly sisters with more frequency and remind them to lock their doors. The fugitive killer had yet to be found. He worried, too, that the twins, Ned and Nora, were taking advantage of the old girls.

"I hope you'll stay for the Hitchcock marathon." Louise broke into his thoughts. She was cutting the spice cake, placing slices on plates (the sisters had brought their own Royal Worchester), and passing them around.

"I'll be pleased to take in the first show," Mr. Bole responded. "Then I'm afraid it will be past my bedtime."

"We thought we'd put on *Vertigo* first."

Mr. Bole clapped his hands. "Oh, wonderful choice."

"There'll be popcorn," said Louise. "Kate has learned to make it herself in the microwave."

"Ned and Nora showed us," Louise added.

Mr. Bole seized the opening. "And how's that working out? Don't you find it inconvenient having the children around all the time?"

The sisters exchanged glances.

"It's no trouble," Emma said.

"They're wonderful children," said Kate.

"They taught us how to make popcorn in the microwave," Louise reiterated.

"It must interfere with your schedule," Mr. Bole ventured. "Amusing them and so forth."

"We have firm guidelines," said Emma. "By invitation only. They're allowed to watch only movies and other entertainments we deem suitable."

"We did allow them to watch one episode of *Criminal Minds*," said Louise.

"It can't be all fluff," Emma added.

"But no movies where we feel their reactions might compromise our own experience," said Kate.

"No blue movies," said Louise.

"Do they make a fuss about that?" Mr. Bole asked. "The restrictions?"

"No," said Kate.

"They've been exceptionally well-behaved," said Emma.

"And they're always jumping up to get us things we want—a can of soda, a cup of tea, the remote control," said Louise.

"I see," said Mr. Bole.

"I know no one likes the children," said Kate.

"They're wonderful children," added Louise.

"Who found themselves in a strange place where no one understands them," Emma finished.

Mr. Bole smiled politely. He gathered the sisters didn't understand the extent of their rudeness to the staff or their treatment of Rudley's frogs.

"They're much like us when we were children," said Kate.

"The adults were always too preoccupied to appreciate us too," said Louise.

"Our father was the emissary to Saudi Arabia," Emma explained. "We met most of the important people of the day."

"And got to ride a camel," said Louise.

"But we were often overlooked," said Kate. "Mama and Papa were simply too busy with official functions to indulge us."

"So we made life hell for the staff," said Louise.

"We were expressing our displeasure about being handed over to nannies," said Emma. "And we had more amusements available than these children do."

"I take it you're quite happy to have them around then," Mr. Bole said.

"Of course," said Louise.

"We appreciate the staff is too busy to entertain them. And their grandparents are too old."

Mr. Bole was somewhat taken aback, although he didn't show it. He guessed the sisters had at least twenty years on the Sawchucks. But he had to agree there was old and then there was old.

"I'm glad you're enjoying their company," he said.

"They're wonderful children," Louise repeated.

They finished the cake. Mr. Bole helped Kate collect the dishes onto the tray. Kate went to the kitchenette to prepare the popcorn.

"Movie time," said Louise.

Mr. Bole watched the opening credits of *Vertigo* and considered what the sisters had said. Perhaps everyone's assessment of the children was wrong, he thought, then reconsidered. No they weren't. The twins were horrible children, rude, selfish. He had met many children who were high-spirited and a bit of a handful. These little miscreants were simply mean-spirited bullies. He was left to contemplate the power of television and video players to alter behaviour and concluded that anything that could turn those rotten children into angels was nothing short of miraculous.

The campers sat around the fire, transfixed by the flickering flames. Crickets chirped, the sound broken by the occasional hoot of an owl.

"That would be the eastern screech owl," said Norman. "The vocalizations immediately prior to that were those of the great horned owl. The great horned owl utters a series of low hoo hoo hoos. Like so." He gave them a rendition. "The eastern screech owl, on the other hand, while it also hoots, emits a gentle trill. Like this." He imitated the sound and smiled. "Once you get used to the pitch, you can easily tell them apart."

"Although I don't know why in hell anybody would want to," Turnbull remarked, picking up a stone and pitching it into the darkness.

"It's a matter of deepening our understanding and appreciation of the creatures whose space we share," Geraldine said in an offended tone. "Norman specializes in owl calls. I have seen voles scurry when he hoots."

"Maybe you should go into the pest control business," said Turnbull.

"I wouldn't mind being able to do that," said Peters.

"Kill bugs?"

Peters gave Turnbull a hard look. "Imitate bird calls."

"I'd be happy to teach you the basics," said Norman. "It's not difficult once you develop an ear."

"Especially if you have a bird brain," Turnbull murmured.

No one heard the comment except Margaret, who was sitting nearest. She changed the subject. "When we were young, we loved sitting around the fire, telling scary stories, acting out frightful movies. What's the scariest movie you've seen?"

"I don't find movies scary," said Turnbull.

"*Halloween*," Miss Miller said. "That child standing on the sidewalk with the bloody knife."

"One can never trust children," Rudley murmured.

"*Silence of the Lambs*," said Gil.

"The old Boris Karloff movies," Norman said.

"Yes," Rudley agreed, "the classics are the best. I find that modern horror lacks subtlety."

"Anything with Vincent Price," Margaret offered. "I'm sure he must be the scariest actor."

"What about you, Mr. Peters?" Geraldine asked.

He hesitated. "I don't watch much horror. Zombie movies, I guess."

Geraldine shivered. "Oh, yes." She grabbed Norman's arm. "They give me the willies too. You'll protect me, won't you, Norman?"

"Of course, Geraldine."

"She's got six inches and fifty pounds on him," Rudley murmured to his wife. "I was counting on her to protect both of us."

"Be nice, Rudley."

An owl hooted. Geraldine tapped Norman on the arm. "Norman, let's see if we can get some photos."

"Let's."

Norman and Geraldine got up and disappeared into the trees.

"What's the trip like tomorrow?" Turnbull asked Gil.

"About the same," said Gil. "The river narrows as we move along, runs faster. There're a few rocks in the next section but nothing we can't avoid." He drew a rough map in the dirt. "This is the only spot on the whole route we'll need to portage."

Simpson was glad they had changed the subject. He seldom watched horror movies. When he was a child, his parents had forbidden him to watch them after he had had nightmares from *The Exorcist*. He was twelve at the time and his friends teased him about it. Elizabeth was aware of this and seemed to think nothing of it. She didn't expect him to be a hero all of the time.

He stared at the embers. It wasn't that he lacked physical courage. He'd played rugger at Chester, his public school, and once stood up to a schoolyard bully. The boy had beaten him senseless. He winced at the memory. He had approached Jack Strachan, who was pummeling slight, bespectacled Terrance Glasspoole, and said: "I don't think it's fair of you to pick on Terrance." So Jack left poor Terrance lying on the playing field, his glasses dangling off one ear and the knot of his school tie yanked under the other, and put the boots to him, Simpson, instead. In fact, Jack never bothered Terrance again. Simpson remained his victim until a new boy, Alfred Tollingate, arrived at school. He was the tallest, strongest boy at Chester and no one dared take him on.

The day Simpson confronted Jack, one of the young boys alerted the headmaster, who came out and ushered him into the dispensary. He had several cuts, multiple bruises, and two magnificent black eyes. His father called him courageous. He didn't remember feeling courageous. He remembered how his voice had quavered when he approached Jack.

Simpson blinked. Terrance Glasspoole went to Cambridge where he was president of the debating society. Alfred Tollingate attended Sandhurst and commenced a career in the military. Jack Strachan went into the seminary. He was unaware of Elizabeth until she touched him on the shoulder.

"A penny for your thoughts."

He looked up and smiled. "Oh, I was wondering if I could perform an appendectomy if the situation called for it."

Elizabeth beamed. "Of course you could, Edward."

Turnbull's voice rose in the silence. "So, have you ever shot the rapids, Peters?"

Peters was feeding wood into the fire. He turned his head and glanced at Turnbull. "No."

"Scared?"

Peters shrugged, but his facial muscles tightened.

"I guess you're glad it's a tame trip."

Peters's hands tightened around his bundle of sticks. With a slight stutter, he said, "Why did you come on such a tame trip?"

Turnbull stretched and yawned. "The timing fit. My girlfriend is in Ireland with her mother. Grandma's eighty-fifth birthday or something. So—" he sighed as if bored with the conversation "—I had a week to kill." He smiled. "Do you have a girlfriend, Peters?"

Peters dropped his sticks. He sat flexing his hands. Then he got up and walked away.

Gil rose, walked over to Turnbull, and hunkered down beside him. "Cut it out."

Turnbull gave him an innocent look. "Cut what out?"

"Picking on Mr. Peters. I think it's gone far enough."

Turnbull rolled his eyes. 'Sorry. He's such a nerd."

"I think you should just leave him alone."

"Sure." Turnbull got up. "I'm going for a walk." He rose and headed down to the shore.

"That was good of you to speak up for Mr. Peters," Margaret said.

Gil smiled. "Sometimes people don't know when kidding turns into harassment."

"I don't understand why Mr. Turnbull is so mean to Mr. Peters."

Gil shook his head. "He really isn't that nice to anybody, but Peters is the only one without a partner here, so I guess that makes him look vulnerable." He smiled. "I'm going down to check the canoes."

"I'm glad you've never engaged in that kind of behaviour, Rudley."

"Sensitivity in interpersonal relations is essential for an innkeeper."

She let that go.

"Mr. Turnbull is a bully. He picks on Peters because he sees him as the most vulnerable."

"Perhaps because he's so quiet."

"Or because his ears are in the wrong place."

"Rudley."

"I'm not approving of Turnbull's behaviour, Margaret, just hypothesizing."

Norman and Geraldine reappeared, smiling.

"We got some super shots of a great horned," said Geraldine. "Our new flash attachment was superb."

"He had just pounced on a mole," said Norman, passing the camera around. "It's the third photo."

"I think I'd rather not see that," said Simpson.

"Edward always cheers for the underdog," said Elizabeth.

Creighton waited at the desk as Brisbois spoke on the phone. It had been a long day but, he reasoned, since it was almost midnight, the day would soon be over.

"What do they think of the new sketches?" Creighton asked when Brisbois had completed the call.

"They think they're great. They're putting them out everywhere. And most of the local TV stations here also reach the northern part of the border states." Brisbois came over to the desk, sat down, and grinned at Creighton.

"What are you smiling about?"

"That wasn't what the call was about. That was Turk."

Creighton looked blank.

"Mel Turk, our lead in Fredericton."

"Oh, yeah."

"He had an interesting story to tell me. A cousin of the jewellery store victim, George Pritchard, came to Fredericton to settle the estate. He's apparently the sole heir. And he wanted to know what happened to his cousin's gun."

"His gun?"

"Yeah, the old man brought a Dreyse pistol back from World War II. It was never registered. The cousin didn't know that. He said the old guy kept it at the store."

"Consistent with the slug?"

"Yup."

Creighton shook his head. "So Pritchard's killer stole the old guy's gun and used it on our John Doe."

"Looks like it." Brisbois beamed. "Told you. It's the same guy."

Chapter Thirteen

Gregoire hustled the last pancake off the grill onto the stack on the breakfast tray. "There," he said, "just as they requested."

"At least as they requested last night," said Tim. "I wouldn't be surprised if they changed their minds just as I presented this to them."

Gregoire gritted his teeth. "If those two brats send back the pancakes, I will be sending them up a box of corn flakes and a pint of skimmed milk."

"With strawberries?"

Gregoire glared at Tim. "No strawberries."

Tim took the tray. "We'll see."

Gregoire was reviewing the plans for lunch when Tim returned. He put the tray, still full of pancakes, on the counter, sat down, and began to eat them. "You'd better call Lloyd," he said between bites, "otherwise the other stack will go to waste...unless you want them."

Gregoire glared. "They have rejected my breakfast," he fumed. "Once again."

Tim shook his head. "No, they aren't there."

"Where are they?"

"I don't know." Tim took another bite. "Delicious. Their beds are made. You know what that means."

"They woke, made their beds, and went into town for breakfast?"

"I can't see them making their beds," Tim said.

"Tiffany must have done that."

"No, they had their DND sign out." He shrugged at the puzzled look on Gregoire's face. "Tiffany may have compunctions about disturbing the little twits, but I don't." He waved his fork, swallowed. "Either they've run away or someone's kidnapped them."

"Then shouldn't we notify the grandparents and call the police?"

Tim lifted the serviette from the tray and dabbed at his lips. "We should probably take a quick look around the grounds first, ask if anyone has seen them." He rose. "I'll do that now. I wanted to have a bite of your pancakes before we have police crawling all over the place."

"They're probably hiding out somewhere eating Tootsie Roll Pops to give us a hard time."

Gregoire took a deep breath when Tim had gone. He was sure the children were all right. They were probably just being disrespectful as usual. He paused in thought. *What if they had gone down to the lake and fallen in?* He went over to the table and sank into a seat. *What if they had taken a canoe out and tipped it?* He stared at the remaining stack of pancakes. Tragic. He picked up his fork and took a bite. Delicious. He dug in.

"You've looked everywhere for the kids?" Officer Semple asked, scribbling in his notebook.

"We haven't checked Outer Mongolia yet, but otherwise, yes." Mrs. Millotte replied, hands on hips. "We've conducted a thorough search—the entire inn, the cabins, the boathouse. We've gone around the grounds and spoken to all the guests."

"And who saw them last?" Semple raised his gaze and fixed her with a suspicious stare.

"Tim, as far as we know. He saw them at nine-thirty last night when he picked up their supper tray."

"And did they say anything about wanting to go somewhere, wanting to get away, meeting anyone?"

"I don't believe so. Not that Tim has said. They gave Tim their breakfast order when he picked up their supper tray. They asked for breakfast to be delivered to their room at ten."

"And that's when you discovered they were missing."

"Yes."

"And no one has seen them this morning?"

"As I said, I've talked to everyone in the place, Officer. No one has seen the children. In fact, I don't think anyone but Tim has seen them since they went upstairs around four yesterday afternoon. I spoke to them on the phone shortly after that to take their order for supper."

"Then who else might have seen them at four yesterday?"

"I'm not sure. I was at the desk when Mrs. MacPherson from the West Wind dropped them off."

Semple flicked her a glance.

"She gave them a ride home from Middleton," Mrs. Millotte continued as Tim and Gregoire entered from the dining room. "They'd gone to town with Lloyd in the motorboat earlier when he went for groceries. When it came time to come home, they refused to go with him. Mrs. MacPherson graciously offered to bring the children home."

"I see." He scribbled in his pad. "Where did Mrs. MacPherson leave the children?"

"Here at the desk."

"And you were at the desk at the time."

"I was."

"And did you actually see the children?"

Mrs. Millotte gave him a scathing look. "Yes, I saw them. Mrs. MacPherson brought them directly to the desk and handed them over to me. She said they'd been acting up in the car, threatening to tell the police that Lloyd had beaten them up. She felt it prudent to escort them to the desk."

Semple stopped writing, shook his pen, and tried writing again. Throwing his pen on the desk in disgust, he rooted around in his pockets. Mrs. Millotte took a pen from the desk caddy and thrust it into his hand.

He continued, "Did you accompany the children to their room?"

"No, I did see them go up the stairs to their room."

"Weren't you concerned something might happen to them?"

"Why would I be concerned something might happen to them from the top of the stairs to their room, a few doors down?"

"Well, something did happen to them."

Gregoire, who had been listening to this exchange, swept his cap from his head and balled it into his fist. "I will have you know, Officer Semple," he exploded, "that from the moment those two arrived here we have watched them like hawks. We have put up with their pranks and kept them at the main inn for additional security. We have not let them go near the boats without supervision."

"Where are their parents?"

"Scurrying from one chalet in the Swiss Alps to another, doing everything in their power to avoid being contacted," Tim answered.

"So the kids are here on their own?"

"They're here with their grandparents," said Mrs. Millotte, "who couldn't manage a cat, let alone this juvenile Bonnie-and-Clyde combo."

Semple paused to review his notes. "Well, we'll activate the amber alert." He glanced up at the three of them. "See anyone suspicious around here?"

"No more than usual," Tim replied.

"Any strangers?"

"There were guests in for lunch and supper."

"People you know?"

"Most of them. People from town and a few from the cottages."

"Names?"

"I'll get the list." He turned back to the dining room, Gregoire in tow.

"Did you advise the children there might be a dangerous fugitive in the area?" Semple asked Mrs. Millotte.

"Of course. We advised all the guests to make sure to keep their windows and doors locked at night and to be alert for anyone who seemed out of place. And we gave them the warning you give to all kids—don't go anywhere with strangers, and if you're leaving the inn, let somebody know where you're going."

"You said Ned and Nora accepted a ride from Mrs. MacPherson."

"Only because Lloyd knew her."

Semple looked again at his notes. "Well, they've gone somewhere. Maybe it was with a stranger and maybe it wasn't." His eyes lifted to the dining room door where Tim and Gregoire had retreated. "Where were those guys all evening?"

"What?" Mrs. Millotte followed his gaze and turned back fiercely. "Well, I never."

Mrs. Millotte was still stewing when Tiffany burst into the lobby.

"Guess what?" Tiffany began. She stopped short. "What's wrong, Mrs. Millotte?"

"Officer Semple, that's what's wrong," she said, tossing her pen down on the desk.

"He's not very good, is he?"

"He had the nerve to suggest Tim and Gregoire had something to do with the children's disappearance."

"Why would he pick on them?" Tiffany asked, then stopped as the realization struck her. "Oh."

"Yes," said Mrs. Millotte. "Officer Semple is a tad homophobic."

"Officer Semple is a deeply flawed man," said Tiffany.

"Officer Semple is an insensitive doofus," said Mrs. Millotte. She picked up her pen. "What were you about to tell me?"

"I took a little drive. After I finished my chores, of course."

"Of course."

"Just in case the children had gone for a long walk and lost their way."

"No luck?"

"No. I did see Mr. Bostock, though. He was paddling along near the West Wind. He had attempted to disguise himself."

"How?"

"He was wearing horn-rimmed glasses and a long black beard."

"Interesting."

"It's very odd."

Mrs. Millotte took the linen inventory from a drawer. "I agree it's odd, but compared to some of the guests we've had over the years, he doesn't seem that insane."

"I realize that," Tiffany said in a worried tone, "but with everything that's taken place here, with the children missing, with a murderer in the vicinity... he could be the murderer."

"I think he's the most boring man I've ever met," said Mrs. Millotte. "I think the dress-up redeems him a bit."

"I'll keep an eye on the situation." Tiffany turned back towards the veranda.

"Yes, do," Mrs. Millotte called after her, "just in case."

Mrs. Millotte paused as she checked the linen inventories. She thought of the murderer reputed to be in the vicinity and of the missing children and wondered how the inn could be at the epicentre of so much misadventure. Nothing like this happened when Mr. MacIntyre owned the inn!

Brisbois slowly walked the perimeter of room 207, checking the locks on the windows. The window overlooking the west lawn he unlocked and opened. He poked his head out and glanced down.

"No evidence they went down the trellis," Creighton said. "Or that anyone climbed in. Nothing disturbed in the flower bed or shrubbery."

"So how would someone get in?" Brisbois murmured.

"Maybe he was already in."

Brisbois continued inspecting the room, brow furrowed. "There's no sign of struggle. A few pictures scattered around." He picked one up and looked at it. "Polaroids. I wonder who took them."

Creighton glanced over his shoulder. "The Benson sisters. See the pattern on the sofa? That's in the Elm Pavilion." He pointed to the lower left corner of the picture. "And that looks like Emma's foot."

"Huh?"

"She wears those old-fashioned lace-up shoes with perforations and an inch-and-a-half heel. Kate wears some kind of flat slip-ons and Louise wears sandals with a closed toe."

"You notice what kind of shoes elderly ladies wear?" Brisbois said, brows elevated.

Creighton shrugged. "Shoes say a lot about a person."

"Is that so?"

"Sure. Emma is no-nonsense and practical. Kate is sort of ordinary, casual. Louise is kind of giddy. She probably wore those little things—you know, the spike heels with the skinny straps—when she was younger. She tries to keep as much style as she can without falling and breaking her neck."

"That's very perceptive, Creighton." He looked down at his feet. "What do my shoes say about me?"

Creighton grinned. "They say you'd probably shine up nice."

"Hmm." Brisbois picked up one of the photographs. "Look at these kids, sitting on the sofa, ankles crossed, hands in their laps. Those wholesome smiles—cherubic smiles. Why would everyone detest them so much?"

"I think it has to do with sabotaging the kitchen, teasing the frogs, running Tiffany's drawers up the flagpole."

"Kids will be kids," Brisbois sighed, turning his attention back to the room. "Who knew the kids were here at the Pleasant?"

"A lot of people. They were all over the place, antagonizing everybody, except the Benson sisters, whose television seemed to bring out their better side. The kids were in town once. Highly visible from all accounts. Acting out. Everybody was talking about them. Maybe somebody assumed they had rich relatives."

"You mean someone kidnapped them."

"Yeah." Creighton shrugged. "Maybe someone casually connected to the Pleasant—a delivery person, say, somebody from town who knew the setup."

"So this person comes to the Pleasant, hides out until everyone's gone to bed, goes upstairs, grabs the kids, and leaves with one under each arm."

"No. Probably someone the kids had had some contact with earlier. Someone who enticed them, told them he was taking them to an arcade or something. According to the staff, they were disappointed Rudley didn't have an arcade."

Brisbois shifted uncomfortably. "Got another theory?"

"The kids sneaked out and got lost?"

"Well, they've either run away and gotten lost or they've run into a bad actor. They sound like pretty savvy kids. They weren't around here long enough to establish a trust relationship with anybody."

Creighton shrugged. "Hey, they're just eight years old."

Brisbois didn't comment further. He didn't want to voice the thought as it was too horrible: but if the kids had encountered a predator or someone like the guy who had left a trail of death across the country, they were probably dead. Instead, he said, "Anything new on the kids' parents?"

Creighton shook his head. "The Swiss police thought they found them at a place in Switzerland called Wengen but they fell off the radar. The Danbys—Ned and Nora's parents, that is—asked the post office to hold their mail."

"What does that suggest?" Brisbois muttered. "They're on a side trip? Maybe a hiking expedition?"

Creighton shrugged. "How big is Switzerland anyway? You'd think they could cover the whole thing in a couple of days with a few patrol cars. Hell, you'd think everybody would know everybody else. You'd think they'd notice foreigners."

Brisbois gave him a long look. "You've really got to see more of the world than a beach and a cold one."

"You've been to Switzerland?"

"No, but with all those mountains, the surface area is huge. They've got thousands of foreigners around—lots of guest workers from Italy, tourists from elsewhere in Europe and North America—"

Creighton snapped his fingers. "Oh, yeah, that's where Tina Turner went!"

"I'm glad to see you're up on current events."

Mrs. Millotte was at the desk when the laundryman appeared. She peered at him over her glasses.

"You're late this morning."

"Yes, I am."

"Back door locked?" she asked, puzzled at his exasperated expression.

"I haven't tried it yet, Mrs. Millotte."

"Tiffany went down just a minute ago. I'm sure if you bring your cart around, it will be open."

The laundryman removed his cap and wiped his brow. "I'm afraid I don't have my cart. I don't have my van either. Someone has stolen it."

Mrs. Millotte stared at him.

"I was making a delivery at the Water's Edge. I parked my van as always and took my cart around to the service entrance. As you know, at the Water's Edge, I am not allowed to bring my van to the front. I have to drive it around to the service road at least fifty yards from the inn, go to the front desk, ask someone to open the service door, then go back to my van. I then have to haul my dolly to the service door."

"That's inconvenient."

"Yes. In the winter, I haul the linens on a sled. A nuisance but this is cottage country."

"And while you were hauling the linens up to the Water's Edge, someone stole your van."

"Yes. I had emptied my dolly and was returning to where I had parked my van, thinking what a beautiful morning it was and how pleasant it was to make the short walk. I arrived at my parking spot and the van was gone."

"Perhaps you left the emergency brake off and it rolled into the lake," Mrs. Millotte suggested. "After all, who would want to steal a laundry van?"

"I know the inclines at the various inns, Mrs. Millotte. I always put on the hand brake. And I always park with the wheels cut so that the van is unable to escape and cause damage. The van is gone and I am certain it didn't roll into the lake."

"Have you called the police?"

"No. I came here because there's often an officer around. And if there wasn't, I was hoping I might come across one on my way or at least someone who had seen the van."

"You're in luck. Officer Semple is around somewhere."

"Semple?" the laundryman repeated. "Is that the officer who always gets injured whenever he answers a call out here?"

"That's the one."

"He should pay more attention to what he's doing."

Mrs. Millotte sniffed. "He's so fond of the way he looks parading around in his uniform he doesn't have the coordination to pay attention to what he's doing. He's probably safe as long as he stays around here."

"True." The laundryman paused. "Does he carry a firearm?"

"Perhaps they don't give him bullets." Mrs. Millotte's gaze strayed toward the door. "Speak of the devil," she said, noting Officer Semple striding across the lawn.

"Officer," Mrs. Millotte said after Semple had stepped into the lobby, "someone stole this man's vehicle."

Semple, who thought the laundryman vaguely familiar, reached into his pocket and took out his notebook. "Can you give me a description of the vehicle?"

"A white commercial van with the words 'MacAvoy's Dry Cleaning and Linen Supplies: Serving the Area since 1925' on the side panels."

Semple frowned. "So, you're the laundryman."

"I am."

"Why would anyone steal a laundry van?"

"I don't know, Officer. Maybe the thief has a thing for the smell of fresh linen."

Semple gave him a stern look. "I mean, why would someone steal a commercial van with a logo on the side? It would stand out like a sore thumb."

The laundryman shrugged. "I can't say I know much about the criminal mind. I only wanted to report the theft, hoping you might find my vehicle."

"I'll get this out right away."

Mrs. Millotte shook her head as Semple made his exit. "I don't think it will take too long to find your van. Whoever took it must have done it as a prank. I don't expect they went far in it. Why don't you have a cup of coffee?"

"Thanks, Mrs. Millotte."

"By the time you finish, Lloyd will be back from town. He'll drive you back to the laundry."

"So who found it?" Brisbois regarded the laundry van.

"Petrie and Howard. Whoever took it drove it onto that old wagon road, lost control on the slope, and ran it into a tree. Then he took off, I guess. There was nobody around."

The crime scene team was crawling all over the van. Sheffield, the forensics officer, stepped over when he saw Brisbois.

"What've you got?"

"Prints all over the place." Sheffield grinned. "And as you can tell, the intruder really stunk up the place. Moldy leaves and soil tramped all over. The linens thrown around and filthy."

Brisbois mulled this information over for a moment, then turned to Creighton. "Okay," he said, "let's have a word with the folks at the Water's Edge."

Brisbois studied his notes a moment, then shoved his notebook into his pocket and marched back to his car. A word with the folks at the Water's Edge had not proven productive.

"It's not as pretty as the Pleasant," Creighton remarked as Brisbois fumbled for the car keys. "A little stiff, I guess, more formal."

"Not as friendly, for sure." Brisbois jammed the keys into the lock. "The staff and the guests—what a bunch of duds."

"Oh, I don't know, Boss." Creighton shrugged. "They were respectful and cooperative."

Brisbois opened the door. "Nobody saw anything. Nobody heard the vehicle coming or going. Nobody even seemed to be aware that the laundry van came every day. Where do they think their towels come from?"

"Maybe they think the laundry is done in-house."

"That's weird, Creighton. I'll bet if you asked anybody at the Pleasant, not only would they know that the linens were delivered from elsewhere, they would know what time they came and where the guy parked his van."

"Yeah, but that's because there's always two or three guests hanging around the desk at the Pleasant. It's part of the entertainment, watching Rudley rant and rave."

Brisbois eased his way into the car. Creighton went around to the passenger's side and got in.

"I guess that's it. Here the guests live in their own world."

"Guess so." Creighton pushed his seat back a notch. "They're also not huddling together and coming up with crackpot theories."

Brisbois put the keys in the ignition but did not start the car. He sat back in the seat, staring through the window. "There's a picture coming together here that I don't like. We've got a serial killer who may have gotten off the bus at Lowertown. We've got some unsubstantiated sightings. We've had reports of thefts, clothes being taken off lines. Now we have two kids missing and a laundry van stolen." He pulled out a cigarette. "Any word on the parents?"

Creighton took out his notebook. "Nothing new. They're supposed to pick up their mail in Wengen in three days."

"At least we know they'll be in Wengen then." Brisbois lit his cigarette. "They don't seem to care if their kids can reach them or not."

Creighton laughed. "If those little shits were mine, I wouldn't care if they could find me either."

Brisbois glared at him. "I don't care if they're the Children of the Corn, we've got two kids missing. Two kids who may have run into a not so very nice person."

"I've noticed as we progress down the river the banks are getting steeper," Rudley remarked, drawing his paddle from the water and stopping to look around.

Margaret drew her paddle in too. "And the forest is getting thicker." She studied the bare rock tumbling to the water. "I've never seen so much wilderness."

Rudley inhaled deeply. "Ah, yes, Margaret, this is the real thing. Makes the environs of the Pleasant seem suburban. And wait until we get to the gorge. I hear the rock face is forty feet high. Sixty feet and completely vertical at some points."

"Formidable."

Rudley nodded. "This is what our forebears came into and, after much struggle, came to embrace—for some foolish reason."

"It's majestic, Rudley. Imagine someone from the heart of London arriving here."

Rudley returned his paddle to the water and drew languidly. "They were sturdy people, our pioneers. Samuel Hearne, Henry Hudson, Alexander Mackenzie, John Franklin and his ill-fated crew reduced to hauling a silver tea service across the frozen tundra."

"In the dead of winter." Margaret shivered, returning her paddle to the water.

"Of course. And there was Champlain arriving in the New World in his Parisian togs to freeze his ass off that first winter."

"Oh, my. In silk breeches and a brocade waistcoat."

"He would have perished if it hadn't been for the indigenous people. They saved him that first winter with food and herbal remedies and later carried him in a basket after his knee was shot through with an Iroquois arrow. The French were allied with the Hurons."

"And we English were allied with the Iroquois."

"A wise choice, Margaret. The Iroquois were renowned warriors."

She smiled. "It was a wonderful alliance, Rudley." Her smile faded as she glanced again at the landscape. "It's overwhelming, Rudley. Forbidding. It's as if nature were drawing you in as you proceed down river and, before you know it, you'll find yourself at the point of no return. Man against nature, and if man is not obsequious to nature, nature wins."

He glanced at her over his shoulder. "You've been watching *Deliverance* again."

She shuddered. "It's a ghastly movie, Rudley, but absolutely gripping. There's a horror about plunging head first into the wilderness but an excitement about what lies around the next bend."

"A nice flat rock to pull up our canoes would be good and perhaps Miss Miller's latest culinary delight."

"Reminiscent of Mr. Cadeau."

"Indeed."

"Apart from the fricasseed frog legs."

"Bite your tongue, Margaret."

Brisbois sank down onto the veranda steps and glanced toward the police dog handler who was crisscrossing the lawn with a pair of bloodhounds. He took off his porkpie hat and pushed his hair back with both hands.

"Tired, Boss?" Creighton sat down on the step beside him.

"Mmm," Brisbois replied noncommittally, reaching for his notebook. "Let's recap. The kids were last seen when Tim took their supper tray away around nine-thirty last night."

"Check. And they left an order for breakfast in bed for ten this morning."

"When they were discovered missing, the staff checked the grounds and buildings, then called in."

"A little over half an hour later."

"Nobody noticed anyone strange around."

"No."

Brisbois scanned the lake. "They checked along the shoreline."

"Yes. The kids were good swimmers."

Brisbois paused in thought. "Nobody liked the kids," he said after a moment. "They were rude, played nasty tricks on Gregoire, ran Tiffany's unmentionables up the flagpole."

Creighton chuckled. "I would have liked to have seen that."

Brisbois gave Creighton a sharp look. "Watch your mouth. The kids' parents are making themselves scarce and the grandparents have no idea where they are and don't seem that worried. The only people who seem to have taken an interest in them are the Benson sisters. The kids were nice to them because of their big television set."

"Semple says the grandparents told him the kids have run away before."

"There's running away and there's running away." Brisbois pulled a pack of cigarettes from his pocket. "There's no evidence of a struggle in their room. The only way they could have gone out was through that front window because all the other windows were locked and bolted."

"Unless someone took them out the front door, lost them, then came back in, bolted the door, then unlocked the window to confuse us."

Brisbois gave him a bleak look as he lit a cigarette. "Why? We're already confused enough."

"You'd think the dog would have barked."

"Albert is so used to people coming and going at all hours, he probably doesn't pay any attention. But you'd think somebody here would have heard something."

"People get murdered around here all the time without anyone noticing."

Brisbois nodded grimly, conceding the point.

"They could have been lured from their room by someone promising a big adventure."

"Maybe." Brisbois blew a plume of smoke in the air. "Or they ran away as a lark, got lost, fell into the lake, or were grabbed by an opportunist."

"Tiffany thinks Mr. Bostock is a likely suspect."

Brisbois flipped through his notes. "Except nobody ever saw him anywhere near the kids."

"Semple ran a background check on him," said Creighton. "He's a teacher with no record whatsoever."

"Sometimes Semple does something right."

"The reason Tiffany thinks he's suspicious is because he goes out in boats in disguises."

"We'll talk to him later." He returned the wave of the dog handler who had tethered the dogs by the van. "Come on, let's see what Corrigan's got." He pushed his hat down on his head, pocketed his notebook, and started toward the van. "Corrigan?"

The dog handler gave him a curt salute.

"How's it coming?"

"Not great," Corrigan replied. "The kids have laid down scent all over the place along with dozens of other people and thousands of animals. They got interested in that place over there." He pointed to the Elm Pavilion. "They were sniffing around, then a squirrel ran out from behind a garbage container. And there was a big cat in the window, hissing."

"The kids spent a lot of time in there," said Brisbois.

"But the dogs picked up their scent again," Corrigan went on. "It led to the end of the dock and disappeared."

"They fell in or someone abducted them in a boat."

"Or a helicopter pulled them up in a basket. I imagine someone around here would have heard that."

"One would think so," Brisbois responded dryly.

"Maybe your dogs need new batteries," Creighton said.

Corrigan shot him an irritated look. "They aren't machines, Detective. And this is a hell of an area to start a search. People running back and forth all over the place. Dogs, cats, every animal under the sun. They got distracted and almost ate a big bullfrog."

Brisbois stared out over the lake. "Well, we know the kids were here and now they're gone."

"That's about the size of it."

"How's the bullfrog?"

"He's okay. They soft mouthed him."

"What now?" Brisbois asked.

"I can try to pick up a scent around the lake and in the islands. It'll take time. Do you have any ideas about narrowing the search?"

"They ran away or they were abducted." Brisbois shrugged. "They left last night after everybody was asleep or they left this morning before anybody was awake. There aren't any boats missing. They could have gone left or they could have gone right. They could be a couple of miles away or they could be halfway to Toronto or heading for the St. Lawrence." He shook his head. "The best I can think of is that you move out from here and see what you can find. If they transferred the kids from a boat to a car they probably wouldn't do it near any of the cottages."

"I'll see what I can do." Corrigan gathered up the leashes.

Brisbois watched the handler and the dogs retreat. "I can't see someone abducting them from the Pleasant."

"The tracks end at the lake."

"Maybe the dogs were confused."

Creighton laughed. "Hungry too. That big bullfrog would have been a nice snack."

Chapter Fourteen

"Do they have a habit of running away?" Brisbois faced Doreen and Walter Sawchuck across the desk in Rudley's office.

Walter looked at Doreen. "They've done that once or twice. Most kids run away from home once in a while."

"How far do they usually get?"

"As far as the mall."

"Where would this mall be?"

"Ithaca, New York," said Walter.

"Not far from us in Rochester," said Doreen.

"Not far enough," Walter muttered.

"That bad?"

"Walter doesn't like our son-in-law," said Doreen.

"He's a hippie," said Walter. "That's why the kids are such brats."

"Now, Walter."

"He has no sense of responsibility," Walter went on. "Running off to Europe like a teenager with a backpack."

"And they left the children in your care," said Brisbois.

"They left them at the Pleasant," said Walter.

Brisbois raised his brows. "Do you think Rudley saw it that way? Perhaps he thought you would be responsible for the children."

Walter gave him a puzzled frown. "The staff here looks after everything. Always has."

"Must be rotten kids if their own grandparents don't like them," Creighton murmured as he and Brisbois stepped onto the veranda where Mr. Bole and Aunt Pearl were enjoying a drink.

"Good to see you, Detectives," Mr. Bole said, rising and offering his hand. "After Semple, you're a relief."

"He was doing his Columbo act," said Aunt Pearl.

"Some of his questions were a bit…obtuse," Mr. Bole clarified.

Brisbois smiled. "He hasn't taken the advanced course on conducting interviews."

"Shows," said Aunt Pearl.

Mr. Bole hesitated before resuming his seat. "I don't think there's anything I can tell you that I haven't told Officer Semple. I last saw the children yesterday morning when I was leaving the dining room. I have no idea about the circumstances of their departure." He shrugged. "They were obnoxious, poorly raised, mean-spirited little trolls, but I wouldn't want any harm to come to them."

"Bad for business," said Aunt Pearl, drawing Brisbois's attention.

"Do you have anything to add to your previous statement?" he asked her.

She shook her head. "As I told Officer Semple, I slept the whole night. Well, I might have been awake for a few seconds. I remember the dock light in my eyes. If I knew anything I'd tell you. Like Mr. Bole, I wouldn't want any harm to come to them. One of them might grow up to discover the cure for the common cold."

"Did either of you happen to meet the parents?"

They shook their heads.

"They were here only long enough to dump the kids and run," said Pearl.

"I was on the veranda when they arrived," Mr. Bole said. "The only impression I got was that they were in a hurry."

Brisbois flipped through his notebook. "What about this Mr. Bostock? Did he ever voice any opinion about the kids?"

Mr. Bole looked surprised. "I don't believe I've ever had a word with him."

"He's a dull fellow," added Pearl. "Not a social type at all. If you say good morning, he acts as if you've imposed. We've never had anyone like him before."

"Strange guy?"

Mr. Bole nodded. "We've had quiet types, even recluses, but never anyone who's been so publicly rude."

"Except Rudley," said Pearl, "and we're used to him."

"Did he have anything to do with the kids?"

"Not that I witnessed," said Mr. Bole.

"I think he held us all in equal disdain," said Pearl.

"I can't wait to interview Mr. Bostock," said Creighton. "Sounds as if he has the personality of an ox."

"Oxen have nice personalities," Brisbois said, glancing at his notes. "What cabin in this guy in?"

"The Pines."

Mr. Bostock answered the door on the first knock. He glared at them. "Yes?"

"I'm glad I caught you, Mr. Bostock," Brisbois said after introducing himself and Creighton. "They tell me you're usually out on the lake."

"Yes."

"I imagine you know why we're here."

"No."

"We're investigating the disappearance of Ned and Nora Danby."

"I gave my statement to the officer."

"I know. We're following up."

"All right, but I don't know anything about it."

"When did you last see the kids?"

"The day before yesterday. Well, I suppose it was Ned and Nora, unless there are other children here. I was never introduced to them."

"Where did you see them?

"Walking the dog across the lawn."

"Did you talk to them?"

Bostock squinted. "No. Why would I?"

"Well, they're kids. You're a teacher."

"I teach cabinetmaking to high school shop students and adults at night school. Besides, they were halfway across the lawn."

Brisbois glanced at his notes. "Mr. Bostock, you've been seen out on the lake in various disguises."

"Is that illegal?'

"No, but in a criminal investigation anything unusual tends to get our antennae up."

"I can see that."

"Any reason why you'd go out on the lake in different getups?"

Bostock eyed him a moment, then shrugged. "I'm interested in architecture. There are some interesting places around the lake. I like to study them in detail, sometimes over a few days. People might get strange ideas if they see the same guy staring at their places day after day. So," he finished, "I figure with the disguises they might not realize it was the same guy."

Brisbois raised an eyebrow. "That's all?"

"Yes." Bostock blinked, then added, "Besides, it amuses me."

"Maybe we should try dressing up," Creighton remarked as they left the Pines. "We could stand to be amused."

"Next," Brisbois barked.

They stopped at the Elm Pavilion and knocked at the door. The sisters didn't answer until the third knock. When he heard a chorus of "come ins," he tried the door. It was unlocked.

The sisters were watching *Rear Window*. Kate pushed the pause button.

"Detective Brisbois."

"Ladies." He removed his hat. "Did you know your door was unlocked?"

"We unlocked it after Tiffany left," said Emma.

"We don't like our door locked," said Kate.

"We could all die and no one would find us for hours," Louise said.

Brisbois frowned. "I'd advise you to be especially careful right now. We have a criminal on the loose. Perhaps in the vicinity."

"Please sit down, Detectives," said Kate.

"Would you care for some coffee?" Louise asked. "And a piece of cake?"

"That would be nice." Brisbois took the chair opposite the sofa. Creighton chose one by the window. Emma bustled into the kitchen.

"It's Gregoire's special red velvet cake," she said, returning with a laden tray.

"Looks delicious."

"Are you enjoying your stay?" Louise asked, as she cut slices for the detectives.

Brisbois smiled. "As always, Miss Benson."

"The detectives aren't enjoying their stay, Louise," Emma corrected as she poured coffee. "They're engaged in an investigation."

Brisbois took a bite of cake and nodded his approval. He set the plate aside and took a sip of coffee. "That's right. We're investigating the disappearance of the twins."

"We've already answered a lot of questions," Kate said.

"When you were here before," Louise added.

"Oh, Louise," said Emma, "that wasn't Detective Brisbois." She turned to Brisbois and whispered, "Louise is always in a fog when she watches Jimmy Stewart." To Louise she said, "That was Officer Semple who interviewed us before."

"Officer Semple?" said Louise. "Did he break anything this time?"

"He tipped over a vase on the way out," said Emma. "It wasn't broken, however."

"Officer Semple is a bit uncoordinated," said Kate.

He's a bit something, Brisbois thought. He settled back in his chair and turned a page in his notebook. "I promise not to keep you from your movie long. I just wanted to follow up on a few things."

"Of course." Emma drew up a chair and sat down emphatically. "Go ahead."

"We have nothing to hide," Louise declared. She looked hopefully at the set where Jimmy Stewart sat frozen in his wheelchair, mouth agape.

Brisbois smiled at the sisters. "They told me you took a special interest in the children, Ned and Nora."

Kate nodded eagerly. "Oh, they're great kids. They come here almost every day."

"Do you remember when you last saw them?"

Louise looked at her sisters. "It was at lunch yesterday, wasn't it?"

Emma made an impatient gesture with her hand. "No, it wasn't yesterday, Louise. It was the day before." She turned to Brisbois. "Lloyd took them into town yesterday, according to Tiffany."

"For a boat ride," said Kate.

"To get them out of Gregoire's hair," said Louise. "That's what Tim said."

"Young people don't have much patience with children," said Kate.

Brisbois cleared his throat. "So you got on fine with the children, but others didn't."

Emma got up, went over to a cut glass decanter, and poured three glasses of sherry. "Detectives?"

Brisbois and Creighton shook their heads. "No, thank you." Brisbois answered. "On duty."

Emma nodded, restoppered the sherry, and placed the tray with the glasses on the coffee table. "What you have to understand, Detective," she said, handing the sherry to her sisters, "is that the Pleasant isn't the ideal place for children. The adults are generally preoccupied."

"Or grumpy," Kate said.

"And unaccustomed to dealing with children," Emma continued, "especially energetic, high-spirited children like Nora and Ned."

Brisbois made a pretense of reviewing his notes. "Pardon me, ladies, but I have numerous reports saying the children were rude, inconsiderate, and mean-spirited."

"Nonsense," said Kate, sipping at her sherry. "They're just full of beans. Like we were when we were kids."

"Daddy was with the diplomatic corps," said Louise, sipping hers.

"In some inhospitable places," added Emma.

"We had to make our own fun," Kate explained.

"Sometimes we got reported to Father," Louise giggled.

"We were high-spirited," said Kate.

"Remember what we did in Bulgaria?" said Louise.

"I think it was in Yugoslavia," said Kate.

"I think it was both," Louise countered.

Emma raised a warning hand. "The detective doesn't have time for reminiscences."

"Not at the moment." Brisbois smiled. "But I'd like to follow up on that later." He took a moment to organize his notes. "So the kids came to watch movies and television."

"And to play those interactive games," said Kate. "We especially enjoy the boxing."

"But not the blue movies," said Emma.

Emma shook her head. "Blue movies aren't appropriate for children."

"You have a few of those?"

"Oh, yes," said Kate. "We have *It Happened One Night, From Here to Eternity*. Very suggestive."

Brisbois thought the children could see racier things on Main Street but said nothing. "Did the children ever say anything about feeling uncomfortable with anyone around here? Did they suggest there was anything that made them feel unsafe or….?"

"Creepy?" Emma supplied.

"There's no one around here who's creepy or unsafe," Louise said, while Kate nodded agreement.

"Well, that's good to know." Brisbois turned a page and flattened his notebook. "Did the kids ever talk about running away?"

Kate laughed. "All children run away."

"They didn't talk about it," said Emma.

"We never did," said Louise. "Remember when we ended up in that back alley in Bombay and were almost bitten by a cobra?"

"Gives me the willies just thinking about it," said Kate.

"I think it was some sort of duck," said Emma.

Brisbois shook his head. "I'll bet you gave your parents a few grey hairs."

"No one here would hurt the children," said Emma.

Brisbois glanced down at his notes. He was making a new entry when Kate said, "Say cheese, Detective." He looked up to see a Polaroid camera aimed at him.

A few yards away from the Elm Pavilion, Brisbois sank down onto a bench. Creighton joined him.

"That was kind of like falling down a rabbit hole," Creighton remarked.

Brisbois removed an envelope from his pocket. "Want to see my picture?" he asked, taking the Polaroid from the envelope.

Creighton looked at it and laughed. "Is that the original Polaroid film?"

Brisbois checked the back of the photo. "No, it's a substitute. Fuji." Brisbois returned the picture to his pocket. "What do you think about Bostock?"

"I think we should stop wasting our time on him."

Brisbois nodded. "He's not at the top of my list. He's kind of a nut." He lit a cigarette. "The kids' scent ended at the dock but they were excellent swimmers so they probably didn't fall in and drown. No word from the parents, by the way. I think Interpol has found members of Al-Qaeda faster than those parents."

Creighton laughed. "That's because Al-Qaeda's not trying to outrun those kids."

Chapter Fifteen

Gil spread the map on the ground. It was early evening. "This is where we are now." He pointed to a spot on the map. "Tomorrow we'll run into a current in the middle of the river, there. It's only moderate but we'll steer clear. There are some interesting rock formations. Some good fishing for anybody who's interested." He smiled at Norman.

"So you've really been up here before," Turnbull grinned.

"I've been up here twice," Gil responded.

"Just asking." Turnbull shrugged and looked toward Peters, who was breaking up sticks for kindling. "What do you think, Peters? Ready for a little current?"

Peters didn't answer. His gaze drifted to the river.

"I imagine we should expect rougher water from here on in," said Simpson. "We've had a rather easy go so far."

Turnbull sniffed.

"I'm rather glad for that," said Simpson. "I think the real pleasure of canoeing is being able to take in the scenery."

Margaret and Rudley were sitting together on a log. "The water's been so calm, it's almost like being at the Pleasant," Margaret said.

"Yes," Rudley murmured out of earshot, "and we have proxies for Tim and Gregoire arguing and for Simpson stepping in to salve everyone's feelings."

"Mr. Turnbull should be ashamed of himself, picking on Mr. Peters and Gil the way he does."

"I understand they train law students to be like sharks in a wading pool," Rudley said. "It seems the training spills over."

"He enjoys picking on Gil and on Mr. Peters in particular."

"That's because they're the weakest swimmers."

"Why, Rudley, that was rather poetic."

"I can be poetic at times, Margaret."

She smiled. "I knew the trip would do you good. To get away from your burdens, to relax, be free of responsibilities."

"I could become comatose in time."

"I imagine your blood pressure has dropped twenty points. By the time we arrive home, we won't have to open the door. You'll be so mellow, we'll just pour you under."

"Margaret," Rudley said, rising from the log, "I have an overwhelming urge to go to the bathroom."

Tiffany was making her way along the shoulder of the highway, trying to look as dignified as possible in an evening dress and high heels. She told herself, holding her chin a little higher, that she shouldn't have agreed to go out with young Mr. Noble—and what an inappropriate name that turned out to be! She had been blinded by his virtuoso performance on the viola at the chamber music performance at the public library the week before and was excited when he invited her to dinner. But on the way home it turned out he expected more than enlightened conversation. When she declined his advances, he promptly pulled the car over and left her at the side of the road. Now, hurrying along the highway, trying to convince herself she wasn't the slightest bit uneasy about being alone on the highway at night, she heard a car approaching. The hairs on her neck stood up as the car slowed. She held her breath, trying to think of how to use a small bag decorated with seed pearls as a weapon. She almost cried with relief when the car pulled alongside and she recognized the insignia of the OPP and a friendly face.

"Officer Stubbs, how good to see you!"

"Can I give you a lift, Tiffany?"

Stubbs was tactful enough not to ask questions. He drove her home and hopped out to open the passenger's door. Tiffany stepped from the car, pulling a lace stole more tightly around her shoulders.

"Thank you, Officer Stubbs. It was kind of you to drive me home."

"My pleasure."

He followed her up the steps to the veranda and waited while she unlocked the door. "Is everyone at the main inn now?"

"Tim and Gregoire are still in the bunkhouse. Lloyd is in the basement. I'm staying in the Rudleys' quarters while they're away. Mrs. Millotte is using one of the rooms upstairs. Mr. Bole and Mr. Bostock have elected to stay in their cabins. The sisters are in the Elm Pavilion."

He tipped his hat. "I'll wait until you're safely in and have locked the door."

"Once again, thank you. It was gallant of you to rescue me."

He blushed. "My pleasure."

She smiled. "Good night, Officer Stubbs." She stepped inside, locked the door, and gave him a wave through the window.

He returned to the cruiser, gave his location to dispatch, and checked his log.

Stubbs was new to the area, assigned to it after successfully completing his probation in Walkerton. He had heard through the grapevine that this corner of Ontario was one of the most lovely and lively detachments in the province with much of the excitement, he had been led to believe, hovering about the Pleasant.

So far he had not been disappointed. Meeting Tiffany Armstrong was an unexpected bonus. He knew she had dated Officers Semple and Owens among the constabulary, plus any number of townsmen. Neither Semple nor Owens nor anyone for that matter had a single bad thing to say about her. He had been introduced to her before and found her charming. The brief trip with her to the inn confirmed his first impression.

Stubbs was about to pull away, then hesitated. Perhaps, he thought, he should do a quick perimeter check. The folks were pretty isolated out here, after all, and there was a dangerous criminal on the loose. He contacted dispatch, declared his intentions, killed the headlights and exited the car.

Tiffany hung her dress over the clothes horse in the Rudleys' quarters. She was about to change into her nightgown when she realized she was hungry. She had had a light dinner and remembered that Gregoire had made a red velvet cake. She pulled her robe on over her slip and tiptoed out into the hallway, leaving the door open, moving softly to avoid waking anyone. She particularly didn't want to wake Mrs. Sawchuck.

She crept down the stairs and turned to scan the lobby, which seemed alien in the dark, the hardwood gleaming in the faint light of the nightlights. She could hear the lake as a vague murmur, the creek of limb on limb of the big maple closest the inn, and the venerable old place sighing in its sleep. She felt melancholy, wondering if this is what the inn would be like once the Rudleys had passed away. It seemed that when Rudley was here, even when he was asleep, his energy vibrated from the front desk.

She took the final two steps and turned toward the dining room.

She paused to contemplate the pale reflection of the moon on the lake through the curtains, then started as a shadow passed the window. But it was only maple branches bobbing on a light breeze.

She took a deep breath of relief and turned toward the kitchen.

Lloyd woke in the basement, his nose wrinkling. Skunk. He didn't mind the smell much. A man had told him once it was good for clearing your sinuses. He could tell from the characteristically strong garlic odour that the skunk had scored a direct hit on someone or something. The last time a skunk had sprayed him, Mrs. Rudley had made him bathe in tomato juice. He turned on his pillow and fell back to sleep.

Tiffany stopped halfway across the dining room. She noticed a sudden strong odour of skunk but also something reminiscent of fetid earth and mildew. Then the scent of skunk again, this time overpowering. A shadow fell across the kitchen door. She screamed.

A filthy ghost hunched in the doorway.

"Who are you?" She barely managed the words.

White eyes stared at her from a grimy face. The ghost bolted past her, strewing cans and bottles. She stepped on a can of peppercorns and fell. Struggling up, dazed, she heard someone hammering on the door to the back porch. Gathering her robe around her, she ran to the door.

"Open up!" a voice called out. "Police!"

She pressed her ear against the door. "How do I know you're the police?"

"It's Officer Stubbs."

She swallowed hard. "How do I know you're Officer Stubbs?"

"Tiffany, it's me. I drove you home tonight."

She hesitated, then opened the door.

Officer Stubbs stood in the doorway, reeking of skunk. "Are you all right?" he asked with as much dignity as he could muster.

She put a hand over her nose. "I'm all right. There was an intruder in the kitchen."

"Where did he go?"

"He went out the front door."

He hesitated. "Stay right here. Don't open the door for anyone but me."

"All right." She locked and bolted the door, then flattened herself against the wall, feeling about for a weapon. She had located the doorstop and was hefting it in one hand when she heard steps on the veranda.

"It's Stubbs."

She lowered her weapon and opened the door.

"I did a perimeter check," he said. "Your intruder came in through the pantry window. He cut the screen."

"Are you sure he's gone?" She put her hand to her nose once again.

"I didn't see him," Stubbs replied. "I've alerted dispatch. We'll have reinforcements here to take a look around. In the meantime, we'll make sure the inn is secured."

She stayed fast by the door. Fifteen minutes later she heard sirens. A short time later, the lobby came alive as the remaining staff, Mr. Bole, and the Sawchucks poured into the lobby.

Brisbois pulled up to the Pleasant, stepped from the car, and stretched his back. Creighton smoothed the brim of his fedora and set it at a rakish angle.

Officer Vance, who was standing by his patrol car, looked up in surprise. "Sir, what brings you out here?"

"I was scanning the police blotter from last night and saw there'd been a break-in here."

"It was pretty routine. It looks as if a homeless guy tried to raid the pantry."

Brisbois glanced around. "How many homeless guys do you think there are out here?"

"Not that many." Vance checked his notes. "Tiffany gave a description. She didn't get a good look at him but she believes he was young, of slender build, and filthy. Sounds as if he'd been living rough for a while."

"Any good prints?"

"He left dirty fingerprints all over the place. And half the forest floor, dirt, needles, leaves."

"Okay," said Brisbois, "let's go see what we can see." Before he could take another step, his cell phone rang.

"What's up?" Creighton asked when his boss had completed the call.

"We've got a ransom note."

"The letter was delivered to the local rag," the duty sergeant told Brisbois and Creighton when they arrived at the local police station in Middleton.

Brisbois examined the letter and envelope in the plastic evidence bag. "No stamp."

"None. A lot of the letters that arrive there are hand delivered. They have a slot in the wall for that."

"And when was this one delivered?"

"Could have been anytime from yesterday afternoon to this morning." The sergeant shrugged. "*The Reporter*'s a small paper. One-and-a-half-person operation. The big story yesterday was the dog show. They were out all day on that. Didn't have time to review all the letters that came in."

"A piece of plain brown paper, torn in half, but kind of a ritzy envelope," Brisbois murmured. "Hand delivered. That means local." His eyes brightened. "Surveillance cameras? There must be at least one surveillance camera in the area."

The officer shook his head.

"Nothing? Not even one measly stationary camera?"

"The only one is at the ATM at the Bank of Montreal. It doesn't show anything beyond the ATMs, the foyer, and the section of sidewalk directly in front of the bank. Nothing else." He checked his notes. "We've got fingerprints from the mail slot so we'll send the envelope and letter to see if there's a match. But we wanted you to have a look first."

"Good work." Brisbois studied the envelope. "This looks kind of familiar."

He reached into his pocket and took out the envelope containing the Polaroid the Benson sisters had given him. "Would you say these envelopes were the same?"

The sergeant studied them. "Looks like it to me."

"Can you get these envelopes around here?"

"Sure. Cowperthwaite's Stationery."

"Cowperthwaite's?"

"Yeah, it's on the main drag between the coffee shop and the lawyer's office."

"Anyplace else?"

"Not around here. I know that because I buy envelopes like these for my wife's aunt. She likes the mint-coloured ones but they all have the same pattern on the inside—little daisies."

"I think they're primroses," Brisbois remarked. He returned the Bensons' envelope to his pocket. "Ask forensics if they can match any prints on that envelope delivered to the newspaper with prints on file from the Pleasant."

"You think the sisters kidnapped the kids?" Creighton asked.

"No. But I think one of their envelopes may have ended up in the hands of the guy who did the kidnapping."

"A lot of people could have bought the same envelope at Cowperthwaite's," Creighton argued.

"Why don't we ask?" Brisbois examined the note again. It was written in crooked print with a pencil. "'Five thousand dollars or the kids die. More later,'" he murmured. "No mention of a date or a drop location. I guess that'll be in the 'more later.'"

"Five thousand dollars." Creighton laughed. "The guy must know the kids. He figures nobody would give more than that."

"Or he forgot to add more zeroes."

Creighton shrugged. "We don't know that much about the parents' finances. The grandparents seem to be pretty flush."

"Although they probably wouldn't think it was their responsibility to pay the ransom."

"They'd think it was Rudley's." Creighton laughed again. "Why don't we just take up a collection at the station? Or maybe we could take it out of petty cash."

Brisbois gave him a sharp look as he headed for the door. "Cool it with the jokes. We're talking about kids here. I'd take the money out of my personal account if that would do the trick."

Creighton jingled some change in his pocket. "Since you've got that much money, you can buy your partner lunch."

Cowperthwaite's was a rainbow of colour. Brisbois and Creighton browsed casually among the lap desks, boxed stationery sets, and multitude of single sheets and mix-or-match envelopes. After several minutes, a slight man in ecru slacks and a blue-and-white striped shirt with matching tie emerged from the rear.

Brisbois turned to greet him. "Mr. Cowperthwaite?"

The man hesitated as Brisbois introduced himself and showed him his police badge. "Actually, it's Fred Lewis. I bought the shop from Mr. Cowperthwaite." He paused. "What's this about?"

Brisbois held up his envelope. "We're trying to track down where this envelope came from. Do you sell something like this?"

Mr. Lewis took a close look at the envelope. "Yes. It's from Cheltham. This particular one is called Chantilly Lace."

"Do you sell a lot of this?"

"No. Chantilly Lace isn't popular nowadays. It's a rather heavy antique ivory. People these days tend to be seduced by the bubblegum colours."

"Can you tell who purchased Chantilly Lace recently?"

"If they paid in cash, probably not." Mr. Lewis sighed. "I don't handle all of the transactions personally and I don't always know the names of customers, particularly summer residents."

"Could you check your sales records?"

"Certainly."

Brisbois expected Mr. Lewis to haul out a dusty box. Instead, he went to a computer at the back of the store and scrolled down a screen. "LB will pick up," he muttered. "Oh, yes." He turned to Brisbois. "We've sold three boxes this year. LB will pick up." He nodded. "All three went to the Pleasant Inn."

Chapter Sixteen

The campers were on the river paddling slowly, glad to be away from the stretch of turbulent water.

"That was rougher than Gil thought," Margaret said.

"I, for one, would have preferred not to have had to be so alert for hidden rocks," Rudley said. "A vacation should be a relaxing experience, Margaret."

"Although Mr. Simpson had trouble keeping Miss Miller from plunging into the worst of it."

"I think that's been his problem from the start, Margaret."

She looked over her shoulder at him reprovingly. "Oh, Rudley, I think Mr. Simpson has always enjoyed Miss Miller's adventurous side. I imagine that's one of her attractions. I suspect he's always longed for adventure but has always been a little timid about undertaking risk on his own. I don't think he realizes how brave he is."

"Consorting with Miss Miller is the definition of bravery."

She gave him a smile. "Now, haven't you always liked my adventurous side, Rudley?"

"I have, Margaret. I've just been smart enough not to be drawn into it."

She started to respond, but a large bird circling overhead caught her attention. "Ooh," she uttered admiringly. "Rudley, look at that magnificent hawk."

"He is a beauty."

"I feel sorry for the little creature he's after."

"Yes, Margaret. Nature is red in tooth and claw."

Seeing no one at the desk of the Pleasant, Brisbois tapped the bell.

"Keep your shorts on, for heaven's sakes," a voice came from down the hallway.

Brisbois peered in the direction of the voice to see Mrs. Millotte's derriere sticking out of the hall closet. Presently Mrs. Millotte's front half appeared. She frowned at Brisbois and said, "What in hell are you doing here?"

Brisbois smiled. "Planning to open your own inn, Mrs. Millotte?"

"I beg your pardon?"

"You're starting to sound a lot like Rudley."

Mrs. Millotte shuddered. "I'm sorry, Detective," she said, recovering her normal tone. "How may I help you?"

"I need to ask you about an order from Cowperthwaite's Stationery." He glanced at his notes. "May twenty-fourth, to be exact."

"Remember it as if it were yesterday," she said. She went to the cupboard behind the desk, brought out a ragged file box, and plunked it down on the desk. She removed a folder, opened it, and eyed the contents. "Nothing unusual, Detective." She handed him a file. "Business forms, number ten envelopes."

"And three boxes of stationery," he noted, reading the list. "Chantilly Lace."

"That was for the Benson sisters."

"Rudley buys stationery for the guests?"

"He provides the usual hotel stationery for most of the units. He gets the fancy stuff for the sisters and bills them for the difference. See?" She pointed to a note. "BD—bill difference. EP—Elm Pavilion."

He frowned. "Why don't the sisters just buy it themselves?"

She looked at him over her glasses. "Because he gets a commercial rate. Rich people don't get rich by wasting money on stationery."

Brisbois and Creighton stood outside the door of the Elm Pavilion, waiting for a response from the sisters. Eventually, Emma answered.

"Detectives." She swung the door open and beckoned them in. "I apologize but we were at a particularly critical part of *Psycho*."

"I'm sorry," Brisbois said.

"Would you like some cordial?" Kate asked.

"Lime or raspberry," added Louise.

"This reminds me too much of *Arsenic and Old Lace*," said Creighton.

Louise tittered. "Oh, Detective, we wouldn't poison you with cordial."

"It would be wrong," said Kate.

"Detectives," said Emma, picking up a carafe. "Perhaps I could interest you instead in coffee and petits fours."

"That would be nice," said Brisbois, watching her pour two cups of coffee.

"Why don't you sit down?" said Kate.

Brisbois and Creighton took the chairs across from the sisters, who grouped together on the sofa. "Ladies," Brisbois began, "if we may ask you a few questions."

"Tsk," Louise said reproachfully. "They're here on business."

"Business and pleasure," said Brisbois, smiling and taking a petit four from his saucer. "It's always a treat to visit the Elm Pavilion." He quickly consumed the pastry and took out an envelope. "Ladies, have you seen an envelope like this?"

Emma glanced at it. "Of course, Detective."

"Chantilly Lace," added Kate.

"We've used it for years," said Louise.

"Our mother always used it," Kate continued. "Mother wrote hundreds of letters. She had wonderful penmanship."

Brisbois took out his notebook. "And where do you purchase your stationery?"

"Mr. Rudley orders it from Cowperthwaite's," said Emma.

"Always Cowperthwaite's," said Kate.

"We wouldn't think of purchasing it anywhere else," said Louise.

Brisbois flicked his pen. "Did anyone borrow any stationery from you or are you missing any?"

"No," Emma replied. "We keep it locked in our secretary." She got up and went over to the antique cherry writing desk at the far wall. She took a key from her pocket, opened the secretary, and took out a box of stationary. "Still here," she said.

"You lock up your writing supplies?" Creighton blurted over his coffee cup.

Emma gave him an impatient look. "We don't lock up the stationery per se. We keep it in the secretary where we keep our valuables."

"Father's stamp collection," said Kate.

"And great-grandma's cameos," said Louise.

"We trust the staff implicitly," said Emma, "but you never know who might be wandering around."

"But you don't worry about keeping your doors and windows locked," Brisbois said in an exasperated tone.

"If someone broke in, we'd hear them," Emma responded crossly.

Brisbois sighed and looked to Creighton, who rolled his eyes.

"Do you remember ever lending or giving some of your stationery to anyone on the premises?" Brisbois pressed.

The sisters regarded each other, then shook their heads.

"I don't think anyone but us would want it," said Kate.

"That's why Chantilly Lace is so hard to find," Louise said.

"People these days don't have a taste for it," Kate added.

Brisbois smiled. "You gave me an envelope."

"Because you're special," Kate sipped her coffee. "Were you thinking of purchasing a supply of Chantilly Lace, Detective? You seem so interested in it."

Brisbois hesitated. "We don't want to upset you ladies. We know you're fond of the children."

"Lovely children," said Louise.

"We received a kidnap note," Brisbois explained. "It was delivered through the mail slot at the local newspaper office. The envelope was identical to the one you gave me. Chantilly Lace."

The sisters gasped.

"What in hell?" Emma muttered.

"We're shocked," Kate dropped her cup in its saucer.

"We were hoping they'd just run away," Emma moved to the window and stared out.

"We thought whoever took the kids might have got hold of one of your envelopes." Brisbois's eyes narrowed. He had a sudden thought. "The kids had some Polaroids in their room."

"Oh, yes," said Louise. "We took dozens of pictures of the children. Do you want to see them?"

"Not right now," Brisbois responded impatiently. "Did you happen to give the kids their pictures in one of your Chantilly Lace envelopes?"

"No," said Emma, turning from the window.

Louise reflected. "Oh, I think we did, Emma."

"Now, Louise, we'd never give the children one of our fine envelopes," Emma countered.

"Children have sticky fingers," Kate reminded her.

"I'm sure we gave them their photographs in a number ten business envelope," said Emma.

"I thought it was a plastic bag," said Kate.

Brisbois sighed. "I was hoping the kidnapper might have come by the envelope through the kids. It might narrow things down."

"I can assure you that would be impossible," said Emma.

"For the sake of curiosity," Kate ventured. "How much did the kidnapper request?"

"Five thousand dollars."

Louise frowned. "Seems low."

"That envelope could have come from anywhere," said Creighton.

He and Brisbois were sitting on the bench near the flowerbed, while Brisbois reviewed his notes.

"It could have been bought by anyone and not necessarily from Fred Lewis at Cowperthwaite's," Creighton continued.

"But the Pleasant connection is the only one that makes sense," Brisbois argued. "I think the envelope was purchased locally and whoever mailed the letter came across the envelope in an indirect way."

"Maybe somebody years ago gave his mother or old auntie a box of Chantilly Lace for Christmas," Cheighton countered, stretching his legs and tipping his hat forward.

"Not just old people write letters," said Brisbois.

"Mostly just old people write letters."

Brisbois sighed. "Possibly the kidnapper got that envelope indirectly and possibly it doesn't have anything to do with the Pleasant, but —"

Brisbois was about to finish the thought when his cell phone rang.

The sergeant at the station in Middleton greeted Brisbois with a smile. "We've solved all your problems, Detective."

"Good for you."

"Come here." The sergeant led him down the hall to the interrogation room and gestured toward a one-way window. "See that guy?"

Brisbois found himself looking at a thin, young man with scraggly, greasy hair, wearing glasses with heavy frames taped together with masking tape. Under a filthy green jacket he had on a T-shirt of questionable colour. A baseball cap rested on the table in front of him.

"Who is he?"

"That," the sergeant replied jovially, "is Johnny Adams. He was caught coming out of a cottage two miles west of Middleton with a knapsack full of watches, the wallet of a guy who reported it stolen from a nearby campsite, a couple of washcloths—I guess he never got a chance to use them—and a silver sugar bowl with the logo of the Pleasant Inn. We're waiting for a fingerprint match from the laundry van. I have no doubt it will be a good one. And he matches the general description of the eat-and-run from the bus station in Lowerton. We'll get him in a lineup for that—unless he confesses, which he probably will."

Brisbois felt a surge of pity. The boy looked alone and hopeless. "You've answered some of our problems, for sure."

The sergeant shrugged. "But I doubt if he's your kidnapper. If he'd touched that ransom letter with those paws, there'd be dirty prints all over it."

"Does he have a record?"

"Possession, minor trafficking, shoplifting, the usual stuff. He just got out of Quinte Detention Centre ten days ago. Shoplifting this time. He was supposed to be on his way to Nova Scotia—he's got family there. He says he lost the ticket his social worker gave him. Probably traded it for Dilaudin. He was hitchhiking. Got a ride as far as Lowerton. I guess he liked the area and decided to stay for a while."

"How old is he?"

"Nineteen."

"Christ."

"I don't think he's your murderer either. He was in Quinte when the old man was killed in that jewellery store in New Brunswick. You're operating on the theory one guy committed all the murders, eh?"

"Yeah."

"He's waiting for his lawyer. As soon as we mentioned the laundry van, he clammed up. I think he's been able to get off lightly so far by throwing himself on the mercy of the court. He knows vehicular theft could land him in the big house."

"They'd eat him alive there."

"Yeah, well, the lawyer'll probably be able to get auto theft knocked down to a joy ride." He glanced at Brisbois. "Don't look so sad, Detective. He'll probably get away with another few months in a provincial facility."

"I hate cases involving kids," said Brisbois.

"Me too," said Creighton, mistaking Brisbois' compassion for disgust. "When I was a beat cop I spent ninety per cent of my time chasing sixteen-year-olds for one jackass thing or another, only to have them smirking at me when they beat the rap." He jingled some change in his pocket. "Give me a good murder any day. At least we get to smirk at them."

Brisbois turned to the sergeant. "Who's the lawyer?"

"Adele Delaney." He checked his watch. "She'll be here in an hour. We should have the prints by then."

"Okay," said Brisbois, "we'll wait."

Late afternoon, with clouds threatening the sky and thunder rolling in the distance, Gil decided to pull the canoes from the water for the night.

"I thought your outfit guaranteed sunny skies the whole trip," Turnbull grumbled when they'd assembled on shore.

Gil shrugged. "Storms come up, sometimes without warning. This one may pass completely. I'm following protocol and pulling out early. In the meantime, I'm going down to check in with headquarters."

Turnbull watched Gil walk down the shore with his satellite phone in hand. "I hope nobody here has a train to catch."

"Now, Mr. Turnbull," Margaret responded, "Gil is being appropriately cautious."

"If anyone has a travel schedule that tight, Mr. Turnbull," Miss Miller said, kneeling to prepare the fire, "they deserve to miss their train." She glanced across the river where a black cloud menaced the trees. "If you want to make the situation as pleasant as possible, why don't you help collect some extra firewood? In case it rains tonight, we might want to have some dry kindling."

"Otherwise it might be dried bread and cold water for breakfast tomorrow," Norman added, favouring Turnbull with a buck-toothed smile.

Turnbull responded to Norman with a twist of the lips and ambled off into the woods.

"I don't think I've ever met anyone so young and sarcastic," said Rudley.

"You weren't like that when you were young, were you, Rudley?" Norman asked in a serious tone.

"Rudley was as sweet then as he is now," Margaret replied.

Norman raised a skeptical eyebrow.

Peters, who had gone into the woods to gather twigs the moment the party landed on shore, appeared now with a substantial bundle. He set it down and went back for more.

"I'll cover those with a tarp," said Simpson.

"Mr. Peters has fit in well," Geraldine observed. "He seemed awkward at first but he's turned out to be an angel."

"I believe he just needed to feel useful," said Simpson.

"Yes," Margaret agreed. "It's amazing how everyone falls into a role. Mr. Simpson helps Gil with the canoes and setting up the tents, Geraldine and Miss Miller cook, and Mr. Peters gathers wood."

When Turnbull returned carrying a bundle of twigs, Miss Miller gave him a smile. "Thank you."

"You're welcome." Turnbull yawned. "What's for supper?"

"Slugs," Miss Miller replied as he flopped down by the fire. "Edward and Norman are going out any minute now to turn over some rocks."

"Elizabeth meant that as a joke," Simpson explained. "I believe we're having pancakes and desiccated sausages."

"With petit pois and carrots, also desiccated," said Margaret.

"I'm going out right now to see what forest greens might be available," said Geraldine. "And I might identify a mushroom patch we can harvest tomorrow."

"I hope Geraldine wasn't involved in that mushroom escapade at the Pleasant," Miss Miller remarked once Geraldine had left.

"Oh, no," said Margaret, "that was Mr. Bole's mistake. He mistook a poisonous variety for an edible type he'd encountered in the Ardennes. Geraldine correctly identified the species."

"I always thought it would have been more useful if she had identified them before Gregoire cooked them up and served them to Doreen," said Rudley.

"Syrup of ipecac is a wonderful medicine," said Margaret.

Rudley sighed. "I wonder what's happening at the Pleasant."

Tim returned to the kitchen and slid the trolley into the pantry.

"How are the sisters?" he asked Gregoire, who was grinding pepper into a white sauce.

"A little tense. Perhaps *The Texas Chainsaw Murder* was a bit much."

"I don't know why. They've watched every horror film ever created."

"They left half their dinner."

Gregoire frowned. "Did Blanche show enthusiasm for her dinner?"

"That cat ate every scrap. But, then, she wasn't allowed to watch the movie. Emma thought it was too violent for her."

Gregoire paused, peppermill in mid-twirl. "She could have a point," he said. "Blanche is several million years old and has a heart condition."

Tim pulled up a stool and watched as Gregoire whisked the sauce. After a moment, Tiffany stepped into the kitchen and pulled up a stool next to Tom. She sat down with a noisy sigh.

"What's wrong with Miss Tiffany tonight?" Gregoire asked.

"Detective Brisbois was around to see the sisters again. I think his repeated interrogations have upset them."

"They left half their dinner," Tim repeated.

"Detective Brisbois is frustrated." Gregoire shrugged. "He is like a bloodhound with all of these excellent scents going in different directions. He has the murders and the kidnappings and the laundryman's van and that filthy guy breaking into my pantry." A look of disgust crossed his face. "I cringe, thinking of him going into my things, putting his dirty hands on my linens, perhaps handling my utensils. I have been over everything with Javex three times and still..." He frowned. "Nothing is normal around here. If the Rudleys were here, none of these awful things would be happening."

Tim snatched a carrot curl from the counter. "At least we're not suspects anymore."

"That was just Officer Semple," said Gregoire. "He has always had a complex about us."

Tim rose from his stool and went to the refrigerator. "I think," he began, removing a block of cheese, "if what's been going on here lately was anything like those past episodes of mayhem we probably wouldn't pay much attention to the investigators. Rudley would be in denial. Miss Miller would have a working theory. Norman would have a different theory." He reached for a tray of crackers and began preparing himself a snack. "Mrs. Millotte doesn't have any interest in the investigation."

"Melba believes one should leave these things to the professionals," Gregoire agreed.

"Speaking of which," Tim asked, "where are they?"

"They have gone back into town."

"I don't know why the detectives aren't taking a greater interest in Mr. Bostock," said Tiffany. "Aunt Pearl and Nick saw him on the lake again today. This time by the Bridal Path. They were sure he was taking pictures. He was wearing a bushy moustache and a baseball cap."

"Maybe he's a developer," said Tim. "He's going to buy up all of the old inns and turn them into luxury condos with swimming pools."

Gregoire rolled his eyes. "I cannot bear the thought of that."

Brisbois left the interview room, walked straight out the back door of the station, and lit a cigarette. Creighton waited a minute, then followed.

"You're going to kill yourself with those, Boss."

"That doesn't sound like such a bad idea right now," Brisbois groused.

"That kid's going to end up back in jail and there's nothing you can do about that."

"I know."

"We did get a few questions answered, though."

Brisbois took a long drag. "We've wasted hours running around after that Johnny Adams because we thought he might be involved in the kidnapping. If anything happens to those kids because of that…"

"Look at it another way," said Creighton. "Now we have more time to follow the other leads." He looked at his watch. "Why don't we catch a couple of hours of sleep and start again in the morning?"

Chapter Seventeen

The aroma of coffee brought the campers to the fire one by one. Gil came up from the shore. He held out two fish, already filleted.

"Nice catch," said Norman.

Gil grinned. "Bass. I caught them right off the rock down there." He hunkered down, moved the coffee pot over on the grill and began to prepare his skillet.

"Are you any good at cooking?" Turnbull said.

"Sure."

"Just asking. It's just that you've never cooked anything for us. Miss Miller usually cooks."

Gil gave Turnbull an exasperated look. "You're right," he said, "I'm not any good at it." He handed Turnbull the spatula. "Maybe you'd like to do it." He picked up the case that contained his satellite phone. "I'm going down to check in."

"What?" Turnbull looked at him as he retreated, then at the frying pan.

"As soon as the butter sizzles, put the fish in," Geraldine advised.

"Well, what about the batter?"

"You don't need a batter," said Geraldine, "unless you want one. Did you have a favourite recipe in mind?"

"No, but…"

Peters smiled as Geraldine took the spatula from Turnbull's hand and said, "I'll look after the fish."

"Fine." Turnbull stomped off toward his tent.

"Oh, dear," said Margaret, "we've hurt his feelings."

"Don't worry, Margaret," said Rudley, "he'll be back as soon as the work is done."

As predicted, Turnbull reappeared as breakfast was being served. Gil returned at the same time.

"Did you ask if they'd heard anything about that poor man who was murdered near the border?" Margaret asked him as he took a plate and sat down.

"I didn't speak with anyone," Gil replied. "I just left a message."

"I wonder if they've identified him yet," Simpson said.

"I'll ask next time I call in."

"I hope the murderer isn't near the Pleasant," Margaret fretted.

"I'm sure he's miles away from there by now," said Rudley.

"I know I'd be," said Turnbull.

Brisbois woke, groggy, when his alarm went off at six, three hours after he had fallen asleep. With his wife still slumbering, he grabbed an Egg McMuffin on his way to work and managed to spill coffee on his shirt. By the time he arrived at the station he was in a bad mood. But a message left for him by the fingerprint analyst turned his frown to a wide smile. He tried to phone Creighton, but to his surprise his partner had already left home.

"I've been over all these fingerprints," the analyst said when he arrived in Brisbois's office. "The ones from the pantry window in the kitchen belong to Johnny Adams."

"Yup."

"And the ones from the laundry van too."

"Okay."

"But Adams's fingerprints aren't on the ransom envelope or on the note."

"We kind of figured that," Brisbois remarked, disappointed.

"There were fingerprints all over the ransom note and envelope but most of them aren't good enough to match," the analyst continued. "Except for one good thumb print and one good index finger print."

"Yes?" Brisbois responded excitedly.

"I matched them with someone on the exclusion list. Melba Millotte."

"I could kiss you!" Brisbois thumped the man on his shoulder.

"Guess whose fingerprints are on the ransom envelope?" Brisbois said to Creighton moments later in the parking lot. "Melba Millotte!"

"You think Mrs. Millotte kidnapped the kids?"

"No." Brisbois flung open the door of his car. "But it proves that envelope came from the Pleasant."

Mrs. Millotte was on the phone when Brisbois and Creighton arrived at the Pleasant's front desk.

"Are you sure you included the prune juice with that order?" She fumed into the receiver. "Well, I've checked everywhere anyone could have inadvertently put it." She tapped her nails against the wood, her face stony. "Believe me, Mr. Gingras," she continued after a pause, "if someone had drunk a gallon of prune juice over the past twenty-four hours, I would know by now." She sighed. "I'll have to take your word for it. If you'll add prune juice to today's order, I'll have Lloyd pick it up this afternoon." She dropped the receiver into the cradle and scribbled a note on the invoice.

"Prune juice trouble?" Brisbois smiled sympathetically to mask his amusement.

"Summer."

"Summer?"

"In the summer, the local establishments hire high school students. Enough said." Mrs. Millotte put the pen aside. "Now, what can I do for you, Detective?"

"Would it surprise you to know," he began, looking her straight in the eye, "that the ransom note that ended up at the local newspaper had your fingerprints on it?"

"Yes."

"Then how could it happen?"

"It couldn't. Unless the letter was mailed from here."

"Could you have picked up a letter someone had to mail while you were making your rounds?"

She shook her head. "No."

"No?"

"Tiffany sometimes picks up letters to be mailed when she's doing the rooms, or Tim, if he's delivering a meal. But I don't."

"So, if a letter ended up here at the desk, how would your fingerprints end up on the envelope?"

"Because I sort the mail."

"Are there a lot of letters going out?"

"Several a day at least."

"Do you take a peek to see where they're going?"

She rolled her eyes. "Of course. We read all of the guests' mail and blank out any derogatory comments about Rudley. But seriously, Detective, all we do is take a quick look to see if they're stamped."

"So if someone addressed something to the local paper nobody would notice."

"Anything to the paper we sort separately for hand delivery," she said. "Lloyd takes them in. The old-timers here correspond regularly with the local rag. They follow everything that goes on. If they put in a new street sign in town, we're talking letters to the editor. Rudley spoils them. If they had to pay postage, they probably wouldn't be so opinionated."

"So everything for the newspaper goes into that envelope marked 'newspaper,'" Brisbois said, gesturing to a battered interdepartmental envelope he noticed on the side of the desk, "And gets hand delivered."

"You've got it."

"So you'd handle any mail that goes in there."

"Unless someone put it in there themselves. Sometimes the old-timers do that."

"Or the staff?"

"Or the staff."

"Thanks, Mrs. Millotte. We'll talk to you later."

"I'm sure you will."

"So anybody who knew the Pleasant's routine could have put that ransom note into the newspaper envelope," Creighton mused as he and Brisbois passed onto the veranda.

"Lloyd's fingerprints weren't on the envelope."

Creighton shrugged. "They wouldn't have to be. Unless the letter in question was on the very top or very bottom. He probably just takes the whole bundle and stuffs them into the mail slot at the paper."

"True."

"Where to now?"

"The Elm Pavilion," Brisbois said. "Somebody must have got hold of one of the Benson sisters' envelopes."

"You're thinking the sisters gave one to the kids with the pictures inside and forgot they did. And the kidnapper got it that way."

"Or the sisters gave it to the kidnapper and don't realize they did."

Moments later, Brisbois was knocking at the door of the Elm Pavilion, but to no response.

"The old dolls probably can't hear a thing over that television." Creighton stepped forward and hammered on the door.

"Just a moment," a voice sang out. After a few more moments had passed, a prim voice invited them to come in.

"Oh, it's Detective Brisbois and that handsome Detective Creighton," Kate greeted them at the door. She turned to Louise. "We must get the gentlemen some coffee."

"Oh, no thank you, Miss Benson." Brisbois removed his hat. "Sorry to disturb you so early."

"I gather this isn't a social call," Kate said.

"Not exactly."

The sisters exchanged glances.

"We have a couple of more questions for you about that envelope. It seems the ransom note it contained was mailed from the Pleasant."

"From The Pleasant?"

Brisbois nodded.

"Oh," said Louise, as Kate looked away and murmured, "How interesting."

"And," Brisbois continued, "the only fingerprints on that envelope belong to Melba Millotte."

"You don't say," said Kate.

"We know the letter originated from the Pleasant and we know Mrs. Millotte's fingerprints were on it," Brisbois continued. "So we wondered if you could think again about anyone you might have given an envelope to or anybody who possibly could have taken one from you."

"I don't remember anything about that," said Louise.

Kate caught Brisbois's eye and tapped a finger against her temple. "Memory," she mouthed.

"I saw that," Louise snapped.

Emma advanced to the sideboard and, to Brisbois's astonishment, given the time of morning, poured herself a sherry. "I think this has gone far enough." She finished the drink in one swallow and addressed her sisters. "We need to tell the detectives what's going on. We can't have Melba implicated in this."

Louise suppressed a gasp.

"Emma—" Kate began, but Emma cut her off.

"We have to trust the detectives. I'm sure they wouldn't assist in anything illegal."

"Emma." Kate spoke through gritted teeth. "We've discussed this."

"Kate, if I may…" Brisbois began, shooting Creighton a stony glance to stop him snickering. "First, Emma's right. You can trust us not to do anything illegal."

"And I'm sure you wouldn't do anything that would bring harm to those children," Emma continued.

"I promise you, we'll proceed cautiously with any information," Brisbois said with growing impatience. "Now, if you have anything to tell us."

Kate interrupted him. "Could we have a minute, Detective?"

"Of course." Brisbois sighed, motioning to Creighton and steering him aside while the sisters huddled. For a few minutes all the detectives could hear was the hum of urgent, whispered conversation.

Finally, Emma nodded and stepped forward, Louise and Kate flanking her, the latter wearing an aggrieved expression. She invited Brisbois and Creighton to take a seat, while she and Louise took their places opposite, on the sofa. She invited Kate to join them, but Kate dithered. Finally, bristling a little, Kate opted for an occasional chair.

"Miss Benson?" Brisbois addressed Emma.

"Detective." Emma appeared to gather her thoughts. "Before I say a word, we have to be assured the information will be used with the utmost sagacity and discretion."

"I guess," Creighton muttered, "if I knew what sagacity meant."

"I assure you it will," Brisbois responded, elbowing Creighton.

"We are deeply concerned that no one come to harm as a result of what we are about to divulge."

Brisbois sighed. "Miss Benson, I can only promise to give what you have to say a fair hearing. But I do have to remind you that to withhold information could expose you to criminal charges."

"We don't want anyone to get spanked," Louise piped up. "We don't believe in corporal punishment."

Brisbois frowned, perplexed. Emma rolled her eyes. "We agreed, Louise, that I was to carry the ball on this one. Now," she continued briskly, as her chastened sister lowered her eyes, "It has come to our attention that the Sawchucks' grandchildren are the subject of a kidnapping plot."

Brisbois glanced at Creighton.

"The story is that the children's parents are on vacation in Switzerland." Emma paused to appraise her sisters, then proceeded. "That is not true."

Brisbois started. "It isn't?"

"No." Emma regarded him sternly. "The children's parents are having marriage problems. The father has lured the mother to Switzerland, promising to work out their differences." She frowned. "In fact, the children's father has a paramour waiting for him."

Creighton's hand went to his mouth to suppress a chuckle. Brisbois kicked him.

"Waiting in Switzerland?" he asked.

"In an undisclosed location," Emma replied, "Possibly Monaco."

"The father—"

"Jim Danby." Brisbois glanced at his notes.

"—has paid an agent to abduct the children and spirit them out of the country."

"How?" Creighton asked from behind his hand.

"In a private airplane." Emma frowned at Creighton. "The children would be taken to an undisclosed location."

"Monaco?" Brisbois asked.

Emma gave him a look that suggested she found him obtuse. "Dubai. Possibly Brazil.

"Once the children are secreted away," she continued, "the father will go out for the proverbial pack of cigarettes and never come back. While his wife searches for him in vain, he'll be in Rio with this Jezebel and those unfortunate children." She crossed her arms to punctuate her final words, fixing Brisbois with a triumphant stare.

"Miss Benson," Brisbois responded, as his notebook slid down his knee, "that is a fascinating theory."

"It is not a theory, Detective, it is fact."

"May I ask the source of your information?" he asked, reaching to retrieve his notebook from the floor.

"The children!" Louise blurted, then covered her mouth as Kate opened hers to remonstrate.

Emma raised a hand. "It's all right, Kate. The cat is out of the bag." She lowered her hands on her knees and leaned forward. "Yes, Detective, the children told us. They're frantic at the prospect of being separated from their mother, from their home, from all that is familiar. They scarcely know the other woman. She's a personal assistant of some sort. A well-paid strumpet is more like it."

"Miss Benson, where are the children?"

"They're safe, Detective."

"That's the best news I've had in days, but where are they?"

"I will tell you under one condition."

"Yes?"

"The children must be given sanctuary. You must be prepared to notify Interpol to get their mother back while their father is detained."

"Miss Benson, I can promise you one thing. The children will be protected until we get this thing sorted out. But first we have to know where they are."

Kate spoke. "Why, they're with Hiram."

"Hiram?"

"Our driver."

"And where is Hiram?"

"He's in Ottawa. He and the children are in a safe house."

"A safe house?"

"It belongs to friends of ours. From Daddy's days in the diplomatic corps," said Kate.

"He was a spy," Louise added.

"So," Brisbois began, seeking to make sense of what he'd learned, "Hiram drove the kids to the safe house in Ottawa …"

"No," Kate responded. "Hiram took them in his boat. After the children told us their story, we called him. He waited until the inn was dark, then picked them up at the dock."

"In his boat?"

"Yes," said Kate, "Hiram owns an island on the lake."

"Ladies, if Hiram owns an island on the lake why is he still employed as your chauffeur?"

The sisters looked surprised, as if they'd never considered the question before.

"He always has been, Detective," Emma replied. "I can't imagine he can do anything else."

"Who do you think sent the ransom note?" said Louise.

"Probably the children," said Emma. "Perhaps to add veracity to their plight." She gave Brisbois an apologetic look. "We gave the children their pictures in a Chantilly Lace envelope. We told a fib about that because we didn't want to betray the children."

"Ladies, if you wanted to make sure the kids were protected, why didn't you call social services?"

Emma gave him a disdainful look. "Nobody pays any attention to what children say."

"Or old people," said Louise.

Brisbois took out his pen, jabbed at his notebook. We're going to need that address, ladies."

Brisbois faced Ned and Nora across the table. He and Creighton had driven to Ottawa through heavy traffic and managed to get lost in the neighbourhood, looking for the safe house. Brisbois was in a foul mood when they arrived to find the kids glued to a television set.

"And you did this why?"

"Because we were bored," Nora said without a trace of remorse.

"Because we were bored," Brisbois repeated tonelessly. "You were in a great place on the lake with boating, fishing, hiking and you were bored."

They shrugged. "They didn't have the Internet."

"They didn't have the Internet," Brisbois echoed, suppressing his fury with difficulty. "Do you have any idea how much this prank of yours cost?"

"It's your job, isn't it?" Ned regarded Brisbois boldly, folding his arms over his chest. "What else do you have to do out there in the sticks?"

"Plenty," Brisbois said. "We had officers working overtime, coming in on their days off, harassing innocent civilians—all because they were worried about two missing kids. We had Interpol scouring the Alps for your parents. If that isn't bad enough, you worried your grandparents."

"Those old farts aren't worried about anything but their bowels." Ned sneered. "They wouldn't have noticed us gone if someone hadn't told them."

"Do your grandparents have any other grandchildren?"

"No."

"Too bad." Brisbois jotted in his notebook. "On top of everything else, you took advantage of the kindness of three old ladies. They believed you," he growled in response to their flippant shrugs. "And they broke the law to help you."

"They're just crazy," Nora yawned.

"No, they have great imaginations. Maybe they were a little bored, too, but they're not crazy."

"Are you going to lock them up?" Nora asked.

"None of your business."

"We didn't mean to make it such a big deal," Ned backtracked. "It was just for fun."

"Yeah," Brisbois murmured as he scribbled in his notebook, "just for fun."

"Can we go now?" Nora asked.

He glanced up. "Are you kidding? We're waiting for social services. They'll be in charge of you until we can locate your parents."

"But grandma and grandpa are responsible for us," Nora whined.

"Didn't one of you say your grandparents aren't concerned about anything but their bowels? I'm afraid you're out of their hands at present."

Nora slumped in her chair. "The story was just supposed to be for fun. We didn't think those old bats were going to call somebody to take us to a safe house."

"We just thought we'd get to stay with them and watch movies and play games for a couple of days," Ned groused. He paused, then asked hopefully, "when Mom and Dad get back, I guess we'll be going home with them, right?"

"That," he told the twins with a smile, "is up to the judge."

Chapter Eighteen

"Rudley, what time is it?"

"Early," Rudley murmured.

Margaret unzipped her sleeping bag and fumbled about for her watch. She held it up, her eyes widening. "Rudley, it's going on six o'clock."

"I can live with that."

"Well, I've slept in. I should be helping with the breakfast." She wriggled into her clothes and took off down the rise to find Miss Miller at the campfire, emptying coffee grounds from the pot.

"I slept in," Margaret greeted her. "I wanted to be getting breakfast on."

"Edward and I got up just a few minutes ago," Miss Miller said. "The coffee was already on, boiling furiously. The handle was so hot I had to get a towel to take the pot off the grill. The coffee had almost boiled away."

"I'll rinse out the pot and make some fresh."

"It's all right. I can do it. It just seems odd for Gil to put the coffee on, then wander off and leave us all asleep with the fire burning."

"He's usually such a stickler for safety," Margaret agreed.

"Edward thought he might have gone fishing at the shore." Miss Miller pointed toward Simpson who was looking up and down the lake with a pair of binoculars. "But his canoe's gone."

Geraldine and Norman joined them. "I'm afraid we slept in," Norman said. "We've gotten used to Gil giving us a call."

"We all slept in," said Margaret. "Perhaps he thought we needed the rest."

Geraldine scanned the shoreline. "Is Gil off getting us some fish?"

"He's taken the canoe out," said Miss Miller.

Norman's face sagged in disappointment. "He told me whenever he took the canoe out fishing, he'd take me with him."

"He must have forgotten, dear."

Simpson came back up the rise, said good morning, and put his binoculars aside. "I didn't see a sign of him, Elizabeth."

"Nothing?"

"Perhaps he's tucked in behind that ledge."

The coffee was on and beginning to perk. Miss Miller opened one of the food containers. "Is everyone up for pan johnnycake?"

"We could have it with dried fruit and desiccated bacon," said Geraldine, as Rudley joined them.

"Gil's not back from wherever," Margaret told him. "We're going to be late getting underway."

"Perhaps we could break down the tents and pack up our gear," Simpson suggested. "That way we won't be too much off schedule."

Norman, Rudley, and Simpson went off to see about the tents. Norman stopped at Turnbull's tent and tried a loon call to rouse him. After several avian variations, Turnbull stuck his head out the flap.

"You can cut it out anytime" he said.

Norman grinned. "I always think it's nice to wake up to the birds."

"Yeah, sure."

"Breakfast should be ready soon," Norman continued. "We're running a little late this morning. We're getting our gear ready to travel."

"What time is it?"

Norman looked at his watch. "Almost six-thirty. We've got to get the tents down, get our gear packed and ready for the canoes, and clean up the campsite." He paused at Turnbull's annoyed expression. "So if you could get your things together, Mr. Turnbull, we can have breakfast and be underway as soon as possible."

"I think I'll get dressed first, thanks." Turnbull retreated into his tent.

"By all means," Norman murmured. He went on to Peters's tent. "Mr. Peters?" He tried his jay and cardinal calls to no avail. "If Mr. Peters doesn't want to get up, he won't get any breakfast," he remarked to Rudley who came by lugging a tent and a duffel bag.

"I can't see that happening," said Rudley.

"I agree." Norman quickened his pace to match Rudley's longer strides. "Mrs. Rudley wouldn't let anyone get away without breakfast." He inhaled deeply. "I can smell the cornbread. That should have Peters up momentarily."

They stashed the gear at the riverbank. Simpson had arrived ahead of them and was once again scanning the river.

"Any sign of Gil?" Norman asked.

Simpson shook his head.

"Let's see how breakfast is progressing," said Rudley.

Miss Miller was apportioning the cornbread when they returned to the campfire.

"No sign of Gil yet," Simpson told her.

"Mr. Peters is still asleep," said Norman. "I couldn't rouse him."

"We'll see about that," she said, heading to Peters's tent.

She returned in a minute. "He's not there!"

The campers stood at the shore, gear packed and ready, scanning the terrain.

Finally, Turnbull spoke the silence. "I don't think they're coming."

"Something terrible must have happened to them," said Margaret.

"Maybe they just got fed up and went home."

"We need to go look for them." Miss Miller ignored Turnbull's remark. "We'll divide into teams, two downstream and two upstream, one on each side." She glanced at her watch. "We'll meet back here in half an hour."

"Why don't we just pack up our canoes and head downstream?' Turnbull said. "Otherwise, we're just wasting time."

"Because they might have gone upstream," said Miss Miller.

"I think he took Peters fishing," said Norman.

They broke into teams, Norman and Geraldine going upstream with Miss Miller and Simpson, the others downstream.

"Well," said Turnbull as he dipped his paddle in the water, "Here's nothing."

"I know something terrible has happened to the boys," Margaret fretted as she and Rudley eased into their canoe.

"I'm sure they're fine, Margaret. They probably swamped their canoe and are waiting for us to rescue them."

"Oh, I hope so, Rudley."

"What do you think that is, Norman?" Geraldine adjusted her binoculars. "I can't seem to get a good fix on it from here."

Norman raised his binoculars and stared off into the trees. "It's an eastern kingbird."

"No, no." Geraldine pointed over his shoulder. "There, near that log."

"Oh." Norman squinted. "It's a shoe." He swept the binoculars to the left. "But if you look closely, Geraldine, in the shallows by that rock, you'll see a nice pair of mallards."

She focused on the shoe. "What do you think a shoe would be doing here, Norman?"

Norman had his binoculars fixed on the ducks. "Probably the same thing large quantities of plastic bags are doing in the Sargasso Sea. The detritus of the human animal is widespread." He frowned. "There's also a hat."

"So," said Brisbois, looking up from the paperwork on his desk, "do we know what we're doing?"

"Don't we always?"

"Sum it up for me just to make sure."

Creighton rolled his shoulders. "Well, we have two very bad kids sending us on a wild goose chase. We have an incorrigible who's really just a scared kid living off his wits—which, in his case, isn't much to live off, if you ask me."

"The waitress in Lowerton picked Johnny Adams out of the lineup right away," Brisbois said. "So what are we left with?"

"Three old ladies and their driver who will probably get a stern talking to."

"And well they should." Brisbois picked up the latest stack of notes, slid half of it across the desk to Creighton, and picked up the phone. "So now we can get back to following up leads on our John Doe."

Reconvened on shore, the campers examined Norman and Geraldine's find.

"That's Gil's hat," said Norman. "His name is on the sweat band."

"And I'm sure this is his shoe," Geraldine added.

"They must have had an accident," said Norman.

"Perhaps the canoe capsized and they had to swim to shore," said Geraldine. "You could lose a hat and shoe that way."

"In that case, they should have made it back by now," said Rudley. "Unless…"

"Unless they were injured and are wandering around in a daze," Margaret worried.

"We need to get help." Miss Miller surveyed the campsite. "Has anyone seen the satellite phone?"

"It should be with Gil's belongings." Simpson walked over and began to sort through their guide's gear.

"He keeps it in that waterproof case." Norman pointed to a padded bag.

Simpson opened it. "It's not here."

"Perhaps he took the phone with him," said Norman.

"I guess," Turnbull said, "if Gil sunk the canoe, we're sunk too."

"Well," said Rudley after a moment's silence, "you've realized your dream, Margaret. We're out in the middle of nowhere, incommunicado."

"The location of the hat and shoe would appear to confirm Gil and Peters went downstream," Miss Miller said. "I think our only option is to continue downstream and keep looking."

"That's sensible," said Norman.

"What if they make it back here and find us missing?" Margaret asked.

"We could leave a trail of breadcrumbs." Turnbull caught their disapproving looks and said, "Look, they're probably fine. That idiot Peters, probably tipped the canoe and…" He trailed off as Margaret frowned.

"We'll leave a note," she said. "We should leave most of our gear here."

"Yes, we'll need to travel light in case we find them," added Geraldine.

"We'll bring the essentials," Miss Miller said. "Food, water treatment paraphernalia, matches, minimal fishing equipment, Swiss Army knives, first aid kit, binoculars. Edward and I will lead the way."

Turnbull snickered. "What a shock."

"Miss Miller is the logical choice," said Margaret. "She's the most accomplished canoeist and most likely to recognize hazards and alert the party."

"I'm not exactly chopped liver," said Turnbull.

Miss Miller studied him a moment. "You're right," she said finally. "Mr. Turnbull and I will take the lead."

"Okay." Turnbull grabbed his life jacket and headed toward the canoes.

"Are you sure this is a good idea, Elizabeth?" Simpson frowned.

"I think it's the best plan, Edward. Mr. Turnbull has proven to be an accomplished canoeist."

"I'd feel better if I were with you."

She gave him a kiss on the cheek. "I need you to look after the others."

"Will do." Simpson gestured to Turnbull, who was stowing his knapsack in the canoe. "Elizabeth," he whispered, "do you trust that man?"

"Not entirely." She smiled. "He's a jackass, but I can handle him."

The door to Brisbois's office opened and an officer peeked in. "We've got something on your John Doe." He handed Brisbois a slip of paper. "A lady called in. She wants you to contact her right away."

Brisbois noted the number the officer had jotted down. "New Hampshire?"

"Vermont."

"Thanks." Brisbois picked up the phone. "We'll get on it right away."

The banks of the river grew higher the farther downstream they paddled. Five hundred yards along, the river narrowed and the current quickened. Leaves, twigs, strips of bark and dead reeds joined their canoe procession. Suddenly, Turnbull shouted, "Look, ahead to your right."

Turning her head, Miss Miller caught sight of a bright orange object snagged on a tree root.

"It's a lifejacket," Turnbull said.

"Hold steady." Miss Miller grabbed the binoculars, took a quick look, then scanned the horizon.

"I don't see anything else."

"We'll have to go in."

"Are you kidding? They got themselves into this mess. Are you going to risk all those old duffers trying to rescue them?" Turnbull gestured back of their canoe where the others lagged a hundred yards back.

She looked over her shoulder at him. "No, I'm not. We're going to paddle back and set them out on their portage. Then we'll go on by canoe." She paused. "If you're up to it."

"You're not the only one who can paddle a canoe. What's up ahead is a piece of cake compared to what I've done."

"Good. Paddle in the water, Mr. Turnbull."

The others listened as Miss Miller laid out the plan. She and Turnbull would continue by canoe downstream through the rough water. The others would go back upstream, portage, and meet them downstream at the shallows past the rapids.

"You may need to go back three-quarters of a mile before you land the canoes," Miss Miller said.

"That far?" Norman asked.

"Unless you want to climb the cliff with three canoes, Norman," Rudley said.

"What if we get to the shallows first?"

"I think that will happen only if we leave the canoes and run like hell, Norman," Rudley remarked.

"Or if Miss Miller and I end up smashed to little pieces on the rocks." Turnbull grinned at Norman's horrified expression. "Hey, that's not going to happen. I can handle water like that in my sleep."

After a silence, Edward said, "At the shallows, then."

"At the shallows," Miss Miller saluted her husband. "Paddle in the water, Mr. Turnbull."

The river took a sharp bend around the scrubbed grey cliffs, narrowed further, and began to drop. As they navigated their canoe through the foaming waters and around jutting boulders, Miss Miller scanned the water and the shoreline. She half expected to find Peters slung over a limb of the one of the trees teetering toward the water, his eyes gouged out like a modern-day Percival, with Gil reduced to a frozen claw stretching out of the water.

Suddenly a bird swooped low in front of the canoe, treaded water, then shot high into the air. She followed its precipitous climb and caught sight of someone clinging to the cliff. "Look," she called to Turnbull and pointed. "Up there!"

Turnbull grabbed his binoculars. "It's Peters!" he shouted. "What did he do? Climb most of the way up before he realized he was afraid of heights?"

They paddled to shore as fast as the choppy water allowed. Jumping out onto a low ledge, Miss Miller quickly secured the canoe and assessed the cliff. "We can scale this easily enough," she said, pointing. "It's only about thirty feet high here and there are plenty of crevices."

She started up the rock wall, Turnbull following and fussing as the gritty surface abraded his knees.

After several minutes of strenuous climbing, they reached Peters who lay pressed against the cliff, holding on for dear life.

"It's going to be all right," Miss Miller manoeuvered beside him. "We've got you."

"My boot's caught," Peters groaned.

"Hang on tight. I'll move your foot to the next toehold once it's free." Carefully, she worked the boot, wedged in a crevice, back and forth. "Is your foot numb?"

"A little."

"Just hang on." She continued to manipulate Peters's foot. Finally it came free and Peters inched his way up, Miss Miller following behind.

"Is the feeling coming back?"

"Yes." He hoisted himself over the rim of the cliff and struggled to his feet, turning to face her as she reached the edge.

"Where's—?" Miss Miller began, the words dying in her mouth as she looked into the muzzle of a gun. She scrambled back down the cliff. A bullet snapped off a branch inches from her shoulder.

"Jump!" she yelled to Turnbull. "Jump!"

Brisbois hovered at the desk of the Pleasant, turning his hat in his hands, waiting for Mrs. Millotte to give him her attention. Creighton, who had picked up a magazine from the lounge, flashed Brisbois a spread featuring a Jaguar.

"I think," Brisbois said, "if you show up in something like that, Internal Affairs will think you're on the take."

"Or have a rich girlfriend."

Brisbois shook his head.

Mrs. Millotte opened a file box and dropped into it the paper she had been perusing. "Detectives." She studied them over her glasses. "I hope you're here to report you've got those Danby children on a chain gang."

"If it were up to me, Mrs. Millotte, that's exactly where they'd be. Unfortunately, they'll probably be going home in a day or so."

"You mean their parents showed up?"

"Yes. As it turns out, they took a little jog off their itinerary. They made a side trip to Zermatt, ended up at the base of the Matterhorn, and fell in love with an old hermit herding five cows and six goats. They spent a couple of days with him, playing at being simple peasant farmers. They didn't know anyone was looking for them until they got back to Wengen." He shook his head. "Now I know what Walter Sawchuck meant when he called his son-in-law a hippie."

"Far out."

"You said it." Brisbois shuffled through a file he'd brought with him. "We've got something to ask you."

"Of course."

"Were you expecting a guest who didn't show up?"

"No."

"Did anyone cancel?"

"No."

Brisbois's face crumpled.

"Should someone have?" Mrs. Millotte raised an eyebrow.

Brisbois pulled a police artist's sketch from the file. "Have you had this guy as a guest recently?"

She studied the drawing. "No, I can't say that I've ever seen that man."

"His name is Vernon Peters."

She frowned. "We have a Vernon Peters, but that's not him."

Brisbois's forehead crimped. "This man," he pointed to the drawing, "has been identified as Vernon Peters. The woman who identified him said he was vacationing here."

"Our Mr. Peters has a long head and thin blond hair." Mrs. Millotte glanced again at the sketch. "That man has a round face and thick black hair."

"Could I speak to this Mr. Peters?"

"Not at the moment. He's part of the group that went on the outdoor trip."

Brisbois thought a moment. "Is his car here?"

"No, he drove his car. Apparently he gets carsick in vans." Mrs. Millotte paused. "I can think of a number of reasons for not wanting to be cooped up in a van with Rudley and Norman, motion sickness not being one of them."

"What make was the car?"

She flipped through the hotel register next to her. "A Toyota Camry. Burgundy. Vermont licence plate."

Brisbois jotted down the licence number. "When did they leave?"

"The same day you wandered in to warn us about the psychopath on the loose."

"Do you have any way of reaching them?"

"They have a satellite phone. I don't have that number but I do for the outfitters." Mrs. Millotte rummaged through the desk drawer, found the outfitter's card, and wrote out the number for Brisbois.

"If you hear anything from them, let me know right away." Brisbois gestured to Creighton, who remained immersed in his magazine. "You have my card."

Tiffany intercepted him as he headed for the door, fishing in his pocket for his cell phone. "Detective, you should know Mr. Bostock is up the lake in granny glasses and a long grey beard."

"See if you can get a picture of that," he said, startled from his thoughts.

Creighton shrugged at Tiffany and followed Brisbois.

"I think the detective is finally taking my concerns about Mr. Bostock seriously," Tiffany remarked.

"That's good," Mrs. Millotte responded absently.

Tiffany frowned. "Is there something wrong?"

"Could be."

Brisbois stopped halfway across the lawn and punched a number into his cell phone. "Get me Inspector Mallen."

"What's up, Boss?" Creighton asked.

"Nothing good." Brisbois raised a warning hand to silence his partner as they neared their car. "I need a plane," he barked into the phone as he slipped into the passenger side.

"Yeah, heads up to North Bay," Brisbois continued as Creighton pulled the car out of the parking lot. "And get onto the outfitters at—"

he reeled off the number. "They should be able to get us a fix on their location."

Creighton gave Brisbois a quick sideways look when he'd closed his phone. "Did I hear you just say that our serial killer is travelling along with Rudley and the gang?"

"Yup."

"I hope we're not too late."

"Hope not either," Brisbois opened his phone again and dialed the Pleasant. "Mrs. Millotte," he said when she picked up the phone, "I'm going to need a complete description of that Peters guy who's on the canoe trip."

"Perhaps we should be getting along now," Simpson said, collecting the remnants of the snack.

The group had stopped to rest for a few minutes, tired from lugging three canoes over uneven ground.

"We just have to wait for Norman," Geraldine trilled. "He's gone looking for that grosbeak he thought he heard."

"I thought he went looking for an appropriate tree," Rudley said.

"He'll be back in a minute."

"Of course—" Simpson was stopped by the sound of a twig snapping.

"That's probably him now," said Geraldine.

"With our luck, it's probably a bear," Rudley muttered.

"I don't think…" Geraldine began, as Vern Peters stepped into the clearing.

"Why, Mr. Peters"—Margaret broke into a smile, as the others regarded him with surprise —"we've been looking for you. What…" She choked on her words and gasped as he leveled a gun at them. "Mr. Peters?"

"Don't move!"

Rudley bristled. "What's the matter with you, you damn fool? We've been looking all over for you."

"Are you all right?" Simpson asked, stepping forward. "Did you hurt yourself?"

"Move back," Peters rasped.

Margaret clutched Rudley's arm. "Where's Gil?"

"Forget about him." He menaced them with the gun.

"Elizabeth and Turnbull…" Simpson began.

"Forget about them too." Peters licked his lips, his gaze drifting over the group. "Where's Norman?"

"He went looking for a bird." Geraldine's voice trembled.

"We'll wait."

Chapter Nineteen

"Move closer together."

They obliged Peters, raising their hands tentatively.

Simpson gulped. "Where is Elizabeth?"

"She's fine."

"You've done something to her, haven't you?"

"She's fine."

Simpson flushed. "If she were fine, you wouldn't be so calm."

Margaret touched Simpson on the elbow. "I'm sure she's all right, Edward."

Simpson turned to her, his face haunted.

"What's this all about?" Geraldine asked fretfully. "What do you want from us? You know we haven't any money or anything particularly valuable with us."

"I don't want anything from you," Peters snapped. "I've already got what I want."

"If you're going to shoot us, why don't you do it now?" Simpson demanded, shoulders squared.

"He's waiting for Norman to come back," Margaret whispered to Edward when Peters didn't reply. "He doesn't want to alert him."

Peters turned on her. "What did you say?"

"I said I think we're in a pickle."

Peters narrowed his eyes. "The first one to take a step forward gets the first bullet."

Margaret stepped forward. "Mr. Peters, I must say I'm disappointed in you."

Rudley clutched the sleeve of Margaret's shirt as Peters brandished the gun.

"We've offered you the hospitality of our home," she continued, "welcomed you on our excursion, broke bread—"

"Step back and shut up."

"Granted, we're in the middle of the forest. Our circumstances, however, are no excuse to abandon civility."

"Margaret," Rudley croaked.

"You're a nice lady, Mrs. Rudley." Peters took a quick breath. "But if you take another step forward, I won't think twice about putting a bullet between your eyes."

"Now see here," Rudley spluttered.

Peters swept the gun over the group. "Now, everybody shut up! You're giving me a headache."

"I don't know why they couldn't have chartered us a plane," Brisbois grumbled. He and Creighton were on the highway, headed for North Bay.

Because we don't need it, Creighton thought. He put on his blinker to pass the car ahead. "The inspector's right. We can drive to North Bay and go from there."

"Maybe we're already too late."

"Boss, we're doing everything we can. The outfitters gave North Bay the last coordinates. They'll have a crew on the ground long before we can get there. Besides, when did you last go trekking through the bush in leather-soled shoes? And I let you smoke in the car, didn't I? So we wouldn't have to stop," Creighton continued when Brisbois didn't respond. "At potential risk to myself and maybe to my unborn children. My clothes will stink. What if I meet somebody nice up there?'

Brisbois rolled his eyes.

"You're the good guy in this. You got the ball rolling. So what if you're not at the scene when they make the collar?"

Creighton kept up the patter. He knew that being the first to yell "Hands up! Police!" wasn't what was bothering Brisbois. He was worried sick about the campers. "You couldn't have moved any faster. You got on it the minute you got ID on our John Doe. What more could you have done?"

Brisbois tugged at his seatbelt. "Maybe I should have notified Rudley and Margaret about the stuff going down—the kidnapping and so forth. Maybe that would have brought them home before anything happened."

"Maybe nothing's happened. If you'd notified them, you might have spooked our imposter. He would have gotten nervous about the police sniffing around and done something stupid. At least this way we have the element of surprise."

"I let my focus get too narrow." Brisbois took out his notebook and flipped through a few pages. "Look at this. Miss Dutton said she was awakened by a bright light in her eyes the night the kids took off. She thought it was the dock light. I've seen that light a hundred times. It isn't bright enough to wake anybody up. The light on Hiram's boat was what she saw."

"What's that got to do with the price of bread?" When Brisbois didn't respond he continued, "You would have ended up spending hours trying to track down every boat in the province and you might not have hit on Hiram's boat. You solved that case by focusing on the envelope. Probably a lot faster."

Brisbois cracked the window and took out a cigarette. He hesitated.

"Go ahead," Creighton said. "My fluffy pinks can probably survive a two-hour trip."

Brisbois lit his cigarette. All the ifs and buts, he thought. What if Vern Peters had planned a trip to Paris instead of a canoe adventure? What if the Rudleys had decided to put the trip off for another year? What if he had decided to go into the plumbing business with his cousin in Sudbury?

"I could have been a plumber, you know," Brisbois remarked.

"Yeah," said Creighton, "and I could have been Prince Charles but I didn't have the ears for it. If you're trying to attract a princess, I guess money helps."

Brisbois let Creighton rattle on. I wouldn't have been any good at being a plumber, he thought. Mary always said that he would have flooded every kitchen in the province. He sighed. Maybe he wasn't good enough at policing either.

Norman stopped and cocked his head. There it was—the distinctive rattle of the belted kingfisher. He glanced around and caught a glimpse of the bird as it darted out of sight. He stopped to get his bearings. The sun was almost directly overhead. Then a large bird soared into his line of vision. He gasped. An eagle! He was wondering where the aerie might be when he noticed a flash of blue between the trees. Elated, he plunged ahead.

He lost sight of the eagle but he found the river. If he stayed near the water, he wouldn't get lost again. Sooner or later, someone would come along. He felt in his pockets. He had two energy bars, one date walnut and one cranberry almond. He supposed he could survive a day or two. He'd done it before. He and Geraldine had spent a day lost in the wilderness. Of course, they'd had a picnic basket of fried chicken and biscuits with them.

He sat down, broke an energy bar in half, started to take a bite, then broke the half in half and folded the remainder back into the wrapper. He finished his treat, watching a pair of chipmunks chase each other around a tree trunk. Thirsty, he took his water bottle off his belt and was surprised to find it empty. He had forgotten to fill it before setting out, which made him realize he'd always depended on Geraldine to share with him if he forgot something. He and Geraldine hadn't spent a day apart since they'd been married. The thought turned his earlier elation to fright and loneliness.

He steeled himself. He knew he would survive. He and Geraldine had taken a course. He knew how to collect dew from large leaf plants and he was sure he could get down the bluff to the river if he had to. He paused. What if he had a heart attack? His grandfather had had one. Of course his grandfather was ninety-two at the time. And he survived to celebrate his ninety-ninth birthday.

Norman rose and walked over to the edge of the cliff. He stared down and teetered in surprise. "Miss Miller."

She looked up at him out of one eye. The other was purple and swollen shut. Her glasses, one lens shattered, the other missing, dangled from their lanyard. "Help," she cried as her hand slipped along a tree root.

Norman dropped to his knees, grabbed the hand that threatened to lose hold, and pulled with all his migh00t. Miss Miller's foot slipped as the rock gave way. Norman closed his eyes, feeling the strain along his arm as she flailed for purchase. "Hang on, Miss Miller."

She gained traction on the next foothold and at last he was able to pull her over the edge.

"What happened?" he asked.

"Water," she gasped. She fumbled for her canteen.

Norman freed the canteen and handed it to her. She gulped the water greedily. "Where is everyone? What are you doing here, Norman?"

"I went into the bush in pursuit of a grosbeak and got turned around. I saw the water. Well, I saw an eagle. But when I came to the edge, I saw you down there. Then—"

"Where are the others?" she interrupted.

"They're back on the trail," he rambled. "I imagine they're waiting for me. Although by this time, I would think they might be looking for me."

"Peters—have you seen him?"

"No." Norman looked at her, goggle-eyed. "You were looking for him, Miss Miller."

"He fooled us, Norman." She gulped the water again. "He probably killed Gil."

Norman's jaw dropped. "Peters? Are you sure?"

"Turnbull and I found him on the cliff. He had wedged his foot in a crevice. We rescued him only to have him turn a gun on us."

"But why?"

"I don't know."

"Turnbull? Is he…?"

"He's down there," Miss Miller gestured toward the base of the cliff. "He's unconscious. I think he has multiple broken bones." She stared at her arm, which was bruised and swollen.

"Mr. Peters doesn't want to kill us, does he?"

"Oh, I think he's quite prepared to kill anyone who crosses his path."

Geraldine plucked at Simpson's sleeve. "Why doesn't he just shoot us now?" she whispered.

"Probably doesn't want to warn the others," he murmured, his eye on the bushes.

"What are you talking about?" Peters demanded.

Simpson cleared his throat. "Mrs. Phipps-Walker was just bitten by an insect," he lied. "She wonders if it might be poisonous."

"Tell Mrs. Phipps-Walker she doesn't need to worry about being killed by a poisonous insect," Peters responded.

"He's insinuating he intends to kill all of us," Simpson muttered.

"What?"

"I was reassuring Mrs. Phipps-Walker that she needn't worry about the insect bite."

"You can all shut up."

"We've been in worse spots," Margaret whispered. She was standing behind Simpson in the huddle.

Simpson smiled grimly. It was true. The regulars at the Pleasant had been in worse spots, but this time he felt more vulnerable. He believed he was correct in assuming that Peters hadn't shot them all straight away because he didn't want to alert the others. The others. His mind raced. When Peters first accosted them, the only one whose whereabouts seemed to concern him was Norman. He'd told them to forget about Gil and Turnbull and Elizabeth. Did that mean he'd already dealt with them? Simpson took a deep breath to overcome a rush of nausea. If he found out that Peters had harmed a hair on Elizabeth's head, he'd kill him with his bare hands. He'd shoot me, of course, perhaps fatally, if I were to make a move toward him, he thought. But perhaps not. Perhaps he'd miss. Perhaps a tree limb would fall on him. One could always hope.

"If he makes a move to fire, we shall rush him," Margaret whispered, echoing his thoughts.

Simpson moved his lips to respond, but Peters pointed the gun at him.

"What did you say, Simpson?"

"Sorry, just a prayer." Simpson's gaze shifted to the ground. He knew no matter what happened, his sacrifice would not be in vain. Some of them would get out of this and this man would not escape justice.

Miss Miller groaned.

Norman turned to see blood running from one of her nostrils. "Oh!" he exclaimed. "I walked you into that tree, didn't I?"

"I'll be all right, Norman."

"You don't look well, Miss Miller. Why don't you wait here? I'll follow the river back. I'm sure to run into the others."

"No," Miss Miller responded sharply. "I just need a minute to recover." She examined her mangled glasses then tried them on.

"Can you see?" Norman asked.

"Marginally worse than without."

"Perhaps you could use mine."

She gave him a wobbly smile. "I don't think that would work, Norman."

"Here, try them." He perched his glasses on her nose. "What do you think?"

"Blurry." She returned the glasses. "I think it's better if one of us can see perfectly."

He looked doubtful but took the glasses back and adjusted them on his nose.

"Now," Miss Miller said after a moment, "we should go slowly and keep our eyes open."

"What do we do if we run into Peters?"

"If we see him first, we'll try to avoid being seen."

"What if he sees us first?"

"Then we may not have to worry."

"You say he has a gun."

"Yes, Norman."

"He wouldn't shoot both of us."

"Not at once."

"Oh!" Norman halted and turned to her. "What does he want, Miss Miller?"

"He wants to get away with murder."

Simpson cleared his throat. "If Mr. Phipps-Walker is not back soon, someone should be released to search for him."

Peters gave him a cold stare. "Nobody's going anywhere."

"Who knows what could have happened to him? He could have fallen."

"Perhaps if I tried some birdcalls," Geraldine piped up. "I could try the scissor-tailed flycatcher. If Norman heard the call of a scissor-tailed flycatcher, he would know which way to go."

Peters's finger twitched along the trigger.

"The scissor-tailed flycatcher isn't indigenous to this area," Geraldine carried on, oblivious. "If Norman were within earshot, he would know it was me."

"The next one who says a word," Peters said between gritted teeth, "is going to lose a toe."

"I protest," Rudley began.

Simpson winced.

"Do you see anything?" Miss Miller whispered, as Norman stopped.

"I thought I heard something."

Miss Miller sensed his tension. "What's wrong?"

He put a finger to his lips to silence her. "Peters," he whispered, hunkering to the forest floor, drawing Miss Miller with him. "He's no more than twenty feet to our left, perhaps fifteen feet ahead."

"Can he see us?"

"He's got his back to us." He turned to her, face ashen. "He's holding everyone at gunpoint."

By the time Brisbois and Creighton arrived at the OPP North-East Region headquarters in North Bay, Brisbois had gone through half a pack of Du Mauriers and Creighton reeked of cigarette smoke. Sergeant Wiskin greeted them at the OPP detachment.

"What've you got?" Brisbois asked.

The sergeant invited them to sit down. He picked up a paper and chewed thoughtfully on his gum. "We've got the last coordinates from the outfitters," he responded finally. "A Natural Resources helicopter spotted a canoe and what looks like a man lying on the ledge above it. Not moving. We've got a search and rescue team in transit."

"Have they spotted anybody else?"

The sergeant moved the gum around with his tongue. "Not yet. If your party's in the bush it may take a while to spot them from the air. We've also got assets on the ground. We've set up a staging area at the end of an old logging road. They're working their way in from there."

"We need to get in there."

"We'll relay you by car."

"That's going to take a hell of a long time."

"I know. We don't have any aerial or aquatic assets to free up for you right now." Wiskin turned to his computer. "That's a good description of the suspect. Kind of an odd looking guy."

"Yeah."

"Armed." He checked his notes. "Old World War II piece. I guess it works."

"We know it does."

"Has he got any other weapon on him?"

"Unknown." Brisbois paused. "Hell, we don't even know who he is."

Chapter Twenty

"We have to get behind him," Miss Miller whispered to Norman. "Is there cover?"

Norman peered to his left. "Mostly. But there's a gap. Six feet."

"Could he see us if we tried to get across it?"

"If he turns his head the wrong way, he will."

"Distract him." Miss Miller groped for a pinecone and pressed it into Norman's hand. He blinked at it. She made a throwing motion. "Over his head."

Norman hesitated, then lobbed the cone into the clearing, where it landed in a bush beside Margaret.

As Peters's head swiveled in the direction of the sound, Norman and Miss Miller scrambled across the gap and into the foliage.

Simpson's eyes widened. Geraldine opened her mouth to speak, then stopped herself.

Peters peered at them. "What was that?"

"It was the cutest little red squirrel," said Margaret, watching the muscles in Peters's face relax. "He dropped a pine cone."

Norman peeked through the shrubs. They were directly behind Peters. "Now what?" he whispered to Miss Miller.

Miss Miller pointed to her ear and mouthed, "Listen."

A helicopter thrashing the air sent all eyes to the sky. But the chopper passed over, a mere patch of metal through the tree canopy, and with it went the promise of deliverance. Everyone was crushed with dismay, but Peters visibly relaxed.

"I really think someone should look for Norman," Geraldine said, stepping forward.

"What did I say?" Peters snapped.

Geraldine flushed and quickly retreated. "If he's out there lost, he'll get dehydrated."

Peters raised the gun and pointed it at Geraldine.

Before Miss Miller could stop him, Norman was up like a shot and into the clearing. "How dare you point that thing at Geraldine?" he squeaked.

Peters's confusion lasted but a second. He turned and fired just as Miss Miller scrambled from the bushes on hands and knees, knocking Norman to the ground. The first bullet went over their heads. The second bullet hit Norman in the buttock and he screamed. The third bullet went astray as Simpson leapt toward Peters. Peters sidestepped neatly only to have Rudley grab his gun arm. With this free hand, Peters punched Rudley in the stomach, causing him to double over, gasping. Margaret and Geraldine, seizing the opportunity, struggled to get the gun. A loud crack rent the air and Rudley fell to the ground. Simpson lunged toward Peters and grabbed his leg, sending him crashing face first to the ground and the gun skittering along the grass. Margaret scooped it up and bent down to a grimacing Rudley.

"Are you all right?"

"Just winded," he gasped. "And shot in the boot."

"Oh, Rudley."

"Don't point the gun at me, Margaret." He pried it from her fingers, removed the magazine, and put it into his pocket. "I imagine the authorities will want this."

"This isn't very elegant," Simpson said. He was sitting on the ground, holding Peters's leg while the stunned man kicked out with the other foot.

Geraldine looked to the edge of the clearing, where Norman was being attended by Margaret, then jumped on top of Peters, grabbing for his arms. "Get the cord from my backpack," she yelled at Rudley as she proceeded to box Peters's ears.

"How dare you shoot my husband?" she demanded. She snatched the cord Rudley held out, grabbed Peters's right arm, and twisted it behind his back. "Get the other arm," she instructed Rudley. She bound Peters's hands behind his back, left Simpson and Rudley to guard him, and dashed to her husband's side.

"Are you in pain, Norman?" She leaned into him.

"Yes," he groaned. "I never imagined he would shoot me." "I don't think it's too deep but it is bleeding a bit." Margaret rose. "I can bind that up from our first-aid kit."

Simpson left Rudley to deal with Peters and hurried to Miss Miller's side. He knelt beside her. "Are you all right, Elizabeth?"

She managed a smile. "I've banged up my arm and I must look awful, but, yes, I'm all right."

He examined her swollen eye and winced in sympathy. "What about Turnbull and Gil?"

She shook her head. "We didn't find Gil. Turnbull's on a ledge about a kilometre downstream. Badly injured. Unconscious."

Margaret had returned with the first-aid kit. She knelt beside Norman and proceeded to dress his wound while Geraldine held his hand and comforted him.

Simpson told Margaret what Miss Miller had told him. "Perhaps we can come up with a way to rescue him," he finished.

Miss Miller shook her head. "We can't move him without causing further damage. We can't risk someone else getting hurt, climbing down. We need to go for help."

Margaret stared off into the trees. "If we follow the river…" She paused. "Miss Miller, Gil said the landscape flattens and the river calms below the rapids. The shallows. If we could get everyone that far, we might have a better chance for rescue."

Simpson nodded. "We could spot a float plane."

"Or that helicopter might come along again," Geraldine added.

"What are we going to do about Mr. Peters?" Margaret glanced to where Rudley sat beside Peters.

"Let's leave him," said Simpson. "We can tie him to a tree."

"That seems cruel, Edward," Miss Miller said.

"When we reach civilization we can send the authorities back for him," he said.

"There are bears out here," Margaret reminded him, "and cougars."

"That man killed Gil. Turnbull may die. He tried to kill Elizabeth. He shot Norman. He would have killed us all if he'd had the opportunity." Simpson ran his tongue over his lips. "He doesn't deserve our consideration."

"Perhaps not," Miss Miller responded. She gave Simpson a quizzical look. "But that's not like you, Edward, to leave a man to be eaten by a bear."

He flushed. "No, it isn't."

The group looked at him, silent.

"All right," he said quickly, "we'll take him with us."

"Can we rest for a minute?" Norman winced.

Geraldine and Rudley eased Norman to the ground and positioned him on his left side.

"He's oozing quite a bit," Rudley said after checking Norman's dressing. "We need to reinforce the dressing." He rummaged through the first aid kit and came up with an abdominal pad and an ACE bandage.

"Imagine putting an elastic bandage on your butt, Norman." Geraldine seemed pleased with this bit of ingenuity. "You might say your butt was in a sling."

"I'm not laughing, Geraldine," said Norman.

Rudley's ears picked up at the sound of a helicopter. He hobbled toward the thinnest part of the canopy, waving.

"Did they see us?" Miss Miller asked.

His shoulders sagged. "I don't think so."

"He might have," Simpson said. "Perhaps he's reporting back to headquarters. I don't imagine he can put down near here." He jerked on Peters's restraint as the man bucked against him. "Be still," he said in a low voice, "or I'll put a leash around your neck."

"I'm sure you're right," Margaret said. "How's your foot, Rudley?"

"Bruised, Margaret."

"Stiff upper lip, Rudley."

"You're looking pale, Norman," Geraldine said a little later when they had stopped for another rest.

"My derrière hurts," he moaned.

Simpson, who had gone ahead for a reconnaissance, returned with some news. "The banks are shallow just a hundred yards from here. If we can make it there, I think there's a good chance we'll be seen."

"Can you make it another hundred yards, Norman?"

Uncertainty flickered on his face.

"I'll get that new ice auger," Rudley tried coaxing him. "You can have it all to yourself and cut all the holes you want for your ice fishing."

"Perhaps I can keep going," said Norman.

Brisbois and Creighton were speeding toward the staging area in an OPP cruiser driven by a young officer named Tulchinsky.

The radio crackled.

"What're they saying?" Brisbois leaned forward.

"Search and rescue has recovered and is in the process of transporting one casualty," Creighton reported from the front seat.

The radio continued to crackle.

"What about the others?" Brisbois demanded.

Creighton exchanged a few words with Tulchinsky.

"They found three canoes and assorted paraphernalia. Search in progress."

"And?" Brisbois persisted.

"Some blood-soaked gauze," Creighton added reluctantly.

Brisbois sank back against the seat, wiping a hand across his mouth.

The campers made their way through a wall of trees and stepped out into a clearing. A flat rock sloped gently to the water.

Margaret and Geraldine lowered Norman to the ground and sank down beside him. Rudley hobbled over and joined them, laying the branch he had been using as a staff beside him. Simpson bound Peters to a tree and joined them.

"I think we need to rest for a while and rehydrate," Geraldine said.

Margaret scanned the sky. "Perhaps the helicopter will spot us here."

Simpson rose and wandered down along the bank. "I think I hear a boat," he called back to them. He climbed up onto a hummock and scanned the river. Geraldine joined him with her binoculars.

"I see it!" she exclaimed.

"He's a rather rough-looking character," Geraldine muttered as the boat drew nearer.

They could hear the man piloting the boat singing over the sound of the motor. Simpson glanced at Geraldine.

"I guess we have to trust him," she said,

Simpson stepped out from behind the bushes. "Here!" he called.

The man started and reached for something in the bottom of the boat."

"He's got a gun!" Geraldine cried.

The man turned the boat toward the bank. He wore chinos, a hunting jacket, and a bright orange cap. He looked them over, the gun held across his body. All at once his wary face, cracked with a grin. "Are you the folks they're looking for?"

Tulchinsky pulled off the gravel road onto a rutted logging road and drove for what seemed miles to an anxious Brisbois. He breathed a sigh of relief when a group of parked vehicles with flashing lights announced the staging area.

Brisbois got out of the car and lit a cigarette, while Creighton remained in the passenger's seat. The radio continued crackling in the background.

Brisbois had finished his cigarette and was reaching for another when Creighton stepped out of the car.

"What?" Brisbois stopped in midmotion.

"Got some news. Some old guy picked up two people off the river. He dropped them at a nursing station." He paused. "It was Miss Miller and Norman."

"How bad?" Brisbois demanded.

"They're waiting to confirm. They'll follow up and let us know ASAP. The guy they pulled off the ledge—that was Turnbull. They're airlifting him to Sudbury. He's regained consciousness. Multiple fractures."

Brisbois's response was aborted by the sight of four officers marching down the road with a handcuffed man so short he barely reached their shoulders.

"That's him?" Brisbois gaped.

"He's the only one in handcuffs, Boss."

Brisbois stared into Donnie Albright's vacant eyes. "I hope you didn't hurt anybody I like."

Creighton tapped Brisbois on the shoulder and pointed toward a second group emerging from the trees. "I think you've got your answer, Boss," he said, smiling.

Chapter Twenty-one

Two weeks later, Detective Brisbois found himself at a table on the veranda at the Pleasant with Miss Miller, Mr. Simpson, and Margaret.

"Your Mr. Turnbull's going to be in a body cast for two months," he told them. "I hear he's not being a very good patient."

"How surprising," Miss Miller remarked.

"I'm relieved to hear he'll make a full recovery," said Margaret.

"What about Donnie Albright?" Miss Miller asked. "Have you been able to get any more information from him?"

Brisbois nodded. ""He's starting to open up. He was practically catatonic when we took him in." He took a sip of his coffee and put the mug down on the table. "With Donnie, it was all about not getting caught. After he killed Pritchard, the old guy in Fredericton, he took the mindset that anyone who might be able to identify him or who interfered with his escape had to go. He was hoping, once he'd killed Gil, that everybody would think the two of them had perished in a canoe accident."

"But then he got his foot caught as he made his escape," Miss Miller offered.

"Right."

Simpson considered this. "But why did he kill Gil? He could have just wandered off."

"He said he was worried about the satellite phone," Brisbois said. "He thought Gil might be getting updates on the murders down here. He was afraid once the real Vern Peters was identified, the jig would be up. He had to get rid of the phone and I guess that meant getting rid of Gil."

"Gil always had the phone close by," Miss Miller said.

"Unfortunately," said Brisbois. "Anyway," he went on, "Donnie caught Gil alone at the shore early that morning. He whacked him across the back of the head with a paddle, pushed his face into the water to drown him, then loaded him into the canoe and dumped him in the rough water downstream. Then he maneuvered the canoe to the base of the cliff, shoved it out, and started to climb the rock face. Unfortunately, for him, he got his foot caught in a crevice in the rocks."

"How could he be sure he could get back to civilization on foot?"

Brisbois shrugged. "Donnie didn't have much of a master plan, Miss Miller. He played it by ear, took whatever opportunity came along."

Margaret sighed. "Is that what happened to poor Mr. Peters? The real Mr. Peters. Simply bad luck?"

"I'm afraid so," Brisbois said. "Like most of Donnie's victims, he was in the wrong place at the wrong time. Donnie was just trying to get to the next town. Mr. Peters said he could drop him in Middleton, then he was going on a canoe trip from the Pleasant."

"The poor man was murdered for his kindness," Simpson concluded.

Brisbois nodded. "As they say, no good deed goes unpunished."

After a long silence, Margaret said, "I feel so terrible about Gil. He was such a nice young man."

The others nodded.

"And Mr. Peters…Donnie Albright, I'm sorry for him too. He seemed haunted at times. And he must have felt desperate at the end."

"He killed eight people, Margaret," Brisbois said gently. "That nice young guide, three elderly people, one of your guests, a young couple on their way to see their family, and a poor guy just trying to make a living."

"I don't think he was a bad boy at heart," Margaret said.

Brisbois smiled but said nothing. He was a bad boy, Margaret. A very bad boy.

December — The Pleasant Inn

Rudley trotted up to the front desk. "Margaret, where's Lloyd? I need him to help me with that door hinge."

"He should be back in a minute, Rudley." Margaret looked up from the note she was writing. "He's gone to pick up a package at the train."

"What did he order this time?"

"I don't know."

"I hope it's not another UFO finder."

"Products advertised in comic books are often disappointing."

"At least the pigeons liked it."

"Yes," said Margaret. "It might have been useless in attracting UFOs but it had lots of little loops and bars for them to perch on."

Rudley glanced at the paperwork next to Margaret's elbow. "How are the Christmas preparations coming along?"

"Splendidly."

"So Miss Miller and Mr. Simpson have confirmed."

"They have. They had thought of spending Christmas with her parents, but it turns out the Millers are spending the holidays with the Simpsons."

"Ah, to be in England at Christmas."

"They're going to be in the Bahamas, Rudley."

"A colony, at least."

"Miss Miller and Mr. Simpson could have gone, but they had their hearts set on snow at Christmas."

Lloyd came in the front door at that moment, carrying a large box.

"What did you get this time?" Rudley asked.

Lloyd set the box at the end of the desk. "It ain't for me. It's just marked for the Pleasant."

Margaret examined the label. "Why, it's from Mr. Bostock."

"Must be a bomb," said Rudley.

"Nonsense, Rudley, packages with bombs tick."

"Very well, Margaret." Rudley took out an Exacto knife, slit open the box, and lifted the contents onto the desks.

"It's a birdhouse," said Lloyd.

"It's the Pleasant," said Margaret, delighted, "with the staff and some of the guests. There's Gregoire with a frying pan and Tiffany with a broom."

"And Aunt Pearl boozing it up on the veranda," said Rudley.

"Be nice, Rudley."

"I must say, it's a perfect replica, Margaret."

She paused. "Do you think there'll be tiny corpses?"

"Only if you let the cat roam."

"Rudley, Blanche is hardly a killer." She peeled off the card taped to the birdhouse and handed it to Rudley with the instruction to read it.

"'Dear Mr. and Mrs. Rudley and staff,'" he began, then stopped and frowned.

"Keep going."

"'Dear Mr. and Mrs. Rudley and staff,'" Rudley began again. "'I hope you enjoy this birdhouse. I usually sell them but I figured you cuckoos could use one. Sincerely, Bill Bostock.'"

After a silence, Margaret said, "Do you think he'll be back, Rudley?"

He returned the note to the envelope and leaned it against the side of the birdhouse. "I think not, Margaret."

About the Author

Judith Alguire's previous novels include *Pleasantly Dead*, *The Pumpkin Murders* and *A Most Unpleasant Wedding*, the first three books of the Rudley Mysteries, as well as *All Out* and *Iced*, both of which explored the complex relationships of sportswomen on and off the playing field. Her short stories, articles and essays have also appeared in such publications as *The Malahat Review* and *Harrowsmith*, and she is a past member of the editorial board of the *Kingston Whig-Standard*. A graduate of Queen's University, she has recently retired from nursing.

"Alguire is clearly of the sly and cosy old-school British detective fiction à la Agatha Christie's Miss Marple. And that's a venerable genre of mystery writing." —*Winnipeg Free Press*

"If a British-style 'cosy' mystery usually resembles a stroll through the dark side of a park, *The Pumpkin Murders* is a 100-yard dash — with attitude. Autumn in Ontario cottage country: scarlet colours, crisp evenings and morning frost — with a female impersonator on the run and some very annoyed drug dealers. More than just pumpkins get smashed at Pleasant Inn this Halloween. The same group of characters from Alguire's first mystery is back, including the owners of Pleasant Inn, cops whose whistles are short of a full blast, vintage card-sharp aunties and murder victims. Snappish dialogue fuels the pace with good one-liners spicing up the tone and revealing a variety of gaudy characters and quaint settings. *The Pumpkin Murders* is a cheery resurgence of the British standby — in Canadian style."
                                        —Don Graves, *The Hamilton Spectator*

ISBN 978-18987109-37-3

Also available as an eBook
ISBN 978-18987109-68-7

Trevor and Margaret Rudley have had their share of misfortunes at
The Pleasant Inn, the cherished Ontario cottage-country hotel they've
owned for twenty-five years. There have been boating accidents,
accidental poisonings, and then there was that unfortunate ski-lift
incident. But this year their hopes are high for the summer season.
However, barely a week goes by before their hopes are dashed. There's
a dead body making a nuisance of itself in the wine cellar, and it's
nobody the Rudleys know.

The guests at The Pleasant Inn, a wealthy and eccentric lot, are dying
for distraction, and one of them, Miss Miller, sets out to solve the
case of the deceased, relying on wild speculation, huge leaps of logic,
and the assistance of her great admirer, Edward Simpson, who is too
smitten to dissuade her from her adventure in detection. Challenging
her in the race to resolution is the disciplined Detective Brisbois,
whose deep-rooted insecurities about his style and status are aroused
by the hotel guests' careless assumption of privilege. When Brisbois
stumbles into peril of his own, the intrepid Miss Miller is the only one
left who can solve the crime.

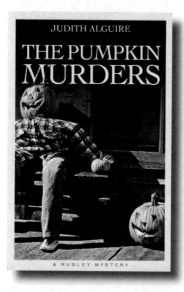

ISBN 978-18987109-45-8

Also available as an eBook
ISBN 978-18987109-69-4

Autumn returns to Ontario cottage country. Leaves redden. Pumpkins ripen. And Trevor and Margaret Rudley, proprietors of the Pleasant Inn, expect nothing more than a few Halloween high jinks to punctuate the mellow ambiance of their much-loved hostelry. However, the frost is barely on the pumpkin when Gerald, a female-impersonator friend of the Pleasant's esteemed cook Gregoire, turns up, dragging his very frightened friend Adolph behind. After witnessing a drug deal in Montreal, they're on the lam, hoping to blend into the Pleasant's pleasant rhythms until the heat is off. Alas, they hope in vain.

As the bodies pile up, the intrepid Elizabeth Miller jumps into the fray, fully armed with her peculiar intuition, her maddening charm, and her devoted swain, Edward Simpson, who proves a useful fellow behind the wheel of a car. Detective Michel Brisbois, in the past bested by Miss Miller in rooting out unpleasantness at the Pleasant, finds himself racing — quite literally — to keep up with his amateur challenger. But when the chips are down — as they inevitably are — it's the laziest creature on earth who ends up saving the day for the kindly and rather eccentric folk of Ontario's most peculiar country hotel.

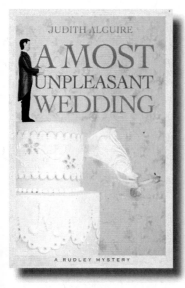

ISBN 978-18987109-99-1

Also available as an eBook
ISBN 978-1927426-07-4

Another summer, and The Pleasant Inn, nestled in beautiful Ontario cottage country, is filled to capacity. This season is especially exciting, as perennial guests Miss Miller and her long-time admirer Mr. Simpson have chosen to marry at the Inn. The guests and staff are clamouring to be involved, particularly Bonnie Lawrence, a young wife adrift while her husband is off fishing. Margaret and Trevor Rudley are delighted to host the wedding, and barring Mrs. Lawrence's obsessive interfering, everything is set to go off without a hitch.

But when a neighbour is found dead in the woods behind the inn, the possibility of a joyous occasion starts looking distinctly less likely. Detective Michel Brisbois, who is heading up the case, is back on the Pleasant Inn's doorstep. Rudley barely tolerates the presence of the police, who are once again on site interviewing the guests as possible suspects. Even though she's prenuptially preoccupied, the fearless Miss Miller refuses to be left out from solving yet another murder at The Pleasant...much to her own peril.